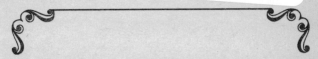

He never meant to kiss her. Even in his deepest drunken state, he would never have thought to kiss her. But he did.

The touch of his mouth to hers, which started as nothing more than a comforting caress, became something utterly different when she parted her lips with the faintest whimper. He tasted her, cider and warmth, felt her gentle giving, and suddenly his free hand was tangled in her curls.

"Grace," he whispered into her mouth. "Good God, Grace!"

By Emma Jensen
Published by Fawcett Books:

CHOICE DECEPTIONS
VIVID NOTIONS
COUP DE GRACE

COUP DE GRACE

Emma Jensen

FAWCETT CREST • NEW YORK

A Fawcett Crest Book
Published by Ballantine Books
Copyright © 1996 by Melissa Jensen

http://www.randomhouse.com

Library of Congress Catalog Card Number: 95-96168

ISBN 0-449-22486-4

Manufactured in the United States of America

First Edition: August 1996

10 9 8 7 6 5 4 3 2 1

For Laura, Susan, and Shannon—
three Graces in their own right.

Prologue

JOAN OF ARC had probably wished for rain.

Staring morosely into the fire at her feet, Lady Grace Granville wished with all her heart for sun. She was sitting as close to the hearth as she dared, watching listlessly for errant sparks. She was freezing, despite a shawl and the relative warmth of the chamber. The cold, she knew, had far more to do with present circumstances than with location. Still, she was chilled to the bone, and should her companion's agitation bode for the immediate future, circumstances were going to get worse.

"I mean it, Grace. I will not marry you!"

"Yes, I heard you the first time, Rafe, and quite believed you. There is no need for you to repeat yourself."

Rafael Marlowe levered his tall form away from the mantel and stalked to the other side of the chamber. He had been pacing back and forth for the past ten minutes, and had Grace not already felt distinctly ill, the constant motion would have made her dizzy.

"Damnit, Grace, I will have none of your games!"

"I am playing none. I never expected you to offer for me. On the contrary, I was certain you would not. You have made your feelings on the matter perfectly clear."

He grunted. "Lot of good it's done me. My God, had I known it would come to this, I would have severed ties with your family ten years ago!"

"Rafe, please . . ."

"As if it were not bad enough that I have your family's

1

expectations to contend with, now I have my aunt's as well. What is it, Grace? A plot to infiltrate and sabotage my life—or simply to send me stark raving mad? Leg-shackling me to you would do both."

Grace pulled her shawl closer around her shoulders and resolutely blinked back the tears that threatened to spill over her lashes. "You have said more than enough. I suggest you continue this discussion with my parents."

Dramatic black brows drew together in a scowl that would have frightened the devil himself. "You will not shrug this one off, Grace. This is not one of your absurd little escapades."

"No, it is not." Grace grasped the arms of her chair and took a steadying breath. "This is a nightmare. I had nothing to do with the matter, and I will not sit here while you insult me. Should you care to continue ranting, you will have to do so at someone else's expense. I am leaving."

"Don't bother!" Rafael slashed his hand through the air. "I cannot believe I even bothered trying to talk to you. You might look like an angel, but you are a devil to the core." He stalked to the door. "Nothing to do with the matter? Do not delude yourself, Grace. You are damn well responsible for every wretched bit of it."

Grace stared unhappily at the spot he had just inhabited and bit her lip. She could not blame him for being angry, really. She simply wished he had managed to display his anger in a slightly less wounding manner.

"Well, you have done it yet again, Grace," she whispered miserably. "Landed yourself neck-deep in the soup."

The truth was that she was well used to being the center of mass approbation. In fact, she had become rather good at ignoring it. The problem, of course, was that it was Rafe who was presently ready to strangle her with his bare hands. She could not fault him. After seeing her at her worst through so many years, he could not honestly be expected to see that she wanted only to give him her best. Quite simply, the matter was hopeless. How nice it would be, she thought glumly, for matters to be different—just once.

Not caring about sparks, she thrust her feet toward the fire.

1

JOAN OF ARC had probably wished for rain.

Gazing wistfully at the smoldering logs, Grace wished with all her heart for sun. She was standing as close to the hearth as she dared, watching listlessly for errant sparks. She had already singed two pairs of slippers and a shawl, and could not hope to replace them before the holidays when she would be allowed to rejoin her family.

The crowded assembly room was unpleasantly cold. No, she amended, it was simply unpleasant. Not that she had ever been enamored of the brittle and brilliant London soirees, but this was beyond depressing. The country assembly ball contained all of the false amicability of London society with none of the amusement. At least one was reasonably certain of encountering Byron, or Brummell, or some such character at Almack's. Or any of the people who were likely to be kind to her.

Here, she had received nothing more than smug queries from the girls her age, and disapproving glances from their mamas. The men filled her dance card, to be sure, but she could read the frank speculation behind their vague smiles. *The chit must have done something damned interesting,* she could almost hear them saying, *to get herself sent here. Wonder if I can get her to do it again. . . .*

It was bad enough to have been sent from Town in disgrace; immeasurably worse to have been sent to Crowborough. She had never hated East Sussex before, but she

4

now loathed the county with a passion that was beginning to border on zealousness. Coventry had nothing on Crowborough. In fact, she was convinced that she had found the supreme purgatory for the disliked and disgraced.

Disgrace. She considered the word with a wry smile. Her mother had become inordinately fond of the word during the Season. *You are a disgrace to the women of our family, Grace. Your behavior, Grace, would disgrace a fishwife.* She had begun to wonder if perhaps her mother had not had some premonition of things to come when she was still in the womb, and had chosen the name in hopes of beguiling fate.

Obviously it had not worked.

Still, to banish her to a relative's house in the country had been the ultimate in punishments. Cousin Bernice was, to put it mildly, an extremely pious woman. To put it bluntly, she was a sour-faced, Bible-thumping crone, who had greeted Grace's arrival with one succinct phrase.

"Hell is filled with those who spurned the way of righteousness."

Now, Grace was reasonably certain she had done nothing of the sort, but she had wisely decided not to argue the point. Instead, she had done her best to keep out of her cousin's way. She had been reasonably successful in her weeks of residence. Other than meals and the requisite premeal prayer sessions, she had seen little of anyone.

Not that there were too many people to see. Crow House was a bleak place. Her cousin's husband had died some years earlier—gone, Grace was certain, to a far better domain—and there was but a meager staff. Bernice had a son who was fifteen, not so much younger than Grace at nineteen, but the young man had proven himself miserable company within a day. Pale and serious, Carston preferred his books to human interaction. Except, of course, when he was filling in for his mother in denouncing the character of ungrateful children. He was one of the blessed grateful; Grace was not.

She had tried initially to tease him out of his somberness,

5

and had received no more than cold stares for her efforts. She had then tried to shock him out of his complacency by putting a mouse in his jacket pocket. It had almost been worth the consequences to see him leap about squawking until the little creature freed itself and scampered off. There had been no way to prove that the mouse had not found its own way into the pocket, but the week of extended and acrimonious prayer sessions suggested that no one had been fooled.

Now, huddled miserably near the hearth, Grace did her best to ignore both the speculative gazes she was receiving from the assembled revelers and Bernice's enviably constant disapproving glare. Why the woman had insisted on attending the ball was beyond Grace's imagining. An evening of lively music and drunken country gentlemen hardly seemed her style. But she had muttered something about noblesse oblige and dragged her unhappy charge through the bitter cold and into an assembly hall filled with colder people.

Grace declined a request for a dance with a singularly unpleasant-looking young man and willed the clock to spin a little faster. She had a far better use of her time in mind, and was rather impatient to get on with it.

A young lady in blinding sapphire satin sidled up a few moments later. If Grace were not mistaken, she had recently been in the center of a knot of young people, all of whom had been staring in her direction, and most of whom had been laughing. The girl did not speak at first, but cast a disparaging look at her pink wool gown. Grace ignored her. She had hardly set out to impress, and warmth had seemed vastly preferable to fashion. The satin was hardly more appropriate for the occasion.

"Are you enjoying yourself, my lady? I vow our little gathering is not what you are used to."

Grace tried to remember the creature's name. Drucilla? Estella? Her sister-in-law had once taught her a rather useful trick: keep trying alternatives until either the right name or something truly diverting came to mind. So, as Griselda

6

waited, Grace tried. It was not working, and the creature was not leaving. In truth, she would rather have conversed with a serpent, but she was a firm believer in the tenet that it was far simpler to be kind than callous.

"I find soirees to be much the same everywhere," she replied, wishing she were a good head taller so that she would not feel quite so insignificant next to the statuesque Prunella. "When one is surrounded by warmth and good cheer, one cannot help but feel at home."

If the girl detected any irony in the response, she gave no indication. "And where is your home, if I may ask?"

Grace sighed. "Staffordshire."

"My goodness! Such a distance. Whatever brought you to our little corner of East Sussex?"

A drafty coach with Charon at the helm sprang to her tongue. She bit it. Sarcasm served no great purpose, and besides, she was fully convinced that Gorgonzola had never heard of the ghoul who ferried the dead across the River Styx to Hades. So she merely said, "My cousin was kind enough to invite me for a visit. And my elder brother's estate is but twenty miles away."

Yes, Jason and his wife lived in East Sussex. And considering the fact that it was nearing the holidays, they should have returned from their trip to Scotland some days past.

If there were any heavenly interventions left in her name, she was saved.

Her brother and sister-in-law would welcome her with open arms and warm hearts. They had been gone for several months and had not known of her plight. In fact, she thought contentedly, both would be suitably outraged by the situation and could be counted on for sympathy, support, and perhaps even a few sharp words for her parents. All she had to do was get to Newhaven.

The smug voice cut into her havenly musings. "How convenient to have relatives to turn to when one is in dis ... enchantment with one's surroundings. You were in London recently, were you not? I believe your cousin said

7

as much. How . . . dull it must be to be there after the Little Season is over."

Grace wondered just what Bernice had actually said. It could not have been the truth, for she did not know it. Still, her suppositions must have been interesting—and vocal.

"Bitter old hen," Grace muttered.

"I beg your pardon?"

"I said, better than . . . oh, Yorkshire, for instance. London is so much more—" she cast a surreptitious glance at the satin "—colorful." *And cruel.* "I imagine you would feel quite at home there." The dismal conversation could not be over soon enough. "I do believe my cousin is beckoning. If you would excuse me . . ."

She fled, cursing herself all the while for cowardice. She was ordinarily not one to decline a challenge, but she was convinced that, sometime during the past eight weeks, most of her spirit had been frozen right out of her.

She did not approach Bernice at all, but took refuge near the refreshment tables. As she watched, Cinderella flounced back to her companions. Whatever she had to impart inspired a wave of giggles. Grace only caught one word. The girl tugged at one of her own raven curls and, in a whisper that must have reached London, announced, "Bleached!"

"Begging your pardon, my lady . . ." Grace turned to find yet one more cup-shot youth leering at her—or rather, leering over her, his eyes sliding from the tip of her blond head to her pink-slippered toes. "I say, would you care to dance?" His hand was already snaking its way toward the midpoint, her waist.

"Thank you, sir," she replied sweetly, and his grin widened, "but I would sooner eat dirt."

Bernice did not say so much as a word to her during the drive home. As a matter of principle, Grace disliked silence, and hated scorn even more. At the moment, however, she was grateful for her cousin's still tongue. Feeling battered, and more lonely than she had ever been, she huddled

8

into her cloak and watched the snow falling outside the carriage window.

Her cousin's silence lasted only until bedtime. Then, as her son sat smugly by, she rounded on Grace, pious indignation etched into her narrow face. "You are a blight on the family name, girl! Did not your unfortunate experience in London teach you anything? The good people at the assembly were all that is welcoming, and you repaid their kindness with pride!"

Grace did not bother responding. It was hardly worth the effort.

"I have been thoroughly humiliated this night!" Bernice continued, clasping a bony hand to her chest. "I will pray for your forgiveness!" Then, smirking Carston in tow, she swept from the room. The boy actually stuck his tongue out at Grace as he went.

She sighed and, in a flash of slightly blasphemous humor, pitied God the harangue he was about to receive. She rather thought He had better things to do than sit in judgment on her crimes against Bernice.

She, too, had better things to do, not the least of which was collecting the suit of clothes she had purloined from Carston's wardrobe and hidden in the library window seat. A few alterations would be necessary, for he was not a slender young man, but she thought she was up to the task. No one would be looking too closely at her stitches, after all. Rolling the oversize clothing into a tight ball, she went off in search of thread. And a pair of shears.

Much later, as she crept out the back door, she thought about heading for the stables, and decided against it. Taking a few items of clothing was one thing; Carston would never notice that they were missing. Taking a horse was another matter altogether. An empty stall was far more glaring than a small gap in a drawer. Besides, she was fully convinced that Bernice would send the magistrate after her if she were to make her escape on an appropriated mount. The most her cousin would do now would be to send a pious note to the earl and countess, informing them of their sinful daughter's defection.

Well, there was a posting house in the village. If she followed the carriage tracks in the snow and walked briskly, she ought to reach it in plenty of time to catch the first coach of the morning.

Walking turned out to be more of a challenge than she had anticipated. The road, where she could see it, was icy, and her low boots, while perfectly adequate for a winter stroll around the gardens, were poorly suited to tramping over frozen and uneven ground. She had had the foresight to take a heavy surtout from a cupboard in the coatroom downstairs and was immensely grateful for its warmth. Its length, however, posed a problem. She held it up as best she could, but ended up tripping over the hem on a regular basis, more than once landing on her nose in the snow.

By the time she reached the posting house, she was cold, exhausted, and grouchy enough to kick the shins of anyone who gave her trouble. Fortunately, the postmaster only took the briefest look at her as she glowered up from under the brim of her filched hat and, after commenting that she must be a "tough lad" to brave the weather, sold her a ticket to Newhaven. The coach arrived late, but she had a seat to herself, and settled down for the journey, expecting to arrive in Newhaven by afternoon. From the posting house there, it would be a simple matter of sending a message to her brother to come fetch her.

She could have sent a letter, of course, requesting rescue, but the wait would have been interminable. She was also of the opinion that Bernice, with any number of pious excuses, would have read any mail she tried to send. It would not do at all for her parents to hear of her plans, even after the fact. As it was, Jason would undoubtedly scold her for being so reckless as to travel alone, and Aurelie would make a fuss over her time in the cold. There was no question, though, that she would be welcome. With that pleasant thought, she pulled her hat lower on her head and prepared to sleep her way to Newhaven.

The coach's shuddering halt brought her abruptly awake. Peering out the window, she saw the driver speaking to a cloaked man on horseback. For an exhilarating moment, she thought that they were being waylaid by a highwayman. Now, *that* would be a story to tell her brother and sister-in-law. But the man rode off soon with a wave and the coach pulled forward again. Grace stifled her disappointment and turned to the older man who was sitting opposite her.

Deepening her voice, she asked, "Are we almost to Newhaven?"

The man shook his grizzled head and chuckled. "Won't be reaching New 'aven today, young man. Snow's a-fallin' again."

"How do you know we will not get through?"

"Oh, I knew it afore we left Crowb'rough. Don't think the coachman knew it, though."

A frisson of alarm ran up Grace's spine. Then it occurred to her that the man might be having a bit of fun at her expense. "Why did you get on the coach if you knew it would not get to Newhaven?"

He chuckled again. "Cause I'm not goin' to New'aven, lad. I'm only goin' far as Lewes. We'll be there afore too long."

And, as it turned out, the thin winter light was fading by the time they reached Lewes, cold and snow slowing their progress. "Sorry," the driver said when he finally opened the door. "You'll 'ave to stay here for tonight. Weather permittin', we'll leave for New'aven in the mornin'."

The older man seized Grace's shoulder as she alighted. "You got enough money fer a room, young man?" He reached into his pocket and Grace stilled his hand.

"I have enough. But thank you." It was the first act of kindness she had seen in many weeks and she wanted to hug him for it.

Remembering her disguise, she merely touched the brim of her hat and, trying what she hoped was a masculine swagger, made her way toward the inn. How difficult could it possibly be to secure a room? She would have a meal sent up and occupy herself as best she could until morning when the coach would leave. If the coach could leave.

There had been little to purchase in Crowborough, even less that Bernice would have approved of, and Grace still had most of the pin money her father had sent. She thought she had enough for two nights, at least, and if the snow had not let up by then ... Well, she would worry about that when the time came.

Her spirits sank when she entered the inn. Dark and dingy, it was completely unlike any place she had experienced in her life, and just the sort of place she knew to avoid. Through a doorway she could see the taproom, filled to overflowing with loud, large men. As she watched, a tankard came flying out, spilling some liquid as it went. A man who might have been its owner came soon after—courtesy, she assumed, of someone's boot to his posterior. He did a surprisingly graceful pirouette before crumpling into a heap at her feet.

He was very still and Grace wondered if he were dead, or merely foxed to the gills. He let out a potent belch then, answering the question and sending ale fumes wafting upward. She wrinkled her nose and took a quick step back, jumping in surprise as a meaty hand clamped down on her shoulder.

"Can I help you, young man?"

The man, obviously the innkeeper, resembled nothing so much as a tree trunk covered with black lichen. His gray-flecked beard reached halfway down his chest, and Grace was convinced she could see the remnants of his last few meals in the bushy depths.

"If you pl ... I mean, I want a room for the night."

"Oh, you do, do you? I don't suppose you have the blunt to pay for it."

She pulled several notes from one of her coat's inside pockets and waved them in his face. "I have the ... blunt."

His eyes glittered under the single black brow that ran across his forehead. "So you do. Well, there won't be a room ready for another half hour. So why don't you go into the taproom and have Meg pour you a drink?"

Grace would have preferred to walk barefoot over live coals, but there seemed to be no other choice. "All right. I'll do that."

"Good lad." The innkeeper slapped her genially on the back. Strength of will alone kept her from sprawling across the floor. "And if you're real nice to Meg there, she might warm your bed later." With a loud guffaw, he shoved her in the direction of the taproom.

Trying to look as casual as possible, Grace slipped through the doorway. And very nearly ran right back out. Not one of the customers seemed to weigh less than fifteen stone, and the shortest one towered over her by a good six inches. She kept her eyes downcast as she wriggled through the crowd toward the bar. She was thirsty, and ale could not be so terribly different from champagne, could it?

A buxom young woman with dark hair and an improbably red mouth was tending bar. Meg, no doubt. Grace tried not to gape at the sight of the woman's overlush form straining at the minimal confines of her dress.

"Like what you see, m'boy?" Meg's voice was much like the rest of her, full and lush and rough edged.

"Aw, leave off, Meggy," somebody said loudly. "The lad ain't got enough to satisfy you for a minute!"

The crowd surrounding the bar applauded this sentiment and Meg threw a kiss into the air. This earned another appreciative howl from the men. "Well, you're not much for size," she purred to Grace, "but you seem a pretty enough lad. How old are you?"

Grace congratulated herself for having had the foresight to rub a light coating of dirt over most of her face. "Old enough," she muttered, "to want ale. Now."

She plunked a coin onto the bar, hoping desperately that it was enough. It must have been, for Meg grinned and the coin vanished into the shadowed depths of her bodice. "Comin' right up." She sashayed to the end of the bar, attracting the attention of at least a dozen pair of eyes.

Grace took the opportunity to study the men studying Meg. She had never seen such a dirty, loutish bunch, let alone stood among them. She suppressed a shiver and prayed that her room would be ready as promised. When Meg reappeared with her glass, she tried to calm her nerves with a hearty sip.

The stuff attacked her throat and burst in her nose. Trying not to cough was like trying to hold back the tide, and she lasted scant seconds before bursting into a series of coughs that rattled her ribs. The group around her seemed to find the whole thing incomparably amusing, and no fewer than four ham-sized fists pounded against her back.

"The lad needs practice!" someone bellowed.

The lad, Grace thought as she valiantly took another sip, *has clearly lost whatever wits she once possessed to even be here.* As far as she was concerned, the situation could not possibly get worse.

She was wrong, of course.

Something scraped against her waist. Thinking that one of the men was crowding her, she took a step to the side. The touch followed, skimming upward. She let out a startled yelp as it hit the lower swell of her breast and spun about to face a hairy behemoth of a man who looked every bit as shocked as she was.

"Bloody 'ell," he shouted. "'E's a she!"

"G'on, Pete," another muttered. "You've 'ad a few too many."

"Feel for yerself," Pete muttered. "Benny said the toff was carryin' a ruddy fortune an' I decided to nip a bit. This ain't no toff. . . ."

As the first of the hands descended, Grace found herself wondering vaguely how such huge oafs could move so fast. And how, in a lifetime full of desirable opportunities, she never failed to tumble headfirst into the worst.

The Duke of Avemar slumped lower in his seat at a corner table and reached for the whiskey bottle. His aim was off, and his fingers merely skimmed the glass surface.

Scowling in concentration, he tried again, wondering when the second—no, third, yes, there were now three bottles— had appeared. He only remembered having ordered one. Well, three was infinitely better.

He tried for the one in the middle and grasped only air. Now he could just see the original bottle. Foxed. Cup-shot. Top-heavy as a loaded mule. That was what he was. Drunk as a bishop and damned pleased with the situation. He made a last grab for the bottle and managed to slosh some of the liquor into his glass. Too much of a good thing was not nearly enough.

As he lifted the glass in the general direction of his lips, a deafening din from the bar caught his attention. Damn buggers couldn't hold their drink. Bad for a man's nerves to have so much noise thundering in his ears.

Then a higher voice rose above the men's roars.

"For God's sake, somebody *help me!*"

Some distant corner of Avemar's brain registered the fact that there was a woman somewhere in the room and that she needed assistance. He downed the whiskey and reached for the bottle again.

A gentleman would see to the matter.

He had become rather adept at ignoring that annoying little voice on the rare occasions when it invaded his brain.

Stepping in here is the acceptable thing to do.

He lifted the bottle.

Now, you clodpated jackass!

"Well, hell," he muttered, and staggered to his feet.

It took some doing to push his way through the rowdy crowd and he was forced to use his fists on more than one occasion. He made it to the center eventually and found the woman. At least he thought it was the woman. She was wearing breeches and a coat—or rather, a tent-sized tarpaulin masquerading as a coat—and was flailing her arms about in a vain attempt to fight off the lout who was holding her.

"Pardon me," the duke said politely, and plowed his fist into the man's face.

As expected, the man released his captive with a muffled roar and covered his flattened nose with his hands. Also as expected, his companions did not appreciate this interruption of their sport and rounded on the interloper. With more speed than coordination, Avemar reached into his coat, removed his pistol, and shoved it under the jaw of the closest figure.

In seconds, the infernal noise had ceased and the crowd backed off. Reaching behind him with his free hand, he groped about for the woman's arm. "Again, gentlemen, pardon me . . . er, us."

Keeping his gun trained on the brute, he backed from the room, pushing the woman behind him. He stopped only when they reached the outer door. "Open it."

She did, and a burst of frigid air enveloped them. Avemar gritted his teeth and headed for the stables, still holding on to her arm. His progress was impeded by the fact that the ground was rolling like waves, and he fell to his knees twice. She went with him and he heard her cry out each time. He had neither the time nor inclination to see if she was all right, however, and focused all his attention on getting them into the stable.

His horse was right where he had left it, saddled and waiting. It took three tries for him to hoist the woman onto the saddle. The difficulty was not due to her size; on the contrary, she weighed no more than a child. But the fading twilight set everything in blurry shadows, his depth perception was off, and she had begun squirming against him.

"Be still," he snapped. "I'm not going to hurt you." He stifled an oath as her foot connected with his thigh. "Can't make the same promise for the crowd back there."

She immediately stopped her struggles and went limp. With a final heave, he got her onto the horse and swung up behind her. She was shaking violently, with cold or shock, he could not tell. Some protective instinct floated up with the whiskey fumes, and he settled her clumsily but firmly in front of him, pulling the flaps of his coat around her shivering body.

16

It was fortunate the horse needed no guidance, for he did not think he was up to the task. But the beast knew the path well and set off for home as fast as the snow would allow. The duke tried to ignore the ominous sloshing of liquor in his gut and concentrated on staying in the saddle.

Minutes—or hours—later they passed through the gates of his hunting box. The horse trotted up the drive and headed straight to the stable. Avemar slid awkwardly to the ground and pulled the heavy door open. Once they were all inside, he closed the door and turned his attention back to the woman. She had stopped shaking some time past and now jumped easily to the floor.

Avemar fumbled with the lantern hanging from a hook on the wall and squinted at his erstwhile guest in the faint light. She had her back to him and he got the impression of a small, compact body and a tousle of short blond curls. Then she turned around, took a few steps closer, and gasped.

"Good heavens—Rafe!"

By this time she was close enough that he could see the heart-shaped face and gold eyes.

"Bloody hell," he muttered. "Hullo, Grace."

Then, with a groan, he let the inviting blackness take over and crumpled to the stone floor.

2

HE CAME TO with a start and, had he been able, would have bolted upright. His body, however, knowing the inevitable result of such an action would be the loss of everything he had eaten that day, refused to cooperate. So he lay on his back, gasping like a netted fish and trying to decide which river he had been pulled from.

"Yes, I imagine it is a bit cold—and damp—but it seemed the most expedient way of waking you up."

Sliding his aching eyeballs upward, Rafe saw the angel and decided he had finally done it, managed to drink himself to death. Or something like it. Fallen off his horse into the river, most likely. He had almost drowned once as a student at Oxford when too much ale too close to the Cherwell made for what had looked to be a wet end until Jason Granville had fished him out. Rafe was a smashing swimmer when sober and would undoubtedly have been able to save himself had he not been floating internally.

Jason was, at the moment, somewhere in Scotland. And it had undoubtedly been the Ouse rather than the Cherwell. Nasty business, ending one's life in something called the Ouse. The Avon would have been far more distinguished—or the Welland. Yes, he could see the announcement now: *Avemar, visiting from his estates near Halland, was unfortunately drowned in the Welland.*

It had a much nicer ring to it than a drunk fool tumbling into the Ouse. Then again, one thing was certain. Dead was dead. How one's obituary read was, by this time, a moot point.

He took another quick look at the golden image above him. Odd that he appeared to have ascended rather than the literally hellish opposite. He rather thought that his behavior in the past year would have doomed him. Must be a law of averages, he thought muzzily. For the first twenty-nine of his thirty years he had been a good enough sort. Apparently it had been enough to promote a bit of divine intervention when that final record was reviewed.

He squinted up at the angel's face. "Funny thing," he mumbled, "you look a bit like someone I once knew. Heavenly irony, I s'pose. She was the most devilish little baggage, not at all—"

The rest of the statement was lost to sputtering as the celestial creature dumped what felt very much like snow onto his face. Startled into some semblance of alertness, he reached up to wipe his brow. His hand came away very cold and very wet.

"Well, damn and rot! What in the hell did you do that for?"

Grace found the rather long and eloquent string of curses that followed quite impressive. Her education and intelligence came to excellent use as she deciphered the meanings of the more obscure terms. It was more than a little disconcerting to hear such things coming from Rafe's mouth, and involving her own person, no less, but it was also reassuring. She had been quite concerned about his head as he had landed quite hard on the stone floor.

The identity of her rescuer had so startled her that she had been frozen to the spot, unable to do more than gape at him as he had fallen. A good thing, probably, because she would have undoubtedly gone down with him had she tried to break his fall. And that would have left two of them prostrate on the cold floor.

She had been too frightened and scattered in the tavern to pay much attention to her savior. By all rights he should have been in Wiltshire, at Margrave Castle. By sheer fortune he had been in Lewes, though she had no idea of what had possessed him to go to that inn. It was hardly his style.

Still, he had been there, an accidental knight in shining armor. Now they were both—somewhere. While she was fully recovered from her adventure and quite herself again, he was an alarming wreck, and she had suffered an icy clutch of fear for his state.

A quick check of his skull had found no blood, not even so much as a goose egg. She had then worried that perhaps one of the rogues in the tavern had managed to hurt him, perhaps with a gun or knife. She had parted his coat and looked as best she could. No holes, tears, or similarly ominous marks.

That examination had taken longer than she had expected, due to the fact that Rafael Marlowe was a very large man. Not fat, certainly, but with a height and breadth of chest and shoulders as to be imposing. Her own diminutive size did not help matters, especially when he was dead-weight against her efforts to move him. She had been ready to give up and go for help when her hands found something curved and hard.

A flask.

To be more precise, it was a very large, extremely ornate silver flask with his family's coat of arms engraved on both sides. And it was empty, save for a few drops of some liquid that made almost no noise when she shook it. The concept of severe bodily injury was waning fast, replaced by the distinct possibility that whatever had once been in the flask was now in Rafe's belly.

Snow had seemed a very good idea at the time as she was not in the habit of carrying smelling salts on her person. Now she was not so certain about the wisdom of her actions. Rafe was awake, proving her assertion that he was merely a bit foxed, but he bore absolutely no resemblance to the genial drunk she had seen on those times when he and Jason imbibed too much. In truth, despite the fact that she had known him for more years than she could count, he was no more familiar at that moment than the men from whom he had rescued her.

It was the same thick, sable hair—too long now and curling over his collar—the same wide, mobile mouth—though grim and hard-looking in its tense line. And the same deep-set, nearly exotically slanted cobalt eyes. Almost. They were bloodshot, bleak, and angry.

"Well, Grace?"

The same voice, deep and elegant, but with an edge now as harsh as a serrated blade.

"I—I thought to revive you. The snow was . . . handy."

"The snow—" he leaned up on his elbows "—was colder than . . ." He shook his head as if to clear it and groaned. "Than . . . well, *snow*, damnit."

"Marvelous simile, Rafe," she teased, emboldened by memories of friendly sparring matches of the past. "I shall be certain to file it away for future—"

"Shut up."

And she did. Not that obeying that particular order was one of her standard activities, common as it was from her mother—though usually phrased a bit more delicately. But this was Rafe, and Rafe had never said anything harsh to her before.

He was Jason's friend, Jason's oldest and dearest friend. He had been a frequent visitor at the Granville homes since Grace had been a small child and, despite the fact that he was more than ten years her senior, had been unfailingly kind. Rafael Marlowe, then Marquess of Holcombe, had been unfailingly kind to everyone, blithe of spirit and easy of affection.

The man below her was not the Marquess of Holcombe. He was the Duke of Avemar. And he was looking at her with something approaching loathing.

Not Rafe. Warm, jovial Rafe. He would never behave so. He was a bit inebriated and merely needed a few minutes to come to his senses. Grace smiled at the thought and waited patiently for him to regain his naturally pleasant demeanor.

It proved to be too long a wait. After some time, when he had done no more than drop back to the floor and close his eyes, she cautiously cleared her throat. He did not move. "Rafe?"

"Are you still here? I'd rather hoped that if I wished it hard enough, you would go away. Blasted rotgut. Makes it damn near impossible to do anything hard enough. I shall try again. Do help me out this time."

He peered up after what seemed an eternity only to find her hovering over him, her lower lip caught anxiously between her teeth. The snow had cleared a portion of the fog from his sight, if not his brain, and he could see the beginnings of a bruise on her cheek. Then he remembered.

"Christ, Grace, what were you doing in that place?"

"I was running away from Cousin Bernice at Crowborough, of course," she announced, as if it made all the sense in the world. "She was horrid."

"Unfortunate, as you'll have to turn right back around and return to her."

She looked different somehow. He could not quite put his finger on the change, but the resolute set of her pointed chin was utterly familiar. "No, I will not. I am going to Jason and Aurelie."

"Wrong. They're still in Edinburgh. Extended their visit. You can be back in Crowborough by morning."

"I am certain Cousin Bernice will not have me."

Rafe did not ask why. He knew enough about Grace to take her at her word. "Staffordshire, then. Back to your parents."

"They will not have me either."

He sighed and closed his eyes, hoping to assuage the pounding in his head. He thought better of the action, however, and peered up just in time to see her reach for the feed pail that she had apparently used to fetch the snow from outside.

"Do it and I will be forced to kill you."

Grace's hand stilled over the pail. He was fully awake, it seemed, and no more pleasant than he had been before. Confused and disheartened, she thought for a moment before saying, "Thank you."

22

"What in God's name for?"

"For rescuing me. At the tavern. It was unbelievable luck that you were there."

He scowled. "It was the devil's own luck. *I* belonged there. You did not."

"What a very odd thing to say. I was there purely by accident. And you surely do not belong among such uncouth ruffians. You are a duke, Rafe."

"Not by my choice," he returned bitterly. "And those uncouth ruffians are perfectly good company as far as I am concerned. They leave me alone to my business."

"Whiskey?"

"Damn right."

Grace could think of little to say to refute him. She had seen almost nothing of Rafe in the past ten months. In fact, she had only seen him on one occasion. He had not been drunk, but he had been in a mood so bleak that she had approached him only to say what words were necessary.

She had heard, through her family and friends in the ton, that he had been in terrible shape since, isolating himself in the country and communicating with few during his brief visits to Town. But never could she have imagined that he had fallen so low as to drown himself with cheap liquor in run-down taverns. The idea was chilling and she shivered.

The reflexive action reminded her that they were both on the very cold stone floor of an only slightly warmer stable. "Do you not think that perhaps we ought to go inside? In your . . . condition, you should probably be in bed."

His scowl deepened. "In my condition, as you so delicately phrased it, I should be snug in my corner of the tavern, well into my second bottle."

The cold was beginning to seep its way into his bones, a firm reminder that he had not drunk nearly enough. A few more shots would have deadened his senses completely. He opened his mouth to tell Grace just that, but she was not there. It took a concerted and painful effort to crane his neck about, but he finally located her across the stable, seeing to his horse.

23

Hannibal, a mean-tempered, exquisitely boned gray whom he had purchased more for the temper than the bloodlines, had a strong tendency to bite and even stronger teeth, all of which suited Rafe perfectly. People were far less likely to get near him when greeted with his mount's flattened ears and wild eyes.

At the moment, however, the traitorous brute was all but wriggling in pleasure as the girl removed his saddle and proceeded to brush him down. Hannibal had little liking for most humans, but Grace had always possessed a great liking for animals, and they seemed to sense it, returning her affection tenfold. Rafe had found that natural affinity beyond charming in the past. Now he found it utterly nauseating.

"I suppose there is no hope of being rid of you tonight."

He thought he saw her shoulders stiffen, but her face was serene when she turned back. "I am sorry you want me gone so badly, Rafe. But no, there is nowhere for me to go tonight. So perhaps we can go inside and see to having some supper."

The mention of food sent his stomach roiling anew. There was a goodly supply of liquor in the house, however, just compensation for having been forced to abandon the inn. He ground his teeth as he considered the fact that his presence would hardly be welcome there in the immediate future. The patrons had been wary enough of him at the onset, a member of the aristocracy in their midst. When he had done no more than drink himself into a stupor, they had relaxed and generally ignored him.

Now that he had robbed them of their sport, they would be far more likely to greet his appearance with fists and knives.

"Blast," he grumbled. It was the only drinking establishment in the area in which he would not be recognized or harassed, and it was no longer available.

The bottle of port on the sideboard was looking better by the second. He levered himself up slowly, not wanting to do any damage with a sudden move. He had almost made it to his feet when the minx came flying at him. His expectant groan turned into a full-throated growl as she barreled into his side.

"What in the devil do you think you're doing?" he asked grimly when she grasped his arm and tried to push him off his feet. It was a puny effort at best. She was a good five stone lighter than he and a foot shorter.

Whatever might have been her retort was muffled as she pressed her face into his coat, and he realized that she was trying to loop his arm over her shoulder to assist him into the house. The image was absurd and his lips cracked into a reluctant smile. "Leave off, Grace. I will manage on my own."

Grace did not particularly want to let go of him, but he had sounded almost pleasant, and acquiescence seemed like a good idea. She moved away and let him lead the way. His gait was by no means steady; he came very close to clipping his shoulder on two stalls and the doorway. The yard posed no real problem as there was nothing for him to run into, but he weaved a distinctly interesting pattern toward the door.

The heavy portal offered a challenge. He eventually got it open by a clumsy combination of hand on the knob and shoulder to the panels. Grace held herself back, certain that any offer to help would be met with snapping sarcasm. She followed as he stumbled across the entryway into the dark hall and winced as some part of his anatomy connected audibly with some piece of heavy furniture.

It was beyond odd that there were neither candles burning nor servants hurrying forward to assist them. But the hall was empty—at least she assumed it was. In truth, she had no idea where they were. Rafe had numerous holdings across England. This must be one of them. As he made his slow way across the floor, she walked toward the wall, running her hand over the furniture she passed. Her fingers located a candelabra on the third table and a tinderbox on the fourth.

It took her a few minutes, but she finally got the branch

of candles lit. She held it high and surveyed the hall. It was not a large space, with no more than half a dozen doors opening from it. There was a pervasive smell of damp, and the meager furniture seemed to take on a gothic twistedness in the flickering light. Then Rafe stepped into view, and Grace had the sudden and chilling sensation that she had somehow stepped into the pages of one of Mrs. Radcliffe's lurid novels.

Every romantic adventure had to have a hero. And a villain. At the moment, Grace was not at all certain Rafe represented the former. His many-tiered greatcoat fell around him like a flowing black cloak, his face appearing unnaturally pale and gray above it. The candlelight caught his eyes, drawing a feral glitter from their depths. Suddenly she could not remember how he had been in the past, nor how he had looked. This figure before her seemed more wraith than man, grim and forbidding, and spectral enough to send icy chills coursing through her. When he extended one waxlike hand toward her she gasped and took an involuntary step backward.

His lips drew back into a wolfish grin. "Afraid of me now, Grace? A bit late, I would say." He lurched toward her and she forced herself to hold her ground, silently repeating his familiar and comforting name over and again. He came to a stop mere inches away, looming over her in such a way that she expected to be swallowed by his coat at any minute. He stood utterly still for a moment before reaching out to take the candelabra from her nerveless fingers. "Come along. I'll show you to a room."

They passed no one on their way to the second floor, and Grace was struck anew by the eerie stillness of the house. "What is this place?"

"Hunting box," was the grunted reply.

As they passed an open door, Grace caught a glimpse of clothing strewn over floor and furniture. "Are you in residence here, Rafe?" she asked.

"Now, that was a stupid question, wasn't it? If I were not in residence, I would not be here."

The little voice chided him for that, and it took him longer than he would have liked to quash it. He was far from obtuse and knew exactly what she was asking. He had no intention of discussing his living arrangements with her, however, and thought it would be far more efficient to stifle her inquisitiveness early on than to waste his time in avoiding the questions.

He was chiding himself seconds later. He should have known better than to think she would be put off by mean terseness. "I meant," she was saying patiently, "to inquire as to whether you were here for an extended stay."

Blasted girl seemed to think he was teasing her. She certainly did not seem cowed. "I am here for the present. Now be quiet while I decide where to put you."

It was not much of a choice, really. It was a small lodge, with few bedchambers. He deliberately chose the one farthest from his own, wanting the distance even the twenty feet would provide. God only knew when the linens had last been changed, and he did not really care. All he wanted was to get the chit settled so that he could adjourn to the study and its resident liquor supply.

"Here," he announced, throwing the door open. "This will have to do." He pulled a single candle from the branch and crammed it into a narrow-necked flower vase that rested on a table near the door. He turned to go, deliberately avoiding looking either at her or the state of the room. He paused, however, for some reason he could not fathom, and said, still not looking at her, "Good night, Grace. Sleep well." Then, on the same breath, "You are leaving for Staffordshire in the morning."

"But—" Grace began, only to be cut off as the door slammed sharply behind him. "I do not want to go to Staffordshire," she muttered to the solid wood. "And I am hungry and cold and my clothes are a wreck."

She almost went after him. Thinking better of it, however, she took the opportunity to study her surroundings. The single taper offered meager light. Not that it mattered. Everything was draped with dust sheets. She made her way over to what appeared to be an elegant, high-backed chair and dropped inelegantly onto the cushions. She was instantly enveloped by a cloud of dust and spent the next several minutes coughing and trying to clear the stuff from her mouth and eyes.

When the air was reasonably clear again, she gingerly drew her legs up and propped her elbows on her knees. Rafe was, she decided, as much in residence as he wanted to be. For some reason, he was choosing to live alone in this cold and isolated lodge instead of the ducal estates in Wiltshire.

So it was true; he was truly consigning himself to hell.

She had heard whispers of it in the past months, but between her ignominious Little Season and subsequent banishment to Crowborough, she had had no opportunity to witness it for herself. The last time she had seen Rafe, nearly ten months earlier, he had shown no signs of impending degeneracy. He had been somber, certainly, and pitifully grim, so very unlike his usual sunny self.

But one would expect little else of a man who had just lost his family in one horrible, bewildering accident.

He had not been at Margrave, the Avemar seat, when the fire had gutted the East Wing. His parents had. The duke and duchess had perished in the blaze, trapped in their beds while the rest of the household stood outside watching in helpless horror as the flames swept through the wing.

Rafe had been there a sennight later, however, when Grace and her family traveled to Wiltshire for the funeral. He had been pale and haggard, his severe black coat sagging about his frame as if he had lost a great deal of weight even in seven days. Each time a servant or friend had addressed him as "Your Grace" he had blinked and shuddered as if his new title pained him. It must have.

There had been a glorious warmth and closeness in his family, one for which Grace had often felt a wistful envy. Her own parents treated her with pinched disapproval, her sister was only distantly friendly, and though her brothers were caring in their own way, she had always referred to Granville family connection as careless affection.

The Granvilles had departed Wiltshire, leaving Rafe to grieve in peace, certain that he would, in his own time, return to Society. But he had not. In subsequent months Grace had heard rumors of his solitude, which was broken only by periodic visits to London, reputed to consist of weeklong descents into the baser activities.

Even as she had scoffed at the tales, she had longed to go to him, to offer whatever solace she could. Such an act was impossible, and while she had not abandoned him at heart, she had been forced to abandon any thought of seeking him out.

Providence appeared to have intervened now in the strangest way.

Ignoring both her damp clothing and the dusty chair, she leaned back into the cushions and began to plan. It was a tenuous and potentially dangerous situation in which she had landed herself, but she was a firm believer in taking full advantage of serendipity. She was here and Rafe was here, and little else mattered.

She roused herself some time later and made her way back down the stairs. Quelling the insistent rumbling of her stomach was the first order of business. Surely there was something in the kitchens. Assuming that she could find the kitchens. She held her candle high as she reached the main hall and decided that the back of the house was the best bet.

A faint light showed from under one of the doors and she paused in front of it. She had no idea what the chamber was, but she was sure that Rafe was in it. She chewed on her bottom lip as she tried to decide what to do. It was quite likely that he would not welcome the intrusion. In fact, he would undoubtedly blister her ears with more of his cursing. But she was reasonably certain that he had not bothered to eat in recent hours, and the mention of food might stall his temper.

Lifting her chin, she tapped at the door. There was no

answer. Either he had not heard her or was deliberately ignoring the sound. The odds were even. After a moment's hesitation, she turned the knob and entered.

She did not see him at first. The room, which turned out to be a study of sorts, was utterly still except for the desultory flickering of a fire dying in the grate. Then she spied one long arm appearing from behind a high-backed wing chair, the hand limp above an empty decanter that rested on its side on the carpet.

"Rafe," she whispered. Then again, slightly louder.

He did not respond, and she crept across the room to stand in front of the chair. He was asleep, his head resting against the padded wing. Perhaps it was only the soft, rosy light of the fire, but he looked far better than he had earlier. In fact, Grace mused with a gentle sigh, he looked warm and peaceful and familiarly, breathtakingly beautiful.

With his tormented, uniquely tilted eyes closed, his dark lashes fanned his cheeks. Women throughout history had coveted such lashes, long and lush. There was nothing feminine, however, about Rafe. He was all bold curves and sharp angles from his cutting cheekbones to his wide, sculpted mouth.

She noticed, for the first time, the faintest glimmer of silver in his earth-brown hair. Leaning closer, she saw no more than half a dozen pale strands just above his left temple. On the day of the funeral, he had thrust his fingers repeatedly through that very area, rough in his agony, and the gray seemed a sad mark of that unconscious action.

Grace's breath caught and a dull ache formed in her chest. Silent, staving off the single sob that threatened to erupt from her throat, she backed away from him. All thoughts of food forgotten, she crept from the room and headed back to the stairs, her resolution building with each upward step.

The Rafe she had known, who had laughed often and smiled almost constantly, who had teased her until she had been torn between kicking him in the shins and laughing with him, was still there, hidden under the hard and bitter mask. It must be. He simply needed to eat more and drink less, to be gently and patiently reminded that, although his family was dead, he was still very much alive. That life was as much a blessing as death was a curse. And it was up to her to do it.

There was no question that she would put her entire heart into the task. She had to. Her heart was already with him, had been even before internal demons had turned him inward and cold. It did not matter what he had become. She had been in love with Rafael Marlowe for more years than she could count, and she could not imagine any number of years so extensive nor any demeanor so vile that it could dim the way she felt.

3

H AD HUNGER NOT awakened Grace early the next morning, she might have slept until afternoon. There was no question of light reaching her. She had debated opening the heavy draperies the night before but had decided that it would be far better to oversleep than to be up all night choking on the dust that would surely be released should she touch them.

The sheets had been musty with disuse, but otherwise clean, and she had slept surprisingly well. She rose from the bed and, padding to the window, gingerly parted the drapes. It was snowing and the wan light hinted at mid-morning. If there were in fact any servants about, they would certainly be up and active. With any luck, some sort of breakfast would be available.

She grimaced as she donned her breeches and shirt, both of which were stiff and torn from the night before. Her small valise was presumably still at the inn and she had no hopes of seeing it again. Not that it mattered. The three gowns she had been able to pack had been of the ridiculous pastel variety appropriate for the Season. None had really been suitable for a cold winter, and besides, she detested pink.

An image of the tavern wench, Meg, trying to squeeze her voluptuous figure into those gowns brought a smile to Grace's lips. She wished the other woman the debatable joy of her clothing and decided to quietly raid Rafe's wardrobe. His things would be far too large for her, but she had discovered that men's clothing was tremendously comfortable and she had no desire to give it up at present. A few rolls and tucks would serve as makeshift alterations.

The thought of Rafe clouded her brow. There was no telling how he would behave that morning. All she could reasonably hope for was that he would be sober. Even if he were not feeling especially pleasant, he would have to listen to her. Once he had, she was certain he would agree to let her stay, even if only for a few days.

Another glance out the window reassured her that he would have little choice. The snow was light at the moment, but the deep drifts and buried hedges hinted at a heavy storm during the night. No one would be going anywhere that day.

Cheered immeasurably, she quit the chamber and went off in search of the kitchens again. The study door was closed and she imagined Rafe had somehow found his way up to his own bed, perhaps not so long ago. She kept going and soon found herself in the kitchens.

It was not a heartening sight that greeted her.

Now, Grace knew little about kitchens, having had little call in her life to be in them, but she knew that the preparing of meals caused clutter, not dust. There was no clutter. The dust, however, covered most flat surfaces and, she noticed with some awe, a few upside-down and curved surfaces as well. She had never seen dust on the outside of a ladle before.

So there were no servants. In truth, she was not surprised. Rafe would be more than capable of seeing to himself, and there was no question that he had chosen solitude over any form of company.

She poked about for a while and came up with a reasonable facsimile of breakfast. There were several loaves of bread, some cheese, and a bit of smoked ham. She would have preferred a nice, warm scone, but her stomach did not, at present, much care what she ate. Even if she were able to locate flour and sugar, she would have no idea how to go about baking scones. Eggs, she thought, and perhaps potato meal. She could find nothing resembling a potato.

Eventually she located some tea and a kettle. Yes, she would manage just fine and would have a respectable repast prepared for herself and Rafe in no time.

She piled some wood into the oven, added a few pages from a several-weeks-old *Times*, and lit it. Moments later, a plume of smoke curled outward. When it blossomed into a thick cloud, completely enveloping her, she decided something was amiss. Coughing, she seized a frying pan and stifled the weak flame. She knew as much about stoves as she did about scones, and could only surmise that something was not quite right with the flue.

She opened the second oven door and, dropping to her knees, took a peek inside. It was dark. Scooting forward, she poked at the back. Her fingers sank into what felt very much like a good four inches of dense soot. Finally she located the flue. It felt clear enough. At least, she assumed smoke would be able to wend its way through the accumulated ash there, too. Well, she would have another go at lighting the fire.

"Bloody hell!"

Grace was so startled that she jumped, knocking her head against the roof of the oven and sending a torrent of soot over her head. Then, before she could react, her ankles were snared in a viselike grip and she was hauled backward, landing facedown on the slate floor. She lay where she was for a moment, coughing and wiping ashes from her eyes. Then, looking up, she gave a bright smile.

"Good morning, Rafe."

He did not look particularly cheerful. In fact, he looked awful. There were shadows under his eyes, darker shadows where his morning whiskers shaded his jaw, and his hair was standing up in diabolical licks. From the deep creases and brandy-colored spots, it was rather apparent that he had slept in his coat. He looked terrible, and Grace found him almost impossibly beautiful.

"Damn it, Grace, what in God's name do you think you are doing?"

She sighed. Unfortunate that his present mood seemed no

more promising than the night before. She decided to ignore it. "I was making breakfast, of course. Do you know how to light the stove? There seems to be a problem with the flue."

There was nothing wrong with the blasted stove. The problem, Rafe decided, was with Grace. She quite simply should not have been there.

An ungodly clamor from the kitchen had awakened him. Had he been in his bed, he would not have heard a thing, but he had fallen asleep in the study and had a crick in his neck that quite rivaled the pounding in his head. Now, thanks to Grace's misadventures with various cast-iron objects, his ears were ringing with enough force to wake the dead.

"Grace," he muttered, "you are a menace."

Unperturbed, she rubbed at her blackened nose. "Yes, I know. My family tells me so all the time. But I really would like a cup of tea. Since you have undoubtedly formed an accord of sorts with this stove, do you think you could see to boiling some water, please?"

Having made this blithe request, she reached up, grasped a handful of his coat hem, and pulled herself to her feet. She was dressed as she had been the night before, in breeches and a ridiculously oversize shirt, both of which were now liberally streaked with soot. Between the smudges, Rafe spied a tear in the linen and remembered the grasping hands from which he had pulled her.

"Damnit, Grace, what are you doing here?"

"I am trying to make breakfast. I told you that." She smiled at him. "You may help."

Same smart mouth. Different Grace—somehow.

The heart-shaped face was the same as always, dominated by the large, not-quite-brown eyes that gave her a look of deceptive innocence. Deceptive. Only those who knew her or could see past the eyes to the strong little nose and determined chin would understand her true character. Grace had always been a sweet enough chit, endlessly devoted to her family and friends, but she also had an extremely sharp wit and a streak of obstinance that would do a mule proud.

Right now she was regarding him with a mixture of amiability and open defiance, almost as if she expected him to turn her across his knee, and was daring him even to try. There was no doubt that she needed a good paddling for rigging herself out like a boy and attempting the journey to Newhaven unchaperoned and unprotected.

He was not, however, the one to discipline her for those transgressions. That was up to her father, who, if she were to be believed, was already out of sorts with her. Her presence in his own home was an entirely different matter, and he was full ready to deal with that sorry situation.

First, though, he had to figure out what had changed about her. Whatever it was irked him like a persistent itch. He studied her impassively, starting at her feet. Long slender legs—well, she had always had those. Softly rounded breasts? She had not always had those, but he had all but watched her grow up, and the transformation from sticklike to pleasantly curved had happened some years before. She obviously had not grown much in an upward direction, leaving her, when standing, somewhere in the vicinity of his collarbone. No, it was something else.

Grace fidgeted under his scrutiny, feeling rather as though she were a bug being examined for extra legs. She was fast learning that Rafe's silences were every bit as disconcerting as his curses. When he was ranting, all of his attention must certainly be turned to the matter of creating such varied and expressive epithets. When silent, there was no way of knowing what was going through his mind.

She was fairly convinced that, whatever it was, it could not be agreeable. At the very least, he was planning a way to send her back to Cousin Bernice or worse, to her parents in Staffordshire. Bernice was not a threat, really, as Rafe had no idea of her direction, and Grace was not about to disclose it. Her parents, too, were inaccessible until the snow let up.

Now, as his eyes finally lifted to her face, she was dreading whatever might leap from his lips. She bit her lip and shoved an errant curl from her forehead, sending a new shower of soot onto her shoulders. She blew a large ash from the tip of her nose and waited for him to speak.

It was not at all what she had expected.

"What did you do to your hair?"

She reached up to touch the short curls again. "I—I cut it."

"I can see that," he snapped. "Why?"

"I was traveling as a young man. And it was . . . liberating." It occurred to her that her hair must now be very nearly black with soot. "Is there a mirror nearby?"

"What?"

"A mirror. I want to see what I look like with raven hair. It is all the rage, you know."

He snorted. "Looks like you went at it with boot blacking and hedge clippers."

She ignored that. As far as she was concerned, she had done a very good job, and the style, falling softly over her ears and to the nape of her neck, was as comfortable as it was fashionable. "So does yours." She knew she was embarking on dangerous waters, but she could not help herself. "You look positively hellish, Rafe."

Instead of taking offense at her words or scowling at her unladylike presentation, he gave a short laugh. "I don't doubt that. I am doing without a valet at present."

"Where is your staff?"

He shrugged. "At the London house. Or . . ." He paused, pain distorting his features, and Grace knew he could not force himself even to say the name of the place where his parents had perished.

"Oh, Rafe," she said softly, leaning forward, hand extended. "I am so sorry."

He jerked back, pained expression replaced by icy control. "Thank you," he snapped. "Your condolences are duly noted and appreciated. You can leave for Staffordshire now."

He could tell that his words had stung her. She withdrew

her hand and clasped it in the other, fingers so tightly intertwined that the knuckles showed white, even through the soot. His intention was not to hurt her, not really. He simply wanted her out of his house, and asking her to leave was not going to do the trick. He knew Grace's stubbornness. He also knew that beneath the blithe exterior was a tender, not very self-assured heart. He was aiming for that weakness.

Her recovery, though a visible effort, was impressive. "I have told you that I cannot go to Staffordshire," she said evenly. "Nor can I go anywhere at all today. The roads are surely blocked and the snow shows no sign of stopping."

"Yes, I suppose you are right. Tomorrow then. I will see you to the posting house."

"And send me off on my own?" She gave a dramatic sigh. "That is a bit like flying from the frying pan into the fire."

"And *that* is no concern of mine. I am merely offering to put you back where I found you."

Now the huge eyes were reproachful. "I wonder that you bothered to help me at all."

"So do I, Grace. So do I."

She did not respond, but turned away from him to poke at the veritable forest she had stuffed into the stove. When she reached for the tinderbox, Rafe decided he might as well do something. Otherwise, she would likely burn his house to the ground. He put a third of the wood in the proper place and lit it. He was out of coffee, but tea would do.

He set the kettle to boil and wandered around the kitchen in search of the tea. He knew he had seen it a day or so past. He looked up when Grace gently cleared her throat. She was holding the tea tin. He snatched it from her hand and dumped a portion into the teapot.

As she had expected, he seemed perfectly at home in the kitchen. There were not many dukes, she mused, who would know the difference between tea and tobacco were it not in a cup or a cigar. Idly she wondered if she could steep tobacco leaves and have them served to the Duke of Earith the next time he called on her father. The man was a truly unpleasant piece of work, always bellowing something about the damned useless youth of today. She watched Rafe preparing the tea, filing the method away for future use.

Rafe was not an ordinary duke. He had received the title unwillingly, and she suspected he would like very much to chuck it into the stove and burn it with the wood.

She was learning. Certain topics were not to be mentioned, not if she did not want him to add her to the blaze—or toss her headfirst out the door.

"The way I see it," she said after a time, "you are stuck with me for the time being. I cannot go anywhere, nor do I have anywhere to go. At least until Jason and Aurelie get back. So you basically have two choices. You can cast me out into the snow. . . ." She gave him her best wide-eyed gaze. "I do not recommend that option. I might be persona non grata with my family at the moment, but I do not think they would take too kindly to my becoming an icicle on your lands." She waited for him to respond. He did not. "I take it then that *you* have no such objections to that happening. Are you perhaps in need of a new piece of statuary?"

Something that might have been a faint smile flitted across his lips. "And the second choice?"

"You can put up with me until my brother returns. I assume it will not be above a sennight if they are to be back in time for Christmas. Aurelie, I believe, is planning a grand fete for the family at Havensgate. You will certainly have been invited."

"Yes, I have been."

She gave what she hoped was a confident smile. "It is settled then. I will stay here till they return, then you and I will travel together to Newhaven. You can stay there through the holidays. . . ."

"No."

Her sooty brows rose. "No to which part? You will not remain at Havensgate . . . ?"

"No to all of it, Grace." Tired beyond imagination, despite having slept longer than usual, and irritated beyond measure, Rafe set the teapot down and towered over her. "You will not be staying here. I will not be staying there. I will not be *going* there."

"But why? They are your friends. Jason is your dearest friend."

He gave an expressive snort. "You are very young, Grace, and very naive."

"Perhaps, but that has less than nothing to do with friendship."

He leaned forward, pushing his face close to hers. "On the contrary, it has a great deal to do with friendship. A man reaches a point in his life when he does not need friends. When he does not need anybody. I do not need your brother, with his unsolicited and arrogant advice. Nor do I have any use for his wife's cloying sympathy." He leaned closer, so close that his breath ruffled the fine curls at her temple. "And I certainly do not need you here, in my sight and under my feet. Can you comprehend all that, Grace?"

Under his fierce gaze, her eyes darkened from gold to deep amber. Her lower lip trembled and she set her firm little chin—staving off, he thought, the tears his words were bound to inspire. She opened her mouth, but whatever words were there stilled on her tongue. The workings of the corner clock seemed unnaturally loud suddenly, and as the seconds ticked by, Rafe felt his conscience edging up from the black depths to which he had relegated it, whispering of his boorishness.

At last she spoke. "I understand perfectly," she said in a tight little voice.

Then, just as he was certain the dam would break and she would begin to cry, she did something completely different and utterly unexpected. She drew back her dainty hand, fisted it, and drove it with all her strength into his jaw.

He staggered backward, more from surprise than the force of her blow, and landed heavily against the edge of the stove. The thing had heated quickly and he jerked away as the metal burned through his breeches. Then, before he could fully recover, she bounded forward and flew at him, hand still fisted. Thinking that she was going to have another poke at his face, he raised his hands to chin level. But she aimed lower, thumping her fist into his chest. He was already off balance and landed awkwardly, half in and half out of the woodbin.

Too stunned yet to be angry, he stared up into her flushed face. "And what was that for?"

"That," she snapped, "was for what you said about Jason and Aurelie!"

"I beg your pardon?"

"As well you should! Theirs, too. If Jason has been offering you advice, it is because he cares about you and is concerned. As for Aurelie, I cannot believe you would call her sympathy cloying. She is the most intuitive, gracious person I know, and would no more hover where she is unwanted than she would ignore someone in pain."

"Damnit, Grace . . ."

"You have insulted two of your dearest friends when I am certain they have been all that is loyal." She glared down at him from her negligible height. Just as he opened his mouth to tell her just what she could do with her righteous anger, she drew back her foot and kicked him in the shin. "They *value* you, you hammerheaded dolt!"

She broke off then, mouth compressed in what he thought was half fury and half pain. Her unprotected toes were far more vulnerable than his shin and must be stinging miserably. As the torrent of her pique waned, his anger rose.

"Sit down, Grace." She did not. *"Sit down!"* She dropped into a chair like a stone. He studied her face and decided that, far from being obedient, she had merely used his shouted command as an excuse to get off her injured foot. He took advantage of her silence to lever himself out of the woodbin. "You will cease these absurd attacks on my person. Is that clear?"

She gave a distinctly unladylike grunt.

"No fist, no feet, no snow. No sharp tongue."

Another grunt.

"I shall take that as an affirmative. Now, have you any idea why I am putting an end to these fits? No? Or are you merely subjecting me to the even more childish act of silent defiance? Well, perhaps you think it is because I do not like to be clouted. That is certainly true, but not the reason. Nor is it because you have the capacity to hurt me." He leaned toward her. "Your blows have the effect of an irksome gnat. The reason, Grace, that you will not attack me again is that it will serve no purpose other than to annoy me and possibly cause damage to whatever part of your fragile anatomy you use as a weapon. You see, nothing you can do or say is going to change how I feel. I do not give a damn about Jason and Aurelie's concern. Nor about yours."

At that moment, Grace fully believed him.

"As to the matter of your presence here," he continued coldly, "you are correct in asserting that nothing can be done today. Tomorrow, however, you will be on that coach."

Her fury dissipated into relief, and it was all she could do not to grin her triumph. He must have sensed it, for his frown deepened and he snapped, "It is a reprieve, Grace, not a welcome. You will stay out of my way for the remainder of the day."

"All right," she replied innocently, "though perhaps you ought to tell me what you will be doing and where—so I can avoid getting in your way, of course." He stared at her suspiciously—as well, she thought, he should. "Really, Rafe—" she gave her best wry smile "—I am gladly accepting the reprieve. Even if for only a day. I assure you that quarantine in your home is far better than what I stand to face in mine."

He did not look fully convinced, but after a time he gave a negligent shrug. "I will be in the study, doing whatever I see fit. You will be elsewhere, doing something else."

Oh, yes, I certainly shall. "Fine. I will see you at luncheon, then?"

"Luncheon?" An alien word, it seemed.

"You know, the midday meal? I shall even prepare it. You cannot drink *all* your meals, Rafe."

"I eat alone."

"Not today, you do not."

He scowled at her. "Are you so confident in your temporary residence here that you feel justified in giving orders?"

"Not at all. I am merely trying to make a compromise."

He should have known that her easy acquiescence was too good to be true. "A compromise?"

"Yes. I will stay out of your way for the remainder of the morning if you will join me for luncheon."

"And if I do not?"

"Really, Rafe, do you wish me to stay? I can always find ways to occupy myself, you know. And you can just ignore me, as you and Jason used to do when I was a child."

Rafe thought back more than a decade and remembered ignoring her. Or rather, he remembered how utterly impossible it had been for Jason and him to ignore her when she wanted her presence noted. The most vivid recollection was of a day they had tried to go riding without her. The rest of the memory involved a string tied taut at ankle level across the stable door and a deluge of rotten apples from the loft above.

He almost smiled.

It occurred to him that she would be very stupid indeed to cross him at present. And Grace was anything but stupid. They were alone in the house, alone in the whole county, for all practical purposes. She was grown and no longer protected by the immunity granted to willful children. True, she was female, and thus protected by some similar code, but he did not think of her as a woman. She was an unmitigated nuisance and he had known her too long. He knew her waywardness and her misguided wit. He also knew her persistence.

"All right, Grace," he said wearily. "Luncheon." She was on her feet in an instant, heading for the door. "Where are you going?" he asked, not really wanting to know but convinced that knowledge would somehow be to his benefit.

"Why, to the cold cellar, of course. I did not think of it earlier. You do have a cold cellar, do you not?"

"Yes, Grace. There is a cold cellar, though I have no idea what you hope to find. . . ."

"Splendid." She continued toward the door. He started in the opposite direction. "Oh, Rafe?" He paused. "Do you not wish for some breakfast? The bread might be a bit hard. . . . No? Some tea, then? I believe I can handle it from here. A nice cup of tea . . ."

Rafe snarled. And headed back to the study and, with any luck, a bottle of brandy.

He did not want to think about what Grace might do to his kitchen. He did not want to think about Grace at all just then. He was far more concerned with trying to remember whether he had consumed all of the liquor in his haven.

4

I T WAS MOST likely a very good thing indeed that he was
not concerning himself with Grace at the moment, for he
would undoubtedly have burst a blood vessel had he seen
what she was doing. Instead of seeking out the cellar as announced, she had crept upstairs. She had located a hunting
knife in a hall cabinet and had already sawed a good foot
off one leg of the breeches taken from his armoire. She
was, at present, hard at work on the second. There was
little she could do about the waist without thread and
needle, but the cravat she had purloined would serve as a
perfectly good belt.

Some time later, having managed to control the stove
long enough to heat bathing water, she surveyed herself in
the cheval glass and smiled ruefully. She looked like a child
dressed up in adult clothes. Even with the sleeves rolled up,
the cashmere coat swallowed her, falling nearly to her
knees. And the stockings, pilfered as well, went nearly up
to her thighs under the loose breeches yet still managed to
bag comically at her ankles.

Well, she was after comfort rather than appearance, and
she was quite comfortable. The ease of breathing and motion that men's clothing provided made her cringe at the
thought of ever again having to don layers of petticoats and
the dreaded corsets. She imagined a good many men of the
ton did wear corsets and stays much like those she had left
at Crowborough. It was no secret that Prinny did. The
squeaking noise that inevitably preceded his entrance left

no doubt as to what he wore under his exquisitely tailored but capacious coats.

There was no such apparatus in Rafe's wardrobe, not that she had expected any. He had never carried much spare flesh, his size due only to bone and muscle, but he was thin now, almost alarmingly so. His shoulders were still broad, his thighs still powerful, but there were hollows under the cutting cheekbones and, she imagined, his collarbone. Her reflection blushed at the thought of actually viewing Rafe's collarbone. Grace stuck her tongue out at her demure half, grinning when it gamely returned the salute.

Yes, she thought, more food was in order for Rafe. She would see to that. She wanted very much to do something about the drink as well, but had no idea where to begin. In her experience, there were three things men took very seriously: their money, their horses, and their drinking. Of course, there were men like her brother who placed their wives at the top of the list, but this was Rafe, not Jason. Rafe would, she was certain, if given the choice between rescuing her or a cask from a sinking ship, risk his own life for the liquor.

She gave a last grimace at her reflection. It was a shame she had had to wash the soot from her hair. She had thought herself quite a dashing picture with black curls, rather vivid and exotic. Now she was just her familiar, unexotic self. She quit the room and headed downstairs. The study door was closed, but she crept by nonetheless, not wanting Rafe to think she had broken their agreement.

True to her promise, she stayed away from Rafe for the remainder of the morning. The cold cellar yielded some rather rigid but usable vegetables. Apparently someone had stocked the lodge at the beginning of winter. Grace arranged her finds on the kitchen table and tried to identify each piece. She was not certain, but she thought there were a few turnips among the potatoes and carrots. She could not remember ever having seen an uncooked turnip.

Nor did she have the foggiest idea how to cook one. She scolded herself for having spent far more time in her father's library than in the more practical areas of the house. Not that she would have been allowed to spend much time in the kitchens, but she was a quick study and would undoubtedly have learned something reasonably domestic. As it was, she was proficient in Greek, Latin, Italian, and French. She had no idea how to prepare coq au vin, but she had read all of Molière's plays in their original form. Having read *The Misanthrope* might serve her well, considering Rafe's current state of mind, but one could not, unfortunately, eat words.

She smiled slightly at the thought. Rafe had said a good many words recently that she would delight in making him eat. A bit of crow would be lovely as well. She could picture him with a black feather sticking out from between his teeth.

Well, there was no crow to be baked, only a pile of motley vegetables and the food she had gathered originally. She rolled up her sleeves. Any woman who could read four languages could prepare a simple meal.

"Now, you behave," she said to the stove, and reached for what might have been a turnip.

He was not coming.

Grace propped her elbows on the table and sighed. He was not coming. The mantel clock had chimed two a good quarter hour past, and her exhilaration had waned with each passing minute.

He had known to be there. She had tapped at the study door earlier to inform him of the time. He had not replied, precisely, but his grunt had seemed enough of an affirmative. And he had promised to dine with her. In all the years she had known him, despite all his past blitheness, Rafe had never broken a promise. But then, she reminded herself, he was an entirely different creature now. Promises might mean nothing at all.

As far as she was concerned, a deal was a deal and she had kept her end of it. In fact, she had done more than that. She glanced around the dining room, cleared of dustcloths now and illuminated by a fire in the hearth and candles in the sconces. There were more candles on the table, their flames reflected in the glossy china and freshly polished silver. Rafe's hunting box might have been in a sorry state, but it was well appointed. Remnants of happier days.

She had done the cleaning herself. Never having had call to polish silver before, she had been startled by how laborious the task actually was. Knives were the hardest; they had a way of slithering out of her hands as she tried to remove the slick polish. When the fourth had shot from her grasp and clattered to the kitchen floor, she had considered abandoning the task. There were, after all, only the two of them dining. At that point she had grimly reminded herself that a job done right was a job done thoroughly. She had finally given up at six sets.

It had taken her a good half hour to remove the polish from under her nails, another hour to get the room set up to her satisfaction. By the time she had arranged the meal on the table, she was tired, hungry, and growing grumpier by the second.

If Rafe was not going to come to her, she would just have to go get him.

The thought that he might well be unconscious somewhere, stewed to the gills, put a momentary damper on her determination. Supper with an alert Rafe might prove a test of her wits and fortitude, but a meal with him propped up in his chair would be nothing at all.

It was not fortitude that settled the matter. Nor was it even her persistent nature. It was, in the end, her heart that set her in motion. She simply wanted, *needed* to see him, regardless of his state. Taking a deep breath, she planted her hands flat on the table and pushed herself to her feet.

The door slammed open, banging loudly against the wall.

Startled, Grace dropped back into her seat and watched, wide-eyed, as Rafe stumbled in, barking his hip against the high sideboard. Her heart sank as she watched him fight for balance. It was touch and go for a moment before he planted a hand atop the sideboard and steadied himself into relative uprightness. He was not unconscious, after all, but he looked well on his way.

"Damn and rot," he muttered, rubbing at his injured leg. "Bloody rug nearly killed me!" He shot a baleful gaze at the floor behind him.

Then, to her astonishment, he straightened and made his way to his seat, his stride firm and directed. He settled himself in his chair, smoothly unfolded his napkin, and deposited it in his lap. His cravat was tied, if not precisely pristine, and he appeared to have run something—his fingers rather than a comb, perhaps—through his hair. Had she not known better, Grace might have thought him sober.

"What are you gaping at, Grace? I have not eaten anything today, so I cannot have food on my face."

Good heavens—he *was* sober. Or at least not completely cup-shot.

"I—I thought," she stammered, "I did not expect . . ."

"That I would show? I very nearly didn't."

No, that was not what she had been thinking, but she was so glad he had come. "Why did you?" she could not resist asking.

"Damned if I know." He surveyed the elaborate place setting with something between confusion and distaste. Distaste took over when his gaze fastened on the glass beside his plate. "What is this?"

"Water."

"I know it is water, damnit!"

To his annoyance, Grace merely tilted her head to the side and studied him through wide, topaz eyes. "Then why did you ask?"

When he snarled, she shrugged and lifted the lid from a tureen. Rafe wrinkled his nose. Whatever it was smelled like charred wood. It greatly resembled charred wood, too, when she ladled some into a bowl.

He accepted his portion with more curiosity than decorum and prodded at a large coallike lump in the center. It sank out of sight, then bobbed back up with impressive force. "Good God, Grace, what *is* this?"

She leaned toward him. "I believe that is a turnip, though I cannot be certain. I have little experience with turnips."

"A turnip." He pushed it aside. The rest of the concoction was distressingly similar. "Just what do you call this particular culinary effort?"

"It is a vegetable stew. I thought to add some of the ham, but I have heard that too much meat is not good for one's constitution." He saw her wince as he held another piece aloft. "That is a carrot."

Rafe tried to return the dubiously gray carrot to the morass. It clung tenaciously to his fork.

"I know it does not look terribly appetizing, but I have tasted it, and it is not all that bad." As if to prove the point, Grace stabbed her fork into her own bowl and lifted a piece of what could have been another carrot to her lips. Rafe heard a distinct crunching.

"Carrot?" he queried.

"No," was the mumbled reply. "Potato."

He could not help it. He gave a choked laugh. She glared at him and took another forkful. There was no crunching, but her eyes widened comically and she reached for her water.

"Had you not taken the first bite, m'lady, I would have thought you were trying to poison me."

Grace took heart at the laughter, despite the fact that it was not a particularly friendly sound. She was convinced that he would be ever so much more pleasant once he got some food in his belly. "Really, if you would but try a bite . . ."

"Damn it, Grace, I will not eat coal!"

"A scone, then?" She lifted the cloth from another dish. "I made my own potato meal for them. Yes, I know, they are a rather odd shape, but they were not nearly so flat when I put them in the oven."

Rafe took one look at the dark brown discs and shuddered. "Potato meal," he muttered to the tablecloth.

"Yes. Very enterprising of me, was it not?"

He did not look impressed.

She shrugged and dipped into her stew again, avoiding the potatoes. They were a bit hard and starchy in the center. She saw Rafe's eyes stray to the sideboard. She had deliberately avoided cleaning the crystal decanters there, but had not moved them. Now she wished she had.

"Are you certain you do not wish to try a scone? I added some molasses as well. At least, I believe it was molasses. . . ." She sighed as he rose from his seat and stalked toward the sideboard. "I really wish you would not, Rafe."

He seized a decanter and returned to his seat. Then he reached for his glass, intending, she assumed, to empty the water somewhere—perhaps onto her own person—and refill it with the liquor. She grabbed the glass and pulled it out of reach.

"Damnit, Grace—"

"You know," she interrupted, desperate for any distraction, "I have considered changing my name to Damnit-grace. That way, whenever I was around my brothers, I could believe they were actually addressing rather than cursing me." Rafe stared at her and she gave him a patient smile. "You see, they seem to feel an overwhelming need to put unrelated words in front of my name. I would spare them the trouble." She tilted her head and pursed her lips in a thoughtful pout. "Though if I were to take my mother and sister into account, I would have to choose Reallygrace, instead. Same tone of voice, same implication. More genteel word."

Again that damned smile. Rafe ground his teeth and tried to think of something to say that did not begin with *Damnit, Grace.* He concentrated on her sleeve, which narrowly avoided dragging in the stew each time she dipped her fork. Something about the russet cashmere seemed familiar. "Damnit, Grace, that is my coat you are wearing!"

"Why, yes, it is. And your shirt and breeches. I had to shorten them a bit, of course. But my own clothing was quite ruined."

51

"That coat," he snapped, "is a Weston."

"Really?" She surveyed the fabric appreciatively. "I should have guessed. It is very fine."

It was, Rafe realized, a far finer coat than the one he was wearing, and in far better condition. He had never paid much attention to dress, but had always demanded freshness. He had been wearing the present coat for a good three days. Bathing was one thing, laundry quite another. He glanced down. The creases were familiar. The potato-sized smudge was not. It took him a moment to realize that he was wearing a print of Grace's hand. He remembered that she had levered herself off the floor earlier with a grip on the fabric. He wondered if the soot would wash out. Then he wondered if one washed wool.

He sighed. And poked at another lump in the bowl. This time, when it bubbled back to the surface, it was accompanied by a rather interesting noise. He almost chuckled.

"You might want to look away, Grace. You don't want to watch me feeding your stew to the dog."

"You do not have a dog, Rafe."

"I shall have to remember to get one. A big hairy beast with fangs."

He thought he heard her mutter something about fleas. Then she said, "Have a scone."

"Shut up, Grace."

"Ah, a variation. Though I do not think it has quite the cadence of Damnitgrace."

As she watched, drinking in the hard planes of his face, a curve appeared. She blinked. What began as a tiny crevice beside his mouth slowly turned into a distinct arc. He was very nearly smiling.

She was entranced.

In fact, she was so consumed by the sight that she forgot to object when he downed his water in a single swallow and refilled the glass with amber liquid. He did not toss it back, however, but sipped meditatively.

"You are an unmitigated jade, Grace. And you are a miserable cook."

"Yes, I am," she replied, unoffended. "But I suppose I will improve with practice."

"Heaven preserve us."

He was still almost smiling as he rose to his feet and disappeared through the doorway. He was back soon, bearing a loaded tray. On it was the bread, cheese, and ham. He plunked the thing down on the table, resumed his seat, and took another sip of his whiskey. "I," he announced after a moment, "am a smashing chef."

She surveyed the cold collation and sighed. "You have always been smashing at everything you do, Rafe."

Pushing her bowl aside, she helped herself to a selection from the tray. The bread was a bit hard, but not too stale, and she assumed Rafe was at least managing to shop on occasion. A few bites removed the charcoal taste from her mouth. A few more quieted her stomach.

She noticed that Rafe had not served himself. "Are you not going to eat?"

He shrugged, then carelessly filled his plate. The decanter, she noticed, was within easy reach of his hand. "Tell me something, Grace."

"Yes?"

"What did you do?"

She speared a bit of cheese and examined it for mold. It seemed all right. "What did I do . . . ?"

"To get yourself sent to Cousin Bernadette."

"Bernice."

"Bernice." She saw his eyes stray toward the decanter. His glass was still more than half full. "Well? I imagine it must have been a coup to end all coups. Your parents have never been so drastic in their measures before, and you have given them ample opportunity."

Grace did not particularly appreciate having her many transgressions thrown in her face. As far as she was concerned, she had done nothing truly awful in her nineteen years, and was past tired of being regarded as something less than seemly.

"You need to change your coat," she commented, deftly

changing the subject. "That one looks ready for the rag bin."

"Fine. Give me the one you are wearing."

"I think not, if you do not mind. I am enjoying its warmth immensely."

"I am certain you are. You really have made quite an art of making yourself comfortable as an unwanted guest, though I hardly think you amenable to that position."

"Really, Rafe. I have become quite used to it. With the exception of my brother's home, I am an unwanted presence everywhere lately."

He stared at her intently for a moment, eyes narrowed. "I don't doubt that. Your pestiness seems to have increased with the years." He sighed as she merely shrugged and poked at the bread on her plate. "You cannot honestly expect me to believe that your parents will not have you."

"Of course they will have me . . ."

"Well, then, what the devil—"

"For a time. Then they will undoubtedly send me off somewhere—a great distance, I would imagine. It would be decidedly difficult for me to escape the Colonies. I suppose I could try, but the next Coventry would undoubtedly be someplace like China, and I am afraid my Chinese is a bit weak. I should have a very hard time trying to commandeer a hack. Assuming they have hacks, of course. I really cannot see myself fleeing on an elephant." She gazed up at him, her eyes deceptively innocent. "Do you know if they have them in China?"

"Hacks?" he queried acerbically.

"Elephants," she shot back.

Rafe ground his teeth. "What do you want from me, Grace?"

She took a healthy bite of bread and chewed, her face thoughtful. Then she took a sip of water. Rafe waited. After a moment, she speared a bit of cheese, following it with a forkful of ham. He got tired of waiting. "Grace," he said warningly.

"Sanctuary."

54

"What?"

"Sanctuary. Shelter from the storm, port in a tempestuous sea . . ."

"I know what the word means."

"Yes, I rather thought you would."

He sighed and started counting. He made it to six. "Do you really expect me to believe your life has become so intolerable that you need sanctuary from your own family?"

The following silence lasted a good deal longer than his six-count.

"Not as a matter of comparison," she replied softly.

His fist hit the table and he saw her wince and edge back in her seat. *Wise girl,* he thought. *Learn to assess the consequences before you speak and you might not end up in China.*

He should have known better than to think she would remain cowed. She straightened and her delicate chin went up several notches. Her gaze, however, remained slightly wary, as if she were waiting for him to shatter either the crystal or her eardrums with a stinging tirade.

He did neither.

Instead, he plied the bottle, pouring until a few amber drops spilled over the edge of the glass and spattered on the tablecloth. Then he took a bite of bread, following it with a glass-draining swallow of whiskey, a bit of cheese, and some of the ham. When at last he spoke, it was with a voice devoid of anger—or any emotion.

"I am in no position to help you, you know. Nor do I have the inclination."

She looked thoughtful. "I cannot comment on your inclination other than to say that I believe you. I can, however, safely say that you are indeed in a position to help me. I need to stay away from Staffordshire till I can go to Newhaven."

"There must be somewhere else you can stay." He followed her gaze to the snow-shrouded window. And sighed. "So what was it, Grace?"

She knew better than to pretend she did not know what

he meant. It was a fair enough question, to be sure, but she really did not want to discuss the mess that had culminated in her arrival at the Lewes posting house. Not yet.

"Nothing worth mentioning, and nothing that should cause you worry. I did not set—" she bit her tongue, horrified at what she had been about to say: *I did not set fire to anything* "—myself to anything as dramatic as pursuing a tryst with the stableboy."

Her blush deepened at the impropriety of the rushed words.

Rafe leaned back in his seat, tapping the arm of his chair with long fingers. "And what do you think your family will say of your presence here? The situation is a Society mama's nightmare: dissolute male, no chaperone for miles, not even a maid."

Again she spoke without thinking. "What rot! Why, you would never compromise me. Even Jason, staid as he is, would not be concerned. Everyone knows I am as safe with you as if I were family—"

His fist hit the table once more, sending one scone skittering from the plate to land on the floor. It made an audible sound against the thick carpet. She flinched. It seemed she was singularly incapable of keeping away from the subject of family. Wishing she could command the floor to open up and swallow her, she peeked at him to see just how furious he was. It was not such a terrifying sight. He merely looked tired.

"You are not family, Grace. Nor would anyone with a grain of sense trust me with any young female relation. Not even Jason." His fingers curved, clawlike, against the tablecloth. "Your safety notwithstanding, you have put your reputation in severe jeopardy by being here. Unless, of course," he amended, "you managed to shred it at an earlier point in time."

"I . . . no, I . . ."

"Face it, m'lady, even if I get you on that carriage before I strangle you, you have dug yourself a ponderous hole.

56

What in the hell are you going to say to your family once you are back in their oh-so-fond embrace?"

"I do not think I shall have to say much of anything, actually. You certainly would not tell them. Would you?" Her hopeful gaze was too much.

"You should know by now that your situation is of no concern to me, Grace, but damnation, use your brain for once! Your absence from your cousin's home will not have gone unreported, no matter how much the woman dislikes you. It does not matter where you have been. As far as the world is concerned, just by not being where you are supposed to be, you have been somewhere unforgivable. Add to that the fact that I do not want you here, and you have yourself in a position for which I certainly do not envy you."

"You really are being a beast, Rafael."

"Well, you are no Beauty, Grace, so do not expect a fairy-tale ending."

He studied her closely in the ensuing silence. She was looking a bit pale, her eyes wide in her face. Ordinarily Rafe would have expected tears. A young woman in her position would be bound to cry, if not fall into a dramatic swoon. But Grace was not just any young woman, and he knew better than to expect anything resembling normal behavior. Still, he waited for her to show fear, desperation—simple *anxiety*, for Christ's sake.

She smiled. Not with her usual sparkle, perhaps, but it was a smile nonetheless.

"It is settled, then. I will stay here till I can go to Jason and Aurelie. After all, as you have said, it does not matter where I am. I'm in the soup regardless. Thank you, Rafe, for solving the matter so logically."

He felt his jaw dropping. He could not possibly have heard her aright. He drew a deep breath, the blistering tirade forming itself on his tongue. And was astounded to find that he wanted to laugh instead. It was not a comfortable feeling.

Seizing the decanter, he pushed himself to his feet and

glared at her. "Luncheon is over, Grace. I am going to the study. You," he added fiercely, "are going elsewhere until morning. Then you are leaving for Staffordshire."

She was still smiling when he spun on his heel and left the room.

Her smile lasted until the door slammed shut behind him. Then she gave a quiet groan and let her head drop forward to rest on the table. "Damnit, Grace," she said miserably, "you really are a fool."

All she wanted was to make Rafe happy, and all she seemed capable of doing was making him angry.

Self-pity was rarely part of her character, but she felt it looming now. How difficult could it possibly be, she wondered, to have a bit of peace and harmony in one's life? Apparently it was far harder than the fairy tales told. Rafe was quite right; she was not a Beauty. He had lumbered off to his lair, bottle in hand, and it seemed she had none of the requisite traits to lure him out.

She could not even manage to feed him into complacency. Allowing herself one exaggerated sigh, she leaned over and retrieved the scone from the floor. Easily as large as her hand, the thing reminded her of a discus she had seen gripped in the hand of a Greek statue. She had no doubt it would fly a good distance, and probably fell anyone who should have the misfortune to get in its way. She dumped the scone into the now-congealed stew and set herself to clearing the table. She knew as little about cleaning kitchens as she did about using them, but she had nothing better to do until bedtime than learn.

5

Hot. So hot. Flames reaching out like greedy hands to seize the two figures at his side just as he was pulling them through the door. Dragging them back into the inferno, leaving him . . . Leaving him.

Rafe jerked upright, sending the already tangled bedclothes sliding toward the floor. "God," he groaned, burying his face in his hands. "Oh, God."

It was instinctive, calling out like that, a habit learned in childhood and never quite lost, even now when he had ceased to believe in anything divine. The dream never failed to invoke such a reaction. He had been having it for nearly a year, and the variations were so small that they were gone seconds after he awoke. Always he got his parents out of the house and always he lost them.

He had long since lost count of the number of times the dream had haunted him. He had thought early on that if he drank enough, induced unconsciousness instead of sleep, he could avoid it. He had been wrong. On those times when it made its way through the liquor, he had woken just as shaky and sweaty as ever, with the added misfortune of inevitably being sick as a dog.

He was weak and chilled now as he reached for the sheet, using it to dry his sweat-slicked skin. Through his window he could see the moon, a faint crescent in the dawn sky. As always after the dream, he climbed from the bed, knowing sleep would elude him. Until the past year, the only sunrises he had seen were those witnessed as he made his drunken way home after a night of revelry. The drunken bit had not necessarily changed; the prelude had. He gave a grim smile and headed across the room for the brandy decanter.

The table was empty. He had come to bed empty-handed after an evening spent not in the bottle but deep in thought. He cursed silently—not at Grace, who, with visions of his own lost life, had consumed his thoughts, but at the necessity of going downstairs to the whiskey decanter he had left in the library. The nearly full decanter.

He might not have felt like crawling into the bottle earlier, but he certainly did at present. The study was as good a place to get sotted in as his bedroom. He knew, having tried out nearly every chamber in the lodge.

His dressing gown was somewhere across the room, and he turned away from the table to fetch it. He had just lifted it from the floor when a draft flitted over his naked back.

"Oh. Oh, my."

Grace. He spun about, clutching the dressing gown in front of him, to find her framed in the doorway, gripping a candle so tightly that he could see it bending in her grasp. She had her eyes squeezed shut and her mouth twisted up in the most eloquent expression of distress he had ever seen.

He shoved his arms into the sleeves of the robe and knotted the belt with unnecessary firmness. "Damnit, Grace," he snapped, "what are you doing here?"

"I—I heard you cry out," she replied, eyes still welded shut. "It was loud enough to wake me and I was concerned."

He was not surprised to hear he had shouted aloud in his sleep. The anguish had certainly been strong enough. "Did your mother not teach you to knock before entering a chamber? For God's sake, open your eyes." She did, slowly, and he immediately regretted the command. The candlelight made her eyes seem larger than ever, and turned them a thoroughly feline gold. "Hell. Did your mother not teach you never to enter a strange man's bedchamber?" She opened her mouth, and he could see the words forming—that he was hardly a stranger. "*Any* man's bedchamber!"

"I did knock," she said after a moment. "Twice."

He must have been so deep in his miserable thoughts that he had not heard her. His first impulse was to tell her to take herself back to bed that very instant. But he did not. Not once in the ten months had he wished for anything but to be left alone. At that moment, however, the presence of another human being seemed like a very good thing indeed.

"Are you all right?" she asked.

"Perfectly. I stubbed my toe getting out of bed." He glared at her. "You cannot stay here."

Grace tried to decide which statement to address first. He was lying about his toe. What she had heard was the anguished cry of emotional distress, not physical. She chose to let it go for the time being, deciding it would be prudent to wait before coaxing him into talking about it.

The second assertion was far simpler—or at least less dangerous. "I cannot leave. You must keep the weather in mind." She mentally crossed her fingers, hoping he had not noticed the snow had stopped sometime during the night. "I have no choice but to stay here."

"I was not referring to the house, Grace. I was referring to my bedchamber." As she sorted through the words, he walked toward her, pointing to the hall. "Out."

"But . . ."

"*Out.* If you insist on plaguing me with your presence, I will meet you downstairs in the study in ten minutes." Then he gave her a reasonably gentle shove and shut the door in her face.

She allowed herself a few skips of pleasure. Far from taking offense at his abrupt words, she rejoiced in them. For the briefest of moments, she had spied a flash of the old Rafe behind his eyes.

She heard the door click. "Grace."

She stopped in her tracks, heart sinking. He had changed his mind.

"Put on some decent clothes," he snapped, and the door clicked again.

She looked down at her garb and blushed. She had been sleeping in one of the fine cambric shirts pilfered, of course, from his wardrobe. When his agonized cry had jerked her awake, she had been too startled and worried to pay much attention to what she was wearing. Her blush deepened. While the shirt covered a good deal more than any chemise, the rolled sleeves coming to her wrists and the hem flapping about her knees, it left much of her legs quite bare.

As she hurried down the hallway, she could almost hear her mother's voice.

Your sense of modesty, Grace, is utterly disgraceful.

"Oh, stow it, Mother," she muttered.

She would risk a goodly dose of disgrace and any amount of embarrassment to spend even a minute with Rafe. She would risk almost anything for one genuine smile.

He was not smiling when she entered the library some nine minutes later. He was scowling fiercely and sending a string of bitter curses toward the hearth as he tried to set flame to the tinder.

"May I help you?" she asked, and he started visibly.

"Must you sneak up on me like that?"

"I was not aware I was sneaking," she replied, unperturbed. "I have never been much of a sneaker. In fact, Mother delights in telling me that I approach with all the silence of a stampeding pachyderm."

"Your mother," he announced tersely as he plied the flint again, "has always been inordinately fond of animal analogies." With his back to her, she could not see his expression as he continued. "She once told me the noise Jason and I made in the gallery put her in mind of a pack of howler monkeys."

"One of her favorites," Grace said, remembering the frequency with which that particular pronouncement had sounded during the Granville children's early years. "How old were you?"

"Twenty," was the bland reply. "Has your mother ever seen a howler monkey?"

She laughed. "Not to my knowledge. What were you doing?"

"Trust me, you do not want to know."

"Oh, but I do."

He looked up briefly. "Allow me to rephrase that. I do not want to tell you."

A vast number of possibilities ran through Grace's mind. His expression forbade further pressing, so she reluctantly held her tongue. He was back at the flint and steel again. She approached and crouched down beside him.

"Perhaps we ought to summon my mother now."

"Good Lord, why?"

"Come now, Rafe. We have a perfectly marvelous animal analogy available here. We would simply point her toward the hearth and vex her into huffing and puffing."

He said nothing for some time. Then, as she watched, a semblance of a smile curved his lips. "Ah, yes . . ."

"The Dragon Lady," they said together.

"I had forgotten," he mused.

"How could you? It is common knowledge, after all, that you were the one who dubbed her as such."

"Are you daft?"

"Not at all," she said, fighting the urge to wink. "Common knowledge."

His eyes narrowed. "Why, you little minx. Now I know why she refused to speak to me for my entire nineteenth year. In the single, blistering tirade she loosed before her extended silence, the word 'dragon' appeared frequently. At the time, I merely thought she had taken an uncustomary dip into the sherry. Now I know better."

Grace gave her best guileless smile. "Whatever do you mean?"

"She must have overheard you using that charming name and taken you to task for it. You foisted the blame onto me. I should have known."

"Perhaps." Now she grinned. "Mother should definitely have known. I was forever shrugging off my transgressions. What I would like to know is what you did to place yourself in her poor graces if she was so quick to let me get away with it."

"Nothing I can recall." Rafe sat back on his haunches. "What *I* would like to know is what I did to deserve being made a scapegoat."

"Oh, nothing I can recall. . . . Of course, it might have had something to do with a game of hide-and-go-seek. . . ."

"Hide-and . . ." Rafe blinked as he suddenly recalled the scene. "That must have happened months before the Dragon Lady incident!"

"I was waiting for the perfect opportunity to strike back."

"For God's sake, Grace, we were going to the Cannock Stud."

"You could have taken me with you," she shot back promptly.

"We damn well could not! We were going to see one of your father's mares bred. Hardly a place for a little girl."

"Well, you could have explained that to me."

"If I remember correctly, we did." Rafe found himself falling easily into the banter. "You refused to listen."

"You sent me off to hide and then you left."

"It seemed the best way. No muss, no fuss."

"I sat in the marrow bin for an hour, waiting for you to find me!"

The image was too much, young Grace surrounded by vegetables and grinning to herself over the cleverness of her hiding place. What began as a hesitant chuckle soon blossomed into a full-throated laugh. Her expression quickly showed the high pique of a thwarted child, and he thought she might cosh him over the head with the fireplace poker. After a moment, however, her lips spread into a rueful smile and she began laughing with him.

The picture of Grace-in-the-bin faded, to be replaced by one of her mother, her usually cream-smooth complexion marred by spots of angry color as she railed at him. If memory served, she had done her best to banish him from her drawing room, house, and county, all the while swatting at him with her tiny lace handkerchief. Jason, blast him, had been skulking in the background, holding his sides in amusement.

When his own sides began to ache, Rafe took a steadying breath and wiped at his eyes. "You have provided me with countless hours of drama, if not amusement, through the years, Grace."

"I have done my best," was her soft reply.

He studied her piquant face and found himself responding to the warmth he saw there. Her presence had somehow managed to banish the night's ghosts, and for the first time in as far back as he could remember, he felt calm and even marginally content.

He did not object when she removed the flint from his hands. Her first several attempts were no more successful than his had been, but at last there was a spark and the kindling went up in a bright blaze.

"And I was all ready to summon Mother," she said, grinning in self-congratulation.

"God forbid."

The swelling flames picked out the deeper strands of gold in her hair. He found himself thinking of a mask he had once seen in Athens, the face of a goddess—Aphrodite, perhaps—the sculpted features framed by golden coils. Idly he reached out and slipped his finger into one of the short curls at her cheek, pulling until it was straight. He let go then and it sprang back into its original shape as if by a will of its own.

"When did you grow up, Gracie?"

His hand was still hovering near her cheek, and she wanted very much to tilt her face into his palm. She had done it; she had made him smile. Now all she had to do was make him love her.

"I am glad you finally noticed," she said on a sigh. "I do not think I could have stood forever being eleven years old in your eyes."

He dropped his hand and rose to his feet. "Nineteen," he remarked, "is not so very different from eleven."

"Goodness, you do not believe that."

"No, I don't suppose I do." He looked thoughtful. "Not nearly as different as thirty from twenty-two."

She sensed that she was losing him to his melancholy. When his eyes strayed to the decanter on the desk, she hastened to distract him again. "I should like to be thirty, I think."

He took his eyes from the brandy. "And why is that?"

"No more pink."

"Pink?"

"Pink," she repeated, and rolled her eyes. "Pink gowns, pink parasols, pink canapes . . ."

He chuckled and held up a hand to stop her. "Surely there is an alternative."

"Of course," was her tart response. "Pale yellow and white." Then, as his hand reached toward the desk, "And when I am thirty, I will be able to laugh with impunity."

"Do you mean to tell me there is a moratorium on your laughter?"

"To be sure. Let's see." She prepared to tick the possibilities off on her fingers. "I must not laugh before dinner. I must not laugh during dinner. I may laugh in the presence of a viscount, but not an earl or duke. I may laugh during a dance if my partner makes an appropriate sally, but if I were to do so after an improper jest, I would certainly be labeled fast and would be forced to retire to Bath. . . ."

She broke off, recognizing the topic that she had just

opened for his convenience, and hurriedly tried to change the subject. "Also, when I am thirty—"

"Ah, too late! So your Bath was Crowborough. Come now, Grace, don't you think it is high time to tell me just what heinous transgression you committed?" He watched as her mouth tightened. "Let me guess. You laughed at the Earl of Hardwin's toupee?"

"No." She shrugged. "Well, yes, of course I did that. . . ."

"But you survived it. Hmm. I know. You trod upon the Duke of Earith's trailing corset strings and suffocated him. No? Pity, that. Did you by chance launch a pink lobster canape at Prinny's waistcoat?" He paused. "I could go on guessing all night. Why don't you save me the effort?"

"Why don't you tell me just what you were doing when Mother invoked howler monkeys?"

He had to give her credit for quickness. In a game of quid pro quo, she had chosen well. Perhaps had he had a half bottle or so of something in his gut, he would not have balked at the question. Sober, and for some reason unwilling to offend her, he was not about to tell her that it had been neither himself nor Jason who had been noisy, but a pair of lively opera dancers they had spirited into the Granville home for the weekend. The "howling," as the countess called it, was the inevitable result of two lush figures trying to squeeze themselves into narrow chest plates taken from the gallery's resident suits of armor. His offer to fetch something with which to grease the ladies' torsos had been met with increasingly loud chortling.

He sighed, temporarily bested. "All right, I will let you keep your secret. For now."

"Thank you."

"Again, it is only a temporary reprieve. You will have to tell me sooner or later." He leaned against the desk and crossed his arms over his chest. "Just as you will have to face your family sooner or later. Sooner, I think—" he glanced out the window "—than later. The snow seems to have let up."

As he watched, she dropped disconsolately to sit full upon the floor. "You are not going to send me home now, are you?"

"Right at this moment? No, I think not. We would still be lucky to make it to Lewes." What he could not say was that he was not quite ready to let her go—not yet. He could barely say it to himself, it made so little sense. "Are you expecting such a cold reception, then? I am certain your family is highly concerned about your disappearance."

"I think it unlikely that they are even aware of my disappearance as yet. The snow . . ." She waved toward the window. "Once they hear from Cousin Bernice, I expect they will begin planning my next banishment. Obviously Crowborough was not enough. Let me think. . . ." She pulled her legs in toward her chest and propped her chin on her knees. "I have already considered the Americas. No, still a degree of civilization there. And China, when one thinks about it, is separated from the European continent only by land. Like a bad pence, I could still come back."

She graced him with a smile that almost reached her eyes. "I have it! They will send me to Australia! Kangaroos and criminals, perfect company for the disgrace of the Granville clan. You know, I have heard that kangaroos box. Wouldn't that just be a perfect penance—to go a few rounds with a kangaroo?" She smiled, but it was a weak effort.

Rafe was silent for a time, wondering how the earl and countess could possibly see their youngest child as a disappointment. Pestiness aside, the girl had always been something of a delight. But the sad truth was that the earl and countess always had regarded her as a squirrel in the family tree. Nor had they bothered to make a secret of it. For the first time since the fire, he thought of his own family with something other than sadness. His parents had never shown him anything but love and pride.

"Put it out of your mind for now," he said with an attempt at levity. "You will not have to worry about being planted a facer by a kangaroo just yet."

More than anything at that moment, Grace wanted to leap to her feet and throw her arms around him. Gratitude was part of the urge, to be sure, but there was more—far more. Even dressed as he was, in shirt, breeches, and frayed-edged lounging robe, he looked like every girl's dream of a white knight in armor. *Dear God, how I love you!* she shouted silently. Aloud she said, "Thank you."

"You're welcome. No doubt I shall regret my benevolence ere long." He reached for the bottle and half filled the waiting glass. "No, don't scowl at me," he muttered, catching her gaze. "I am going to drink this, and only this. I need it, after all this night has been."

She remembered. "It was a bad dream, wasn't it?" He grunted. "Will you tell me about it?"

"No."

He spoke the word softly, but with enough force to make her bite her tongue. She wanted to make him smile again, not frown into a series of brandies. "Well, perhaps we could do something. . . . I could . . ."

She thought furiously of something to get his attention and please him. Unbidden, the image of Meg-from-the-tavern flashed into her mind. She would no doubt know how to take a man's mind from the blue devils. "I could . . ." *What—climb onto the desk and wiggle my . . . arms? Bat my eyelashes and sing a bawdy tune?*

She turned a desperate gaze to Rafe. He was holding his glass up toward the fire. The logs had caught and the flames licking at them gained strength by the second. He was not drinking, but was slowly twirling the glass's stem in his fingers, gazing into the amber depths. When at last he spoke, his voice was low and rough, edged with fatigue.

"Do you think we could just sit quietly for a time? Stare into the fire? Can you do that with me, Grace?"

Her heart swelled. "Yes. I can do that."

* * *

They were still sitting quietly several hours later. Rafe had, as stated, done little but stare at the hearth. Grace normally hated silence, but as he had not reached for the bottle, she did not complain. She also hated sitting quietly and was not very good at it, despite her assertion to the contrary. In fact, the only way she could abide it was to read. So, after enduring a torturous half hour, she had crept to the decently stocked bookshelves and grabbed the volume nearest to her hand. It had turned out to be a copy of the *Canterbury Tales.* Forbidden fruit.

She was so engrossed in the tale of the lascivious miller's wife that she literally jumped when the pounding started. Her jaw, which had been completely slack, closed with a snap that rattled her teeth.

She turned to Rafe, who was already heading toward the hall. "Stay there and be quiet," he ordered, and closed the study door firmly behind him.

Never having been one to obey unexplained commands, especially terse ones, Grace hurried to the door and pressed her ear to the stout panels. It was impossible to hear much through the oak. She could make out Rafe's deep voice and one other, also male, but no words. After mere moments, she heard the outer door close. She promptly scuttled back to her seat.

It seemed an eternity before Rafe returned. He was holding a sheaf of paper, and judging from the black scowl on his face, it did not bring tidings of great joy. He stalked across the room and dropped into his chair. Grace waited for him to speak. When he did, his voice was rife with irony.

"The ever-so-thoughtful postmaster rode all the way out this fine morning to give me my mail."

So the roads were open. Grace's heart sank. She did her best, however, to smile nonchalantly. "Did you receive anything of interest?"

"Define interest." Rafe fanned the letters. "Let's see. There is an invitation to the Lewes Christmas assembly ball. I do not believe I will be attending." He crumpled it and tossed it over his shoulder. "A letter from the local vicar's wife, very prettily worded, inviting me to tea and to become an honored contributor to the church charity fund." The prettily worded letter joined the invitation. "Stupid of me to think my presence here would not be noted."

Grace squirmed uneasily in her seat as he continued. "Another invitation. Squire Trilby. I believe he has a daughter of marriageable age. The man must be truly desperate to be rid of her if he's angling after me. . . ."

"Rafe . . . " She reached out, but a blast from cobalt eyes stopped her hand.

"Now, here is something: several missives from my solicitors in London and one from my steward at Margrave, all intended to apprise me of the estate's condition in my—" he peered at one of the pages "—'understandable but lengthy absence.' Tell me, Grace, does that sound like a polite reprimand to you? I can only assume Messrs. Thurston, Biggs, and Pollan have settled on this as the best way to remind an errant duke of his responsibilities while not directly offending him."

"Oh, Rafe."

This time he actually jerked away. "This—" he tossed yet another paper in her direction "—might be of interest to you. It is from Jason. It appears that he and Aurelie arrived at Havensgate last week. Thoughtful as always, informing me of their whereabouts when I could not care less. Of course, they do not know you have gone missing, but I imagine they will soon enough."

"I don't care—" She broke off with a startled gasp as he abruptly surged to his feet.

"Stay here," he commanded once again. "And I mean it, Grace. You will not even move so far as the door!" Then he was gone.

Grace had no idea if he knew she had tried to eavesdrop, or if he simply knew her well enough to guess. This time she did obey him. She really had nowhere to go.

It took him even longer to return this time. And when he did, he was holding not paper, but a bundle of cloth, which he dumped into her lap. "Put them on."

Grace stared blankly at her coat and boots. "But, Rafe . . ."

"Now. We are leaving."

Biting her lip to stave off helpless tears, she did. Then, as she tried to think of something, anything, to say to him, he seized her arm. He all but dragged her out the door and across the yard. She began to struggle as they neared the stables. He merely cursed and hefted her off her feet and over his shoulder. He was no more gentle when he tossed her onto the back of his already-saddled horse.

She would have slid right back off had he not, apparently sensing she would try just that, anchored her firmly in place with one arm. Then he swung up behind her and urged the horse out of the stables. The animal seemed impervious to the deep snow and plowed relentlessly toward the main road. Grace turned her head and watched as the hunting box disappeared behind a copse of snow-shrouded trees. It was not until her cheeks began to sting that she realized she was crying, and that the bitter cold was all but freezing the tears.

"Why are you doing this?" she asked miserably. He did not answer. "What did I do . . . ?"

"Shut up, Grace," was all he said.

She huddled into the dubious warmth of her coat. The garment was warm enough, but she was chilled to her very core. She had known that she would have to leave Rafe eventually, but she could not even begin to understand the harsh suddenness. It seemed that only moments ago they had been sitting companionably by the fire. He had even been smiling. But now . . .

Too battered to think, she simply leaned back and felt nothing but the soon-to-be-lost magic of Rafe's arms.

He knew the moment she fell asleep. He wished he could relax with such utter abandon. There was no chance of that.

72

Not only was he suffering with the soft pressure of her bottom against his loins, but he was aching with the knowledge of what was very likely to come.

His present course was a palliative, no more. He had known the moment he had read her brother's letter that he had to get her out of his house, as soon as possible. Perhaps had she not mentioned elephants, or kangaroos . . . But no, he simply could not let her remain in his house, and booting her out quickly had seemed the only choice.

Delivering her to Dickerdean was the least evil of the possibilities, but far from ideal. Grace was going to have hell to pay, later now, perhaps, rather than sooner, but hell nonetheless. He knew she deserved better, better than what her family would give her, and far better than anything he had or would. But she had made her choices. He had made his.

You could save her, you know. The voice was back.

"Not bloody likely," he growled in response, keeping his own voice low so as not to awaken her.

You could.

"I cannot."

You mean you will not.

"Fine," he agreed tersely. "I will not."

He knew his abrupt actions had confused and hurt her. He could not concern himself overly with that. She could not stay with him. He did not want her around. Even as that thought formed, he realized how, despite the fact that he had never wanted her around, he had never regretted her presence in the end.

Grace, despite the coldness of her parents and his own varied abuse, was a creature of warmth and light. She was certainly a nuisance, too strong of will and too short of common sense, but she was also lovely, clever, and dauntlessly free with her affection. Whatever odd impulse had induced Lady Heathfield to name her daughter Grace had been a splendid one.

She makes you feel human again.

He did not even bother responding to the blasted voice,

73

merely quashed it. And filled the passing miles with counting the myriad reasons why, with friends like Grace and the rest of the Granville clan, a man needed no enemies.

At last the gates of Dickerdean came into view. Rafe halted Hannibal and jostled Grace awake. She blinked at him sleepily as he lifted her to the ground, then shook her head as if to clear it, setting tousled blond curls in motion. She spied the gates and asked, "Where are we?"

"Dickerdean."

"Where?"

"My great-aunt's home."

"But I thought . . ."

"You thought wrong. No questions, please, Grace. I do not feel like answering them."

Of course, she ignored him. "Why are we not riding up to the house?"

And he answered. "You will be walking to the house."

"Walking? Why?"

"Because I will not be accompanying you." He raised his hand to stall her protestations. "Aunt Myrtle will be absolutely delighted to have you, and you will not have to explain where you've been since Crowborough. After a day, she will forget that you haven't been with her for a week. You will contact your family, and perhaps no one will ever be the wiser."

"Except for us." Her voice was little more than a whisper.

"Except for us," he agreed. "But we will forget."

With that lie, he suddenly could not find anything else to say.

She stared at him for a long moment, too much heart showing in her eyes. "I thought . . ." She bit her lip. "I know. I thought wrong."

She leaned toward him, and he expected her to fall into his chest, even braced himself to catch her and hold her away. But she did not. She straightened her shoulders, lifted her chin, and turned away from him.

"Good-bye, Rafe."

Good-bye, Grace, he said silently, and watched her make her way up the snow-shrouded drive.

6

"REALLY, DEAREST, I find pink to be a splendid color."
Lady Myrtle Hammond completed the pronouncement by beaming cherubically at her guest. Grace
did her best to smile back, chiding herself for having muttered her distaste for the color aloud. Myrtle's grasp of reality was a bit faulty at times; her hearing was not.

Grace had no wish to distress the older woman with her
careless tongue. Rafe's aunt was a dear and had welcomed
her with open arms, a good deal of gauzy fluttering, and
not so much as a blink of an eyelash at her men's garb and
tear-streaked face. A full four days later, she had not commented on Grace's appearance at her home, other than to
repeat how pleased she was to have such a charming young
visitor to lighten the dreary days.

The gown, one of Myrtle's own, had been altered by the
lady's maid to fit Grace. To call it pink was not quite accurate. Rafe's aunt had a proclivity for muddy half colors,
mostly mossy greens and taupes. This gown, commissioned—as Myrtle informed her—in a fit of fancy, was
more of a grayish mauve. It was surprisingly flattering,
even in its matronly style, but as far as Grace was concerned, pink was pink.

In the spirit of her hostess's kindness, she did a dutiful
pirouette before dropping into a curtsy. "Thank you,
madam, it is a lovely gown."

Myrtle clapped her hands in delight. "Very prettily done,
my dear. You always were the most pleasing little angel."

Grace managed to keep from grimacing. She and the

lady had met but a dozen or so times over the years, and she was well aware that her behavior on many of those occasions had been anything but pleasing or angelic. Still, Myrtle's memory was, in the lady's own eyes, infallible. Considering her own situation, Grace was not about to gainsay her.

"Yes," Myrtle continued, "I remember one particularly lovely day at Havensgate when we were all playing at charades. You and Rafael were paired, acting out *The Taming of the Shrew*. Your talent was such that you had him quite speechless in admiration."

Grace, of course, remembered a slightly different version of the story. Rafe's speechlessness had been the result of her fist tangled in his cravat. It had seemed an entirely appropriate action for the shrewish Kate. Had Rafe not always insisted on wearing his cravat shamefully loose, she would not have had so much fabric to grab. She had not meant to cut off his air.

"And of course, there was the time . . . oh, perhaps a year back, at Margrave, that you quite had us all on tenterhooks waiting for Rafe to make an offer. How lovely it would have been to have united our two families." She peered at Grace owlishly. "Whatever were you thinking, dear, to leave before the dear boy could take care of the matter?"

Grace had no answer for her. She had been to Margrave exactly once in her life, ten months earlier for the funeral. And Rafe would unquestionably have come closer to indenturing himself to His Majesty's Navy than he ever would have to offering for her. The thought was as laughable as it was unbearably sweet.

Whatever Myrtle thought she recalled had nothing to do with her. Grace did not want to consider that Rafe might have considered marrying someone else. She sincerely hoped Myrtle's mind would flit elsewhere.

It did, although the subject was no better.

"Now that you will be suitably attired," the lady chirped, "I expect you are ready for our trip to Havensgate."

"Yes," Grace replied as expected, "I am."

As ready as I would be for a trip to Hades.

She had not been surprised to hear that Aurelie and Jason had invited Rafe's aunt to pass the holidays at Havensgate. After all, Rafe was Myrtle's only close relative now, and he could not be counted upon for appropriate familial company. But Grace, for all her earlier enthusiasm at the prospect of seeing her brother and sister-in-law, was not ready.

There would be so many people, after all. She had become used to quiet and seclusion. The noise would undoubtedly rattle her senses. Then, too, was the issue of facing her parents. She felt confident that they would accept her story of having come directly to Lady Hammond. After all, they had no reason to doubt her. But she was equally confident that their reaction would be somewhat less than pleasant nonetheless.

She had not entirely been joking when she had mentioned to Rafe the possibility of being sent to the Colonies. Her mother had a cousin of sorts in Boston, and the woman's not infrequent letters hinted at an eagerness to have any member of the Granville family for a visit. Any titled member, one could read between the lines. So why not send the hoyden? She did, after all, have a title. And should her behavior so scandalize the distant family, they could always send her back—someday.

Boston did not seem like such a bad place, really. In fact, she had heard it was quite lively. Lively was good. Thousands of miles away was abominable.

The simple truth was that she could face the noise, her parents, even the threat of being banished to the Americas. What she could not face was being without Rafe.

"Now, dear, perhaps you will play the pianoforte for me. No, no more of your modest excuses. I know you are quite splendidly proficient. Why, I remember one breathtaking Haydn sonata. . . ." Myrtle captured her elbow in a surprisingly strong grip and led her toward the dreaded instrument of torture.

Grace had not been modest when she had called her

playing less than breathtaking. In fact, her talent was close to nonexistent. Her older siblings were all dab hands at it, and their mother had retained the elderly Monsieur DeLange to provide instruction to Grace when she reached her eighth birthday. She had frightened him off within weeks. Her energetic but maladroit playing had been part of his defection, certainly. The earthworms in his peruke had merely clinched the matter.

His parting shots, directed at a resigned Lady Heathfield, had quickly deteriorated from English to rapid French. The final word, *"Honteuse!"* had been delivered with special, red-faced emphasis. Grace, her grasp of French only slightly better at the time than her talent at the pianoforte, had been forced to ask her older sister to translate.

"Honteuse," Catherine had informed her smugly, "means *disgraceful,*" before flouncing off to console their mother with a perfect rendition of Bach's Little Fugue in G Minor. Grace, knowing her future as a musician was hopeless, had vowed to improve her French.

Now, not wanting to disappoint her kindly hostess, she settled herself on the bench. It had been years since she had played, and the keys might very well have represented mathematical symbols for all the sense they made. She sighed and closed her eyes. A Scottish reel, perhaps. At least she would be able to repeat lines over and again.

She hit an opening chord, then peered at Myrtle, who promptly beamed back. Well, so far so good.

Launching into a lively tune, she found her fingers flying almost with a will of their own. *Hah,* she thought triumphantly, *I am not nearly as bad as all that.* After a time, she was even confident enough to divert from the safe refrain to a creative chord combination. Feeling quite proud of herself, she finished with a flourish and prepared to launch into Bach's Little Fugue.

"Grace, dearest," Myrtle said.

"Yes, Lady Hammond?"

"Are you warm enough?"

Grace was, in fact, more than warm enough; Myrtle had

a tendency to keep her rooms heated to somewhere around tropical. "Perfectly warm, thank you." She reached for the keys again.

"Are you certain, dearest? I would not want you feeling compelled to lie on my behalf."

"Quite certain, madam. Why do you ask?"

"Well . . ." Myrtle settled her own diaphanous wrap more firmly about her shoulders. "I am convinced that your dear little fingers are chilled. One cannot expect to hit the correct keys, after all, with stiff hands."

"No, madam," Grace replied with a resigned sigh. "One cannot."

Unaware that she had just blasted a brilliant talent, the older woman smiled, her eyes taking on a now familiar opacity. "I will never forget the time in London when you quite astounded all those present at the Biddington soiree with your lovely interpretation of Mozart. . . ."

The Biddington soiree two Seasons earlier had been an unmitigated disaster. Grace had indeed quite astounded the gathering, but she had been nowhere near a pianoforte at the time. She winced at the memory, which involved a trellis on the balcony. Its ladderlike slats and profusion of climbing roses had seemed the perfect vantage point from which to watch Rafe entertaining a merry widow in the shadows. There had been no way for her to know that the thing was not anchored firmly to the wall—nor that, when it did fall with her clinging tightly, it would land in front of the open French doors, in full view of the salon.

Her mother had vowed never to forgive her. Lady Biddington had vowed never to invite her to another fete. Grace, worried that she might never be able to look Rafe in the eye again, recovered, albeit temporarily, when she realized he had not seen a thing. He had been gone by the time the trellis collapsed, gone with his merry widow through the shadows and away into the night.

All in all, the fiasco on the trellis had been a sobering experience.

Myrtle was busy at her knitting again, some long, shapeless, fluffy object that looked as if it could swallow and smother a small child. She had provided Grace with needles and yarn earlier, but to her credit, had not objected when the items found their way unused back into her work basket. The Hammond library was extensive if outdated, and Grace spent much of her time buried in a book.

She was deep into *Tom Jones* at present. It was yet one more book her parents had not allowed her to read, and she had expected similar disapproval from her hostess. Rafe's aunt, however, had either not read the book or had long ago forgotten its contents. When she had cheerfully asked about it, Grace had replied, "It is a lovely story about a young man in love with a squire's daughter."

True enough. She had felt no need to mention poachers, prostitutes, and drunken debauchery. Myrtle had merely smiled, replied, "How nice, dear," and gone back to her woolly child-trap.

Poor Tom was, at the moment, lamenting the loss of his beloved Sophy's regard. Grace found Sophy charming, but dense. If the foolish girl could not see past Tom's devil-may-care demeanor to his true and constant heart, she did not deserve him.

"Why don't you read aloud to me?" Myrtle requested some time later. "You seem so very engrossed in the story. I am certain I would find it most diverting."

Most distressing was more like it, Grace decided. Tom was presently dining in the company of a woman whose virtue was, to put it mildly, debatable. "Actually, madam, I was just thinking to switch to Mr. Pope. Would that suit?"

Myrtle clicked her needles together in delight. "What a marvelous idea! I do so love 'The Rape of the Lock.' "

Grace suppressed a groan as she set Tom aside. Why had she not said Donne, or even Swift? Cursing herself eloquently, she dutifully went off in search of Alexander Pope. Minutes later, she was launching into his "heroi-comical poem" about Belinda and her ringlet's unfortunate encounter with a pair of shears.

As she read, she tugged at her own short curls. In her

opinion, the baron wasted a choice opportunity in only severing the one lock. With Belinda intent on playing the coquette, he had ample occasion to collect a good deal more of the sable curls he so desired. A shorn Belinda would be far wiser and, with the freedom cropped hair afforded, could spend more time on improving her vapid mind and less on gazing adoringly into the mirror.

When the butler arrived in the middle of the fourth canto to announce supper, she gladly set the book aside. Belinda, she knew, would remain essentially unshorn, and the baron would suffer from excessive inhalation of snuff. It was a thoroughly unsatisfactory ending and she was happy for it to wait. If the evening went as usual, Myrtle would be dozing into her yarn by nine, leaving Grace to her assignation with the dashing Mr. Jones.

"That was lovely," the older woman commented as they made their way toward the dining room. "You have the most angelic voice. We shall resume after supper. I should like to hear Canto Three again, if you would be so kind. 'Tis some of Mr. Pope's finest rhyme."

"Of course," Grace agreed, vowing as she did to see that Myrtle's wine goblet was kept full throughout the meal. A few glasses and she ought to be asleep by the third finely rhymed line.

Unfortunately, her hostess was more inclined to prattle than tipple. "Your sister sent me the most charming letter not a month past. She thanked me most prettily for the christening gift I sent. A silver cup, if I remember correctly . . ."

Catherine's last child had been born more than five years earlier. A lively little boy, Freddy had most likely reduced the cup to a tarnished lump by his first birthday. Grace was rather looking forward to seeing her nieces and nephew. They were among the more accepting of the family. True, seven-year-old Phoebe had a distressing habit of informing her each time she got a spot on her gown, but certainly did not think less of her because of the spots. Michaela, who was now ten and unfailingly gracious, would stick to her like a limpet, hiding any tears or stains with her own skirts.

"And your brother Richard is still at Oxford, is he not?"

"Yes, my lady, he is." And for once, her agreement was true. Rickey showed no inclination to be done with his studies, much to Jason's disapproval. It was Jason, however, and not Rickey who would someday be the earl. The younger Granville brother was far better suited to the life of dilettante scholar. Charming, blithe, and utterly lazy, he seemed more than content with his life. As long as their father continued paying the bills, he would be at Oxford.

"Would it not be lovely to learn that Aurelie is increasing? Jason is a dear boy, but he has been most lax in providing himself with an heir."

It was Aurelie, Grace mused dryly, who would ultimately do the providing. And if, in fact, her sister-in-law was not yet with child, it would not be due to lack of opportunity. Jason and his wife were almost obnoxiously in love. One could very nearly see Cupid flitting above whenever they were together.

"I am near to despairing with Rafael. His heir at the moment is a rather odious cousin, far more concerned with tying his cravat properly than matters of estate. He would make the most foppish duke." With that grand pronouncement, Myrtle turned her attention to her crimped salmon, and Grace hoped that would be the end of the discussion of Rafe's procreative failings.

She was not to be so fortunate.

"Perhaps I ought to write to the Countess of Shiveley. I believe her daughter is of marriageable age. A terribly plain girl, if I remember correctly, but extremely healthy. Yes, she would do quite nicely. There is an excess of good looks in Rafael's bloodlines. Even a plain wife could produce comely offspring."

Grace was not about to inform her that the countess's daughter, Zelda, had been married off during her first Season to Lord Jarmyn, nor that she had recently produced a healthy and, by all reports, beautiful son. Should Myrtle in fact take it upon herself to play matchmaker, she would be temporarily thwarted in that quarter.

The thought of Rafe marrying was enough to rob her of her appetite. The excellent stewed greens could have been wet paper for all she could tell. In truth, she missed the hard bread and cheese that had seemed ambrosia. Even more, she missed simply being at the dusty, drafty lodge. With Rafe.

She had never, as far back as she could recall, found it easy to be away from him. Nor had she ever been as happy as she was when they were together. It had occurred to her of late that she had never been quite as miserable, either, and wondered at the quirks of love. Was it truly better to be unhappy with someone rather than without him?

That was a philosophical quandary that she was not about to tackle at the moment. Maybe later, when she had been sent somewhere else in disgrace, pondering her muddled life would give her something productive to do. Until such time, she preferred to contemplate the possibility of fulfilled expectations.

When Myrtle had at last taken her last bite of trifle, they repaired to the drawing room. The older woman seemed thankfully to have forgotten about Belinda and the baron, but she did not appear tired in the least. Grace, with deceptive thoughtfulness, added several logs to the already blazing fire, hoping to induce some heat-inspired drowsiness. It was she who was blinking heavy eyelids a half hour later.

"Are you fatigued, dear?" Myrtle asked when *Tom Jones* landed heavily on the floor. "Perhaps you ought to retire. We will be traveling tomorrow, after all, and you want to be fresh and bright for your family."

Grace retrieved Tom and tried to find her place. "I shall be fine," she replied with little conviction. The journey in itself would hardly be wearying. She could not say the same for the reception. In all likelihood, her father would bark and her mother would enact a dramatic swoon— without actually fainting, of course.

She did not need to be bright and fresh. She needed to be encased in armor.

"How pleased you must be with the prospect of going home. It was so kind of your dear parents to send you to me for our lovely visit, but home is where the heart is, after all."

Home, Grace amended sadly, *is where the havoc will be.*

"And your entire family will be there. All the better for you."

All the better for all to witness yet one more thunderous scene of which I will be the center.

"Family is such a blessing. How nice it is to know one will be loved regardless of one's faults."

Grace darted a quick look at the older woman. For a second she was convinced she saw perfect sharpness in the bright blue eyes. Then Myrtle beamed her seraphic smile and announced, "Horatio and I always lamented not having children of our own. Now that he is gone, all I have is Rafael. If the dear boy would simply settle down and breed some children, I would be in heaven."

She looked at the mantel clock then and sighed. She did not, however, take herself off to bed. As the knitting needles clicked rhythmically away again, Grace fought off encroaching drowsiness and turned her attention back to Tom. At the rate he was going, he was never going to make his way back to Sophy. Not, she decided, that it was such a tragedy, but she was in the mood for a happy ending.

Soon enough she was once again engrossed in the tale, and looked up in surprise when Myrtle clapped her hands sharply. "Lady Hammond?"

"Oh, splendid. I was beginning to worry. I do hate having to wait like that. It is so very taxing on the nerves."

"I beg your pardon?"

"Of course, you are too young to worry about such things. It is the province of the aged to be set to fits by weather and waiting." Myrtle was hastily shoving her knitting into its basket. "I cannot complain about much, of course. My person seems to be holding up rather well with the passing of the years. My nerves, however, are beset far too easily these days."

Grace waited for an explanation. None, apparently, was forthcoming. "I am afraid I do not understand," she offered helpfully.

"Well, of course you do not. You are young." Myrtle patted her gray curls and smoothed her skirts. "And you look lovely, as always."

"I . . . thank you, madam." Grace tried to remember just how much wine the older woman had imbibed. Very little. "Should I open a window, perhaps?"

"Whatever for? Really, dear, it is freezing outside. I know you young things relish the fresh air, but it would not do at all for you to catch a chill. . . . Yes, Garrowby, I know."

Grace spun around to see the butler standing in the doorway. She had not heard him enter.

"It seems my presence is already known," a voice said from behind him. "No need to announce me."

"Well, it is about time!" Myrtle announced brightly. "We have been waiting all evening."

"My apologies, madam. The road has become appallingly muddy. Hello, Grace."

"Rafe," she gasped, and promptly dumped Tom onto the floor.

7

H E DID NOT look at her again, but stalked across the room to warm himself in front of the fire. Grace watched him, her heart swelling to near-painful proportions. He had come back to her.

"I daresay you have brought winter inside with you," his aunt commented tartly. "Garrowby, have my maid bring me another shawl."

Rafe turned from the fire, brows raised in a sardonic arc. "Really, Aunt, I daresay you have brought the tropics to Sussex."

"Dearest Grace thoughtfully added several logs to the fire not long ago. I imagine she knew you would be chilled after your ride." Dearest Grace was, at the moment, watching the scene openmouthed. Myrtle regarded her curiously. "You look a bit befuddled, my dear. Oh my, I did not forget to inform you of Rafael's arrival, did I? I did. Good heavens. Well, it must have slipped my mind in the anxiety of waiting."

"You said today, Aunt," Rafe remarked with a sigh. "You did not specify a time."

"Quite right, dear boy. And I do thank you for accepting my invitation to accompany us to Havensgate."

He was to be at Havensgate. Grace's already flying spirits soared even higher.

"Your invitation, madam, was not an invitation. It was a royal summons."

Her spirits dipped slightly at his words. Myrtle, however,

appeared entirely unperturbed. "The important thing is that you came. It was ever so gracious of you."

"I came because, as you so dramatically informed me, you refused to leave for Newhaven without my escort."

Rafe saw the animation fade from Grace's face. He quite believed she had not known of his aunt's summons, nor of his impending arrival. Her expression upon his entrance had convinced him of her innocence in the matter. She had looked startled, disbelieving, then surpassingly gratified. It was the gratification that directed his tongue now. She needed to know that he would not have returned had he had the choice.

"While your message was a bit melodramatic, Aunt, I saw no reason to doubt its earnestness."

"Wise of you," Myrtle replied pleasantly. "I was entirely in earnest. Grace and I must go to Havensgate, and you must accompany us. It would not do at all for us to travel without male escort in such weather. Why, what if we were to be stranded along the road? Or worse?"

He wanted very much to remind her that Havensgate was but fifteen miles away, and that her driver and footman would be more than adequate help should anything happen on the way. The worst-case scenario, after all, was trouble due to inclement weather. There had not been a brigand in their sleepy little section of East Sussex in a good twenty-five years.

None of this was likely to have much of an effect on his dizzy aunt, and he well knew it. The important thing had been to make sure Grace got to Havensgate, so he had grudgingly prepared to do just that. He had even managed to maintain a degree of bitter resignation during the ride. The fact that an angelic face with tousled blond curls had consistently invaded his pique had not helped.

Now here she was, dressed in a smoky rose gown, looking at him with something akin to reproach in her eyes. He did not take kindly to being reproached. "Divine gown, Gracie. Makes you look like a lady."

She flushed but did not respond. Myrtle, however, could

ever be counted on to fill silences. "Yes, it is a lovely gown, is it not? It never suited me half so well. But you did not comment on Grace's hair, Rafael. Is it not beyond charming? And so very fashionable."

"I have already seen—" He cut himself off with a silent curse. Despite his aunt's flightiness, it would not do at all to let the proverbial cat out of the bag. "Charming," he muttered. "No, beyond charming."

Grace, already feeling decidedly battered by his coldness, flushed anew. True, he was merely covering his near gaffe, but she wished he had done so with less acerbity.

So, Myrtle had summarily demanded his presence. And he had responded. She did not really wonder why. It was clear he wanted nothing more than for her to be back in the bosom of her family and well away from him and his.

"It was kind of you to come," she said softly, hoping to assuage some of his annoyance.

He merely grunted.

Grace bent to retrieve her book, laying it gently on the table. "If you will excuse me, my lady . . . Rafe, I believe I will retire now."

"Of course, dear." Myrtle held out her arms for what had become a familiar good-night embrace. Grace clung to the older woman for a moment, needing some warmth, then moved away.

"Grace." Rafe's voice stopped her as she reached the door. "Sleep well. It appears you are leaving for Havensgate in the morning."

She hurried from the room, knowing she would either scream or cry if she stayed a moment longer. Screaming would be quite pleasant, actually, but she knew it would up-set her hostess. And she certainly did not want to cry—not in front of Rafe.

As it turned out, she did neither. Instead, she stared up at the canopy of her bed and silently cursed the happy cherubs who rioted there. Cupid's dart, she decided, was poison tipped. Either that, or he had appalling aim.

* * *

"I believe you upset her, Rafael." Myrtle was busy unraveling a portion of her knitting. "And you are getting mud on my carpet."

Rafe glowered at his boots. Glowering at his aunt served no purpose whatsoever. "I do apologize, madam."

"Whatever for? Grace is upset, not I."

He discreetly and deliberately ground his heel into the floral Aubusson. "I was referring to your carpet. There is very little I can do about Grace. She has been upsetting *me* for a good fifteen years now." He added quickly, "I imagine she has done the same to all of Jason's friends."

"Yes, well, she is a charming little minx, is she not?"

Rafe felt an answer was neither required nor wise. There was a bottle of something across the room and he decided to avail himself of its comfort. The ride to Dickerdean had been easier than it had been four days earlier, but it had been no warmer. He was cold, tired, and thoroughly out of sorts. A drink was in order.

It occurred to him as he reached for the bottle that he was not entirely certain what *in* sorts was lately. The closest he had come was only in the midst of blithe sparring matches with Grace in the past week. The fact that he had been in a tolerable mood a mere two or three times over the past ten months did not sit well with him.

A drink, of course, would sit quite well, indeed.

He unplugged the stopper and was immediately met with the aroma of sherry. He detested sherry. Always had. He returned the bottle to the sideboard. "Have you any brandy in the house, Aunt?"

Her plump face creased into a thoughtful frown. "I must, dear, but I could not tell you where."

"I imagine the wine cellar would be a strong possibility."

She beamed at him. "Why, yes it would! How clever of you, Rafael. But you always were such a bright boy. Why, I remember the time you decided that your mother's rosebushes would bloom through winter if only they were brought inside the house. I must say, I was most surprised by the amount of dirt each required. . . ."

90

Rafe sighed. He loved his aunt. Really. But her reveries tended to be a bit wearing on one's patience. He, too, remembered the rose incident. If he was not mistaken, he had been six at the time. His mother had, to her credit, been quite understanding, even appreciative of his efforts to give her roses year round. His father had not been so kind. It was not the act itself that had bothered him, but the fact that Rafe had used his best hunter to transport the bushes. He had given his son a stinging lecture on the uses of fine horseflesh, then denied him access to the stables for a week. And of course, made him clear up the mess without the aid of a blooded Thoroughbred.

All in all, it had not been such a terrible punishment.

Rafe actually caught himself smiling. His parents had been wonderful people, encouraging and supporting him even when his goals did not quite coincide with their idea of proper deportment of a future duke. Then he sighed. God, how he missed them.

"Yes, dear, I know."

He looked up to find his aunt regarding him with sympathetic eyes. Damned if the old hen did not find the worst times to be astute.

"I believe I will go raid your wine cellar, Aunt."

"As you wish, dear, but you will have to find Garrowby first. He has the keys."

Rafe blinked. "You keep the cellars locked?"

"What an odd question. Of course I keep them locked. Otherwise, Percival would have gone through every bottle there."

It took a great deal of self-control, but Rafe managed not to groan aloud. Percival, an ill-named, half-witted brute of a mastiff, had, indeed, had a taste for liquor. In fact, the dog had become impressively adept at pawing bottles onto the floor where he would proceed to lap up every last drop without so much as nicking his tongue on the glass. Then he would weave his way through the house, knocking over whatever persons and furniture should have the misfortune to be in his path before finally collapsing into a snoring heap somewhere. As a youth, Rafe had found the whole thing vastly entertaining.

"Madam," he said patiently, knowing it was not terribly sporting of him to be saying anything at all, "Percival has been dead a good seven or eight years now."

Myrtle pursed her lips. "Yes, he has, hasn't he? My, how time flies. I rather miss that dog. He had such a charming way of putting his head on one's knee."

The beast's ham-sized head had covered a good deal more than anyone's knee. And he had invariably soaked the object of his affection with his copious drooling. Well, at least his aunt had not replaced Percival with a whining, piddling lapdog. Rafe had had countless pairs of boots christened by walking hairballs displeased with his presence in their mistresses' homes.

"Well, dearest, now that you have safely arrived, I shall take myself off to bed. I cannot handle the hours you young things seem to find so civilized." His aunt rose to her feet and peered at him expectantly. He dutifully escorted her to the stairs and planted a kiss on her plump cheek.

"Sleep well, Aunt. I trust we will leave for Havensgate before noon."

"As you wish, Rafael. Now, do not stay up too long yourself. I do not fancy having you sleep all the way to Newhaven. Bad enough that those legs of yours take up half my carriage. The least you can do is entertain us."

Rafe refrained from telling her that his legs would be comfortably outside the carriage. She and Grace would have ample room. He would be riding.

As it turned out, he did not stay up long at all. In fact, he was in bed less than an hour later. Thinking that perhaps his aunt's memory of locked cellars was on the faulty side, he had gone looking. Then he had gone looking for Garrowby—and the keys. The butler, drat his elusive hide, had been nowhere to be found. And the cellars had remained locked.

Rafe contented himself with the knowledge that, despite the fact that Havensgate was going to be Hades incarnate and that he would have himself away at first opportunity, his friend Jason kept a smashing, *unlocked* cellar.

"I do not imagine you are aware of the fact, Grace dear, but you are twisting pleats into your skirts." Myrtle smiled benevolently at her charge and patted her hand. "It is understandable, to be sure. You must be quite beside yourself with the prospect of seeing your beloved family again, but we cannot have you looking frowsy when we arrive."

Grace removed her clenched fingers from her lap and dug them into the seat. She was quite beside herself at the prospect of seeing her family, but it was hardly with pleasure. They would be reaching Havensgate at any moment, and she was a wreck. Myrtle's chatter had been effectively distracting for approximately the first two hours. Then Grace had started thinking. About her parents, who would be about as welcoming as angry bears, and about Rafe, who had said almost nothing to her before their departure and who had been riding outside the carriage since. He ranked only slightly above her parents on a scale of people who appreciated her presence.

Thank heavens for Jason, Aurelie, and the children. They, at least, could be counted upon for a bit of genuine affection. Grace wondered who else would be present. Aurelie, when she entertained, did so on a grand scale. Perhaps Noel and Vivian, Earl and Countess of St. Helier, would be present. Noel was as old a friend of Jason's as Rafe, and his wife was a delight. Yes, if she were very fortunate, the St. Heliers would be present. All things considered, the numbers were in her favor. The problem, of course, was that Disapproval had as much a presence as a veritable army.

The carriage lumbered through a familiar bend in the road, and Grace steeled herself. It was not an easy task. They passed through the stone gates, and with each foot they traveled up the drive, her spine became more like water. Myrtle had to all but prod her out of her seat.

The front door of her brother's house flew open and

servants streamed into the drive. To Grace's vast relief, her sister-in-law was right behind them.

"Grace!" Aurelie promptly gathered her into a warm embrace. "We were so worried about you! Your parents received a letter from your cousin just as they were leaving to come here. . . ." She pulled back and said softly, "Whatever anyone says, I have met Bernice and I cannot say I blame you in the least for running away."

"The dear girl did not run away! What an absurd thought! She came to me for a visit."

Aurelie smiled over Grace's head. "Lady Hammond. I am so pleased you could come."

Myrtle patted the viscountess's cheek and swept up the stairs. "Absurd," she muttered, then paused to plant a kiss on the cheek of the man who appeared in the doorway. "The very thought! Preposterous!" she informed him, then disappeared into the house.

Jason Granville, Viscount Tarrant, gazed bemusedly after her for a moment. Then he turned back and opened his arms. Grace ran into them without a thought. "You will be the death of us, sprite," he scolded. Then, "But damned if I'm not glad to see you."

Grace burrowed into the comforting strength of her brother's arms. If she tried very hard, she could imagine that his regard, and his wife's, was all that mattered. For the first time in months, she felt truly at home. She tried not to sniffle into Jason's cravat even as she knew he would not mind.

Rafe watched this display of family devotion with something less than indulgence. Tarrant had been a rather splendid fellow until his marriage, remote and stern. Aurelie had changed all that. True, he had found Tarrant's reserve alternately annoying and amusing at the time, but he mourned its passing now. The sod looked ready to embrace *him*, too.

"Do not even consider it," Rafe muttered as he handed Hannibal over to a waiting groom. He ignored Aurelie's frown of consternation. "Hullo, Aurelie . . . Tare. Wish I could say I am pleased to be here."

Tarrant did not appear overly insulted. "I wish you could say it, too, Rafe. But welcome nonetheless."

"Thank you. I will not be staying long."

"That is too bad," was his friend's sincere reply.

Aurelie was not so philosophical. "Nonsense. You will stay through Christmas, and that is all there is to it!" She fixed him with a sharp, silver gaze. "Now, you may frown all over the stones if you like, Rafe, but it is cold out here. May I suggest you bring your glower onto the drawing room rug instead?"

He very nearly smiled. Aurelie had that effect on a person. He shrugged instead. "What is on the drawing room sideboard?"

"Dust," she shot back, and grabbing her husband with one hand and her sister-in-law with the other, disappeared into the house.

Now, Rafe was fairly certain there was little, if any, dust to be found. He was sure, however, to find himself a more than acceptable drink. So, maintaining his best glower, he followed.

Grace knew he was somewhere behind her; she could feel him. At the moment, though, she was deriving only slight comfort from his presence, only slightly more from Jason and Aurelie's. The drawing room loomed and she could hear her father's voice altogether too clearly.

"Came to you!" he bellowed, she assumed at Myrtle. "Damned gel will be the death of us all!"

He did not sound angry, really. The truth of the matter was that Lord Heathfield tended to bellow all his statements. But Grace's knees shook nonetheless. She could not hear her mother at all, and that boded far worse for her future. She could handle her father's shouting; she had developed a basic immunity through the years. She had never quite managed to do the same with her other parent's silences.

"Chin up," Aurelie whispered into her ear, then pushed her into the room.

Grace had been right about her mother. She was not

95

saying a thing. In fact, she was draped gracefully across the divan, eyes closed, looking for all the world as if she were in a deep swoon. Grace knew better.

The moment she crossed the threshold, the countess's eyes snapped open, fixing her with an ice-blue gaze that would have frozen molten lead. Slowly she raised one elegant hand to her brow, gave a soft gasp, and waved her free hand toward her younger son.

Rickey gave his sister a harassed smile as he hastened forward with a glass of sherry. Lady Heathfield managed to take several sips from her reclined position without spilling a drop. She was prodigiously good at things like that. Then she turned her attention back to Grace.

"Now that I have seen you are not cavorting with a Gypsy caravan somewhere, you will take yourself elsewhere."

"But, Mama . . ." Grace began.

"Really, Mother . . ." Jason added.

"Now!" Lady Heathfield waved at Rickey again. He thrust his fingers through his blond hair and looked helpless.

Grace cast a wary look at her father. His eyes, warm golden brown like hers and her siblings', were unreadable under the dark shelf of his brows. He shrugged. Knowing better than to think she was being given anything more than a brief reprieve, Grace bit her lip and headed for the door.

"Grace!" Her mother's plaintive cry stopped her just as she reached the hallway.

"Yes, Mama?" she said hopefully.

"Whatever possessed you to do such a horrible thing to your hair?"

"Comfort," Grace muttered under her breath, and, chin high, marched away.

It would have been a splendid exit indeed had she not, quite literally, run into Rafe. He made no move to get out of the way. Had Grace been able to see where she was going, the collision could have been easily avoided. But her eyes were filmed with tears, allowing her no more than the briefest, blurry view of a misbuttoned waistcoat before she bumped against it.

"I must ask, Gracie," came Rafe's drawling voice from above, "would now be a good time to ask your parents just what you did to get yourself sent to Crowborough, or would you recommend I wait a bit?"

Grace would have liked more than anything to plant him a facer he would feel for weeks, but the tears were flowing now, and she did not think she could hit water if she fell from a boat.

"May I ask you something?" she managed.

"If I say no, will you refrain?"

She ignored him. "I would simply like to know, Rafe, if being cruel truly serves to make you feel better—or merely makes me feel worse."

Then, quivering chin again in the air, she pushed past him and headed for the stairs.

Rafe was temporarily stunned. "Foolish question, Grace," he muttered after a moment, then entered the salon.

Lady Heathfield was still on the divan, but she was sitting erect. As far back as Rafe could remember, he had been thoroughly intimidated by his friend's mother. She looked no different than she had twenty years earlier, her hair still pale blond, her posture still perfect. She was, to put it mildly, a formidable woman. Upon spying him, she thinned her lips, but did not wilt in the least. Not that he had expected her to do so. He had done nothing to upset her—or rather, nothing she could know. And even if she had known that her daughter had spent several days alone with him in an isolated lodge, she would not have truly fainted.

Over the years, Rafe had seen Lady Heathfield swoon in dozens of places, in dozens of impressive manners. He doubted the woman had ever actually lost consciousness in her life.

"Avemar," she said regally.

"My lady." Years of being a reasonably polite fellow took over, and he nodded to her husband. "Sir."

Lord Heathfield grunted. At that moment, Rafe quite liked the man. The earl always grunted his greetings, manners bedamned. Rafe knew he had a good many years of practice ahead of him if he were to develop the same panache.

Lady Heathfield's decidedly ladylike grunt did not make her more endearing, however. No one had the right to treat Grace badly, he decided, except him. The very irrationality of that statement struck him, but he had no time to analyze it, for Lady Heathfield was addressing him.

"You have looked better, Avemar."

"Well, I feel just marvelous, madam," he returned dryly.

"Humph. Your hair is far too long. You look like a Gypsy."

And your daughter has been cavorting with me. . . . He reluctantly swallowed the words. As much as their many years of acquaintance made the countess feel justified in speaking so to him, they prohibited Rafe from replying as he would have liked. He forced a smile. "We shall have to furnish Grace with a pair of shears, then, and let her hack away."

In the corner, Rickey chuckled. "Here, here," he announced. And received five quelling glances. His father was staring at the hunt scene over the mantel, and Myrtle was smiling at no one in particular. A reasonably intelligent and likable young man, Rickey had absolutely no control over his tongue. It was, Rafe knew, a Granville family trait.

Jason, the only Granville with any reserve, cleared his throat. "I believe it is time for . . . for . . ." Rafe was amused to see him floundering.

"Tea," Aurelie said firmly, and reached for the bellpull. "After your journey, you must be ready for some refreshment."

Rafe had not missed seeing the amber-filled decanters. Nor did he miss the desperate look Aurelie sent her brother-in-law as Rickey gamely proffered a glass. So, she was concerned about his drinking. He could not have cared less.

Aurelie Carollan Granville was a smashing creature,

lovely and intelligent, and he had always liked her. But she could damn well take her tip-tilted Irish nose and poke it in someone else's business. Rafe accepted the brandy with his first genuine smile of the day and tossed it back. Rickey, splendid chap that he was, plied the decanter again.

"Dashed good to see you, Rafe," he gushed. Rafe toasted him. "Can't believe the crowd Aurelie's got descending on us. Enough to drive a man to serious drink, I say."

"That bad, hmm?"

"Beyond imagining," the younger man lamented. "St. Helier's a goer, but the rest . . ." He rolled his eyes for emphasis.

"Richard!" his mother snapped. "That is quite enough. And you, Avemar, should not encourage him. Aurelie has planned a lovely week, and I will not allow you to spoil it with your reprehensible attitude." She gazed toward the open door. "If we could only count on Grace to comport herself with a modicum of decorum . . ."

No one even bothered to look at Rafe when he gave a hearty snort and relieved Rickey of the brandy decanter.

8

GRACE LAY ON her back in the middle of the familiar bed, staring up at the familiar canopy, and felt completely at home. It was not just that she had spent most of her life at Havensgate, her family's home until her father had succeeded to the earldom and they had moved to Heathfield Hall. No, it was more that she was in the utterly familiar position of being in disgrace. And she had been in the house for mere hours.

Some things never changed.

Unfortunately, Rafe was not one of them. He changed like the weather, cold as the dead of winter, then, briefly, warm as . . . well, very early spring, perhaps.

It had been a hard enough task, trying to make the blithe, jovial Rafe of old fall in love with her. How on earth was she going to manage now? In the midst of her family, where she never failed to be at her very worst, it was hopeless. Her siblings were kind, certainly, and Aurelie did everything in her power to help, but the fact remained that the Granvilles were, in general, to her image what bright light was to a flawed piece of art. Every fault was glaringly illuminated.

Deciding to change the familiar view a bit, Grace rolled onto her stomach and buried her face in the counterpane. It did not help overmuch, simply hampered her breathing.

When the knock came at the door, she ignored it. Not that it mattered. Moments later, she heard feet treading across the carpet.

"I do not suppose it would matter if I were to tell you that one cannot breathe through velvet."

There was no mistaking the American voice. Vivian! Grace promptly removed her face from the bed and launched herself at her friend. "Did you just arrive? Oh, I have missed you! How is Noel? I was worried you would not come!" She gasped as she encountered the viscountess's rotund form. "Good heavens, Vivian! You're . . . you're . . ."

The lovely countess grinned at her. "As round as a turkey and walking like a duck, or so my beloved husband says. He is ever so proud of himself."

Grace sat down heavily on the edge of the bed. "Good heavens."

"Yes, well, Noel refuses to give any credit elsewhere, heaven included." Vivian, Lady St. Helier, studied her friend intently. "You have cut your hair since I last saw you. . . ."

"And you have grown another person!"

Vivian laughed. "Really, Grace. I came in here to have a nice, serious bit of girl talk, and I cannot keep a straight face."

"Please, no serious talk. I do not think I could abide it."

"Oh, dear. Aurelie said it was a bit tense here." Vivian sank into a facing chair and pushed her own ebony curls off her face. "If I say 'this, too, shall pass,' will you throw something at me?" She grinned again, emerald eyes sparkling. "No matter, whatever you threw would just bounce off anyway."

To Grace's great mortification, she responded to her friend's wonderful, affectionate, irreverent banter by bursting into tears. Vivian, perfect creature that she was, did not say anything, did not try to make Grace say anything, and did not flutter about uselessly. Instead, she moved over to sit beside her on the bed, offered a handkerchief, and waited.

"Sorry," Grace snuffled eventually, knowing no apologies were necessary.

"Nonsense. We all need to cry on occasion. In fact, I might very well cry right along with you."

Grace peered up. "Whatever for? Do not tell me you are unhappy."

"Not at all. I am expecting. My emotions have been running amok for several months now." Vivian smiled gently. "Though I am not at all happy to see you so miserable." She watched as Grace made her shaky way to the washbasin and splashed water on her face. "I saw Rafe."

Grace promptly showered the front of her gown with cold water. "I beg your pardon?"

"Oh, Gracie . . ." Vivian began. Then, after a moment, "It is so good to see him . . . socializing again."

She knew. Grace was stunned. Vivian knew how she felt about Rafe. She turned and scanned the lovely face, looking for pity, even amusement. All she saw was understanding and she had the disconcerting feeling that Vivian had *always* known. The temptation to let go, to spill her heart into her friend's lap, was strong, but not strong enough.

Vivian would never, ever be cruel, but she would not be able to remain impassive or inactive. She would either cry right along, as promised, or take herself downstairs to blister Rafe's ears with a tirade that would be heard in London. Both were reasonably appealing to Grace's current state of mind, but neither was going to be of much help.

"Rafe," she allowed herself to say, "is . . . different now." Then, to avoid saying anything she would later regret, she surveyed her bodice. The water had succeeded in turning Myrtle's mauve gown a rather dark brown. "Oh dear, it is almost time for supper and I have had no chance to seek out other clothing. I left everything at the i— in Crowborough." She mentally kicked herself at the near slip, then hastened to cover it further. "I ran away from my cousin, you see. I was in such a hurry to get to Lady Hammond that I did not pack. . . ."

Vivian silenced her with a wave. "What a clanker, Grace. I know exactly how your gowns came to be left behind."

Grace's heart stopped. "You do?"

"Of course. You left them quite deliberately. We all know how you detest pink and white!"

"Would green do? Or perhaps aqua?" Aurelie appeared in the doorway, her arms filled with clothing. "They shall all have to be shortened for you, but my maid will see to that." She tossed a leaf-green muslin gown at Grace and draped the rest over a chair. "Try that one."

Grace touched the beautiful embroidery at the neck. "But these are yours. . . ."

Aurelie was busy sifting through the garments her maid was holding. "I specifically remember taking the pomona-and-cream kashmir shawl. . . . Yes, here it is. There is a wool gown among the lot, but I thought the muslin better for supper. We shall simply wrap you warmly on top of it." She caught Grace's frown. "Whatever is the matter?"

"These are *your* gowns. If they are shortened, you will not be able to wear them again."

Aurelie laughed. "We are sisters, Grace. We share. Besides, I shall have a whole new wardrobe soon enough." She touched her stomach.

"New . . ." Grace's eyes shifted from Aurelie to Vivian, then widened. "You, too?" Aurelie grinned and nodded. Grace promptly thrust the gown aside and embraced her. "When? You are still so slender!"

"Sometime in May. It appears I shall be missing the Season."

"As if you cared! Oh, Aurelie, does everyone know?"

"Everyone who is here. We told your parents when they arrived."

Grace gave a rueful grin. "No wonder Mother did not come at me with the fireplace poker."

"Yes, she was very pleased. She is already suggesting names."

"Oh, dear."

Her sister-in-law nodded. "Horatio seems to be at the top of the list. Followed by Reginald, Godfrey, and Milward." From across the room, Vivian gave a choked laugh.

"Family names," Grace offered, "which Papa would not

allow for his sons. Have you countered with any of your own?"

"Of course," Aurelie answered saucily. "Hortense, Regina, Godiva, and Millicent. Now, here is a fresh chemise. Let's get you into that gown."

When she descended the stairs an hour later, flanked by Aurelie and Vivian, Grace felt at least marginally ready to face the firing squadron. The maid had done a very good job with the gown, and it fell in soft folds to the top of her kid slippers. Emerald ribbon gathered the material just under her breasts and banded the long sleeves, and a matching ribbon was threaded through her hair.

She knew she looked well enough. The problem, of course, was how she would look when the evening was over. Rather like a ship after a full-force gale, she imagined.

Vivian's husband was the first to greet them. Always a handsome man, Lord St. Helier was positively blinding in the smile he gave his wife. Yes, he was certainly very proud of himself—and very much in love. He did notice Grace after a moment, and the smile he gave was a good deal less fervent, but warm nonetheless.

"A golden grace to go with the red and raven." He bowed over her hand. "Hullo, Grace. You are looking quite splendid this evening."

As if it had been mere days since they had last met. She was very grateful for the casual, friendly greeting. "Hullo, Noel. And thank you."

As he stepped aside to claim his wife's arm, Grace scanned the room. The costumes and placement had changed a bit, the players and atmosphere had not. Her mother, garbed now in ice-blue silk that exactly matched her eyes, was ensconced regally in a Sheraton chair, deliberately looking at a wall. Her father was lounging on the settee, Myrtle by his side. Jason did send a bolstering smile from his position at the mantel, but she barely noticed. She was looking for Rafe.

She heard him before she saw him. In fact, the neighbors must have heard him. His deep, resonant laugh was loud enough to rattle the paintings. He was joined almost immediately by Rickey, whose laughter sounded distressingly like a braying mule.

Grace knew her brother. Rickey only sounded like that when he was utterly disguised. Rafe mumbled something and Rickey laughed again. There was no doubt about it. They were both drunk as bishops.

"Oh, dear," she heard Aurelie whisper.

Her own sentiments were far stronger. Not that she had counted on receiving much support from Rafe anyway, but there was no hope for it now. If she was very lucky, he would ignore her. If fortune was smiling on her as was usual, he would be downright unpleasant, then would proceed to tell her family exactly where she had been during the past week.

He did not ignore her.

"Grace," he saluted from the corner, "nice of you to join us! And another new gown. Blink, if you would, please. You rather resemble a grasshopper at present."

"Really, dearest," his aunt chided. Rickey guffawed.

Grace very nearly spun on her heel and left the room. Aurelie's grip on her arm stopped her. Jason, looking decidedly pained, gestured toward the sideboard. "Would you ladies like some sherry? Lemonade?"

"Lemonade," Vivian and Aurelie replied in unison.

"Sherry," Grace said grimly. At the moment, she actually envied Rafe and Rickey their intoxication. A few glasses of champagne would have been very welcome just then.

The thought brought to mind the last occasion she had had a bit too much champagne. It was not a pleasant memory, as it had led to her subsequent banishment to the country. She hazily recalled weaving her way up St. James's. . . .

"Here you go." Jason's voice cut into the reverie. She accepted the sherry with a tight smile and took a hearty sip. She would take her fortitude where she could get it.

"That is a lovely gown, my dear," Myrtle announced. "I myself am far more inclined toward moss green, but the young must have their dewy colors. You know, Aurelie, I

105

am reminded of the time when you were a child and you got grass stains all over your gown. How clever you were, rubbing the whole of it with grass. I do not believe anyone would have noticed had your dear mother not known that you did not have a green gown in your wardrobe. . . ."

Grace turned to Aurelie, who smiled and shook her head. Apparently Myrtle was remembering someone else's childhood. It was not an uncommon occurrence.

Rickey broke the ensuing silence. "I say, Mother, remember the time Grace decided to play Anne Bonney? Rigged herself out in Jason's clothes and cast his raft into that old pond near the mill? Good thing Reverend Biggs was riding by to fish her out when she went tip over ar—tail. Might have been the end of her otherwise. If I remember right, both you and the reverend were a bit green all over, Gracie. Nasty, slimy stuff, algae."

Rafe chuckled. Lady Heathfield moaned quietly. Grace, for her own part, wanted to howl, but it was not worth the effort. Rickey was merely doing what he always did, affectionately casting the brightest light possible on her flawed life.

He turned his attention back to his glass then, and it appeared the matter would be allowed to pass. She should have known better.

"What a charming story!" Myrtle chirped. "You always were a lively little thing, Grace, dear. But who is Anne Bonney? I cannot seem to place the name. Is she a relative of yours?"

Lady Heathfield sighed again. The earl grunted.

Rafe answered. "Anne Bonney was a pirate, Aunt. She terrorized the waters of the West Indies a century ago with her lover, Captain Calico Jack Rackham. Quite a paragon of female virtue."

"A pirate, hmm?" Myrtle was silent for a moment. Then her plump face creased into a delighted smile. "A pirate. I have always said that a family is nothing without a good scoundrel or two!"

If the Tarrant butler thought it odd to be walking into a

completely silent room, he gave no indication. He merely bowed toward Aurelie. "Supper," he intoned, "is served, my lady."

Midway into the first remove, Rafe decided Havensgate was not such a terrible place to be after all. The food was good, the wine was better, and there was an ample supply of both. True, he could have done without the company, but it could have been worse. Rickey was proving himself an entertaining fellow, far more genial than his older brother. Rafe wondered why he had not noticed this before and silently speculated that perhaps he had spent a lifetime being chummy with the wrong Granville.

Yes, Rickey made a decent drinking companion. He certainly believed in keeping the glasses full. The rest of the family could take themselves off to the nether regions as far as Rafe was concerned. Even Aurelie. She had been casting surreptitious glances at his glass since the first course, and he had even caught her giving a small shake of her head when a footman had stepped forward to offer a refill. He had silently set her straight on the matter, holding the glass aloft himself.

Lady Heathfield, seated to his right, had said nothing whatsoever to him during the meal. No great loss, that. To his left, Vivian had done her best to maintain a polite conversation, but he had done nothing to help. Eventually she had given up, and was presently engaged with Lord Heathfield in a lively discourse on the increasing power of the Colonies. She might have married an English earl, but she was an American through and through.

"I would suggest graceful concession, sir," her husband said genially to Lord Heathfield. "My wife has cajoled you into an argument you cannot possibly hope to win."

"Colonials," Heathfield grunted, but he patted Vivian's hand.

"Brits," Vivian replied sweetly, and patted right back.

Grace, watching her father's craggy face break into a grin, wished she could handle him with half as much skill.

And spirit. She rather liked her gruff father, and had spent the better part of her life trying to make him show even a modicum of affection. He was genial enough with Jason, but she half suspected that was due to the fact that his elder son and heir looked a great deal like him, from the mahogany hair to the topaz Granville eyes.

She had those eyes as well. They all did. And that fact was quite probably the reason her mother did not look upon her with favor. They shared the golden hair, certainly, but the countess's pale blue eyes were hers alone.

At present, Lady Heathfield's pale blue gaze was directed somewhere toward the far wall. Grace was certain Aurelie had invited at least one other matron. It was always wise to provide the countess with suitable company. Rafe's aunt, of course, was marvelous company for everyone else, but never failed to send Lady Heathfield into disapproving silence. The great irony was that Myrtle seemed to regard the countess as great fun, and addressed her with constant familiarity. Grace had long ago decided that, despite her flightiness, Myrtle's quizzing of her mother was deliberate, and utterly lucid.

"How delighted you must be, Lady Heathfield," she was saying now, "to know that dearest Aurelie is increasing at last. I, of course, never doubted her capacity in the matter, but it seemed to have been distressing you grievously. I have often wished to offer some comfort but refrained, you understand, out of respect for the delicacy of the subject."

Trust Myrtle to broach a topic inappropriate to supper with such sincere gentility. Grace hid her reluctant smile behind her napkin and waited for her mother's response. It was decidedly disappointing.

"Quite."

Myrtle, if she comprehended the dismissal behind the clipped tone, gave no indication. "Yes, to be surrounded by one's glorious children and their progeny is life's greatest blessing, I have always said. Do you not agree?" It was clear Lady Heathfield was not about to respond, but Myrtle scarcely allowed time for a reply. "With the elders married

108

and Rickey off at school, how grateful you must be to have dearest Grace close at hand. Are you not excessively grateful?"

"Aunt," Rafe said warningly.

"Why, of course you are! Silly of me to so much as mention it." She beamed at Grace. "What a joy you are to your parents, dear girl."

"Aunt," Rafe said again. Ordinarily he would not have interfered, but Lady Heathfield was looking a bit white around the mouth, her husband was gradually turning a faint shade of purple, and Grace's gold-flecked eyes were wide enough to flag passing ships. Another moment and his lovely intoxication would be completely spoiled.

"You have something to add, Rafael?" His aunt clapped her hands in delight. "I know you are ever so fond of Grace. Do feel free to share an anecdote of your time together. I am certain we would all enjoy it ever so much!"

The wine, which had so recently cast a warm glow, began to roil in his gut. There was no way Myrtle could know that it was he who had delivered Grace to her door, but the old hen was unwittingly treading on very thin ice. "I confess, Aunt, I would be hard put to remember any childhood tales at present."

"Childhood? Pah! Why, the angel has done countless charming things since childhood. . . ."

Grace made a small, choked sound. Then, from the head of the table, Tarrant offered, "You know, I read the most interesting account of the Spa Fields demonstration in the *Observer*—"

"Oh no, you will not distract us with political faradiddle," Myrtle interrupted, fluttering her hands at him. "That nasty Orator Hunt and his common followers are not fit conversation for the table. Terrible, how they were allowed to gather like that. I will hear nothing of the rabble and near riots. No, no—we must have more cheerful talk!"

"Here, here!" Rickey announced, lifting his glass. "And I have just the shtory." His words were decidedly slurred. "Remember, Grashie, the time you climbed the trellish at

Lady Biddington'sh? Dashed funny, that, though I can't fathom what you hoped to look at in the garden at that hour. Birdsh were all gone . . ."

Lady Heathfield sniffed, Lord Heathfield grunted, and Grace, wanting nothing more than to drown her brother in his turtle soup, groaned quietly. A quick glance at Rafe made her want to drown herself in the soup. His black brows were raised to dramatic levels and his jaw was slack. Then, before she jerked her eyes away, she saw his mouth curve into a catlike smile. He knew the event, and had clearly gone from considering her presence on the balcony to recalling his companion in the gardens.

"You know," Vivian said, her tone overly bright, "I am certain I spied a peacock on our way up the drive. It was dark, of course, but I did point it out to Noel. Did I not, my lord?"

Her husband, when everyone turned to him, gave a weak smile. "Did you, my dear? Why, yes, I believe I recall your mentioning something of the sort. Have you peacocks now, Tare?"

Grace knew full well that there were no peacocks. Jason hated the creatures, had always joked that their strident cries put him in mind of a rather peevish governess who had tormented the young Granvilles years back. At the moment, however, he was clearly considering lying. Jason, of course, never lied. Grace appreciated the gesture, but wished he would get on with his decision quickly.

He cleared his throat. "No, we do not have peacocks, but there are some very large grouse about. . . ." Grace saw Aurelie roll her eyes. "I suppose you might have seen a *very* large grouse. . . ."

"Very large, you say?" their father all but bellowed. "Never had much luck with fostering large grouse in my time here. Demmed good hunting, it could be."

"Of course, sir," Jason replied. "I shall arrange it."

" 'Twas not a bad season in eighty-seven, if memory serves," the earl muttered. "We might've had some *moder-*

ately large birds then, but not *very* large. Do my soul good to have a crack at the real big 'un. . . ."

No one seemed inclined to mention the fact that grouse season had been over for several months. Grace had no taste for the hunt in general, but she would gladly have discussed *husband* hunting at the moment. No, she amended wryly. That was not a subject she wanted to touch with a barge pole. Her mother, on the other hand, would certainly break her stony silence should the topic be raised.

She tried to think of something brilliant to say about grouse.

The butler appeared then, and crossed silently to Aurelie. "I beg your pardon, my lady . . ." Grace could not hear precisely what he said next, but she caught, ". . . have arrived."

Aurelie's lovely face immediately broke into a wide smile. "Oh, good! I was beginning to wonder."

"It is a bit late for arrivals, is it not?" Myrtle queried. "Why, to travel after dark on these roads! One is surely courting grave danger."

Aurelie hastened to reassure her. "I promise you, madam, the only danger is to be found in the weather, which I am certain is the reason this party was delayed. I suggested that people arrive either today or tomorrow. . . ."

Myrtle was not listening. "I fear I recounted a false tale to you, dearest," she said to Grace. "I do apologize."

"It is of no matter, madam," Grace replied, curiosity piqued against her better judgment. "It does happen."

"Oh, but I do so hate those persons who cannot get a tale right! I see where I erred clearly now." The older woman beamed as she gestured toward the open door. " 'Twas not you for whom we expected Rafe to offer. 'Twas Lady Chloe!"

All eyes turned to stare at the petite redhead who had just entered the room. She gave the table a bright smile. "I am so sorry to be arriving now. The roads are in an appalling state and Dunstan would insist upon driving himself." Then she fixed her lovely hazel gaze on Rafe. "I thought we had agreed, Your Grace, that we would keep the matter just between us."

Now everyone turned to regard Rafe, who was still regarding Lady Chloe. After a moment, he lifted his glass. "Quite right, my dear," he replied, toasting her. "We did agree and I have not changed my mind. You may continue to consider the matter just between us."

9

THE MATTER WAS just between them. Grace smiled grimly. Just between Rafe and Chloe, and sixteen other people—nineteen if one counted the children. And one could not, after all, discount the children. Trying to keep gossip-worthy news from children was as futile as trying to keep news of the Prince Regent's infidelities from his wife.

And she had forgotten the servants. Careless. Not that most of the staff gave a fig about the matter, but the news certainly would have traveled throughout the house. So it was now upwards of forty people who knew what was between Rafe and Chloe. Or at least knew something was between them.

In the time following Chloe's arrival, neither she nor Rafe had said a single word about the initial scene. A full day later, the rest of the guests had arrived, and with the party complete and lively, there had been little time for anyone to think much about it.

Anyone except Grace, of course.

She had thought of nothing else. When Chloe, a longtime acquaintance, had regaled her with the latest Society *on dits*, Grace had wanted only to ask if she and Rafe were betrothed or even if the possibility had arisen. Fear of the answer, and the certainty that her heart would spill out with the words, had kept her from asking.

When her mother had scolded her roundly at supper the evening before for arriving at the table in a wool gown whose hem was still damp from her walk in the snowy gardens, she had merely flushed into her quince-stuffed turbot.

She could not have informed everyone present that she had been too caught up in thinking about Rafe to remember that changing for supper was de rigueur.

And when Rafe had stumbled over the edge of the drawing room carpet, losing his grip on his glass and spraying her with brandy, she had not so much as blinked. She had been far too busy imagining children with Chloe's flaming hair and his glorious sapphire eyes.

It would be an appropriate match, certainly, at least as far as Society was concerned. Rafe was a duke. It was only fitting that he marry the daughter of another duke. Chloe's father would certainly condone the match. The man would care a good deal less about Rafe's present debauched state than about the fact that unmarried dukes were as scarce as hen's teeth. Rich, unmarried dukes were to be seen as akin to manna from heaven.

Chloe, blithe and irreverent as she might be, could do far worse. She had often lamented that her despairing sire would undoubtedly end up marrying her off to the first lofty peer who so much as expressed an interest. The two girls had been reduced to helpless giggles each time they had considered the possibilities. The Duke of Tilsby, with his rheumatism and false teeth? The Marquess of Friers, with his quizzing glass and penchant for puce waistcoats?

It appeared the Duke of Earith had chosen the Duke of Avemar.

"Aunt Grace?"

Grace turned away from her blind contemplation of the frosted window. Her niece Michaela was standing mere inches away, gazing at her with familiar topaz eyes. "Yes, sweetheart?"

"You are sad," the girl announced. Grace's sister Catherine, for all her vain selfishness, had produced distressingly astute children. "Would you care to talk about it?"

Grace suppressed her smile. Ordinarily such an offer from a girl of ten would seem laughable. From Michaela it

was only to be expected. The child was mature quite beyond her years.

"I am not sad," she lied, "merely feeling stifled. I do not
believe it has stopped snowing for so much as a minute today."

"I do not mind so much. Miss Thurston is indisposed, so
Aunt Aurelie was teaching us to play vingt-et-un. She says
it is ever so popular at the gentlemen's clubs."

This time Grace did smile. Catherine would have a fit, or
would have if she ever paid any attention to what her children were doing. "And now?"

"She has gone to lie down." Michaela's smooth brow
furrowed. "She says she needs naps more than Freddy does
lately."

Freddy, at five, was an adorable little boy, but he drove
his governess to fits with his boundless energy. He had
snuck out of bed the night before and made his way downstairs to the salon, announcing his intention to have port
with the rest of the gentlemen. The haggard, decidedly ill-
looking Miss Thurston had arrived hot on his heels, and
Freddy had proceeded to skip wildly through the room,
evading her grasp. In the few moments before a single
snapped command from his grandmother sent the boy flying into the governess's arms, Grace had spied both Jason
and Noel watching him with an amusing combination of
masculine delight and sheer terror. Both had then snuck surreptitious glances at their wives' midsections. Aurelie and
Vivian had grinned broadly.

"Where are Freddy and Phoebe now?" she asked
Michaela.

"I am here!" Seven-year-old Phoebe flounced into the
room, all but glowing with her own consequence. While the
other two children had their father's pale hair and Saxon
features, Phoebe was pure Granville, all raven curls and
flashing eyes. Michaela was lovely; Phoebe showed every
promise of becoming an incomparable beauty. And a complete hoyden. "Here I am!"

"Hello, minx," Grace greeted her, accepting the enthusiastic, slightly sticky embrace. "Where is your brother?"

"Climbing the draperies, I s'pose," was the unconcerned reply.

"Oh, dear," Grace and Michaela said in unison. Freddy's proclivity for drapery climbing had led to countless tense situations. "Where?" Grace asked. Phoebe shrugged.

Michaela, ever dedicated to her self-appointed role of siblings' keeper, was already twisting pleats into her pinafore. "We must find him, Aunt Grace, before Grandmama does. She said that if she ever caught him climbing again, she would have him pilloried."

Grace sighed. "She did not mean it." Inwardly she was not so certain. "Phoebe, sweetheart, where did you last see your brother?"

"In the conservivitory," Phoebe said. "What's pillowried? Will Grandmama stuff Freddy with feathers?"

"No, sweetheart, of course not," Grace replied, adding under her breath, "She could never hold him still long enough." Then, "Come along, ladies. We must go on a quest for Sir Frederick."

Michaela nodded and squared her shoulders. Phoebe clapped. "Oh, good! I shall be Lady Galahad. When we find Freddy, will you give us a broom, Aunt Grace?"

"A broom?"

"Yes, for my act of squalor."

"Ah, a boon for your act of valor. Yes, I suppose one could be arranged. What would you like?"

"A diamond crown," Phoebe answered immediately.

Grace smiled. "Would you settle for cakes and lemonade?"

The child thought for a moment. "With icing?"

"What, you want icing in your lemonade?"

Phoebe giggled delightedly. "On the cakes, goosey!"

"Oh, on the cakes. Icing it is then." The three headed for the conservatory. "Phoebe," Grace asked as they crossed the great hall, "where did you hear about Galahad?"

"Lady St. Hillier. She told me all about King Arthur and

116

Galahad. And she said there was a woman named Vivien who trapped a pow'ful magician under a rock." Phoebe paused to stick her tongue out at a portrait of a singularly ugly Granville ancestress. "Then Lord St. Hillier told her she had a vivid imaginatium and said I would be just like her when I grow up. I like him. He's almost as nice as Uncle Jason."

Approval from the king himself was not worth a pence compared to that. Grace hoped Noel felt suitably honored.

"I hope you did not bother Lady St. Helier, minx."

Phoebe shook her dark curls. "She said I was absolutedly splendid. Then she went to take a nap." She skipped splendidly ahead.

At first view the conservatory appeared to be empty. "Sweetheart, are you quite certain—" Grace began, then gasped.

Freddy had been climbing the draperies. And quite successfully. He was, at the moment, seated in an alcove a good fifteen feet above the floor, clinging for all he was worth to the marble bust of Bach who was sharing the space. The scene was enough to make her heart lodge in her throat.

Then she heard the curse.

The scene below the boy made her jaw drop. Struggling against the weight of the harpsichord, muttering vague invectives, was Rafe. He looked up at Freddy long enough to say, "Hang on there, soldier," before leaning into the heavy instrument again.

As Grace and Michaela stood gaping, Phoebe skipped over to offer her assistance. Instead of pushing at the harpsichord, she butted squarely into Rafe, wrapping her arms about his legs. Thrown off balance, he stumbled, smacking his jaw soundly against the top of the harpsichord. Grace expected him to turn about and snarl at the girl.

Instead, he gave an audible sigh and suggested, "Perhaps if you were to push at that side—" he gestured to the far end of the instrument "—we would manage it."

With a sharp salute, Phoebe did as he indicated. It was

debatable whether she was actually helping or hindering the process, but with a final shove, Rafe got the harpsichord against the wall under Freddy. Phoebe promptly tried to scramble upward. Rafe gently pulled her back.

"As I am a bit taller, mademoiselle, I think I should be the one to do the actual climbing."

By this time, Grace had recovered her wits and hurried forward. Rafe gave her a wry smile. "A bit late, Gracie. Miss Phoebe and I—"

"Lady Galahad," Phoebe corrected.

Rafe quirked one black brow. "Been consorting with Vivian, have you?" He sighed. "*Lady Galahad* and I had to move this behemoth ourselves." Then he boosted himself onto the harpsichord.

"Rafe, why didn't you simply get a footman and a ladder?"

He looked down at her from his high perch. "If you had not noticed, my dear, Noel's mother arrived recently. Every servant in the place has been set to dealing with her baggage. Master Frederick would have reached his majority before a footman became available."

Grace could not dispute the truth behind the statement. The Dowager Countess of St. Helier was well known for traveling with staggering amounts of baggage in tow. The woman was such marvelous company, however, that no one ever thought to complain.

"Is there anything I can do?" she asked. Rafe did not look entirely steady, and she could not help but wonder whether or not he was sober. "I could—"

"Stand back."

"But, Rafe—"

"For God's sake, move back! And take the girls with you."

His tone brooked no dissent, so Grace did as he ordered, pulling a reluctant Phoebe with her. Michaela, ever sensible, had taken herself nearly to the door at Rafe's initial command.

"All right, Freddy," Rafe said, stretching his arms up,

"let go of Herr Johann, if you would, please, and give me your foot."

Now, Freddy had been pulled from enough alcoves and valances to have a great deal of trust in whichever adult should be doing the rescuing. Whether it was the height at which he sat, or his own doubts regarding the stability of Rafe's position atop the harpsichord that dictated his present actions, however, Grace was not certain. He did thrust one foot toward Rafe's hand, but he did not relinquish his grip on the bust.

"I've got you," Rafe said. "Just come at me slowly now."

Everything happened so fast that Grace barely had time to blink.

Freddy jumped toward Rafe. Herr Johann came with him. The marble bust glanced off Rafe's shoulder and crashed to the floor. Just where Grace and Phoebe had been standing moments earlier. Michaela screamed, Freddy shouted, and Rafe said nothing at all.

He barely felt the impact. Rather, he barely felt the first impact. He was completely aware of Freddy hitting him full in the chest and the subsequent sensation of falling. Then he felt his back hitting the parquet floor. Hard.

He lay where he landed, seeing stars and gasping for breath—with little success. It was small consolation that he had managed to protect the boy by keeping him clasped to his chest. The boy, he was convinced, had shoved his rib cage right out his back. Then, with a grin, Freddy thumped his chest. Breath came back with a whoosh.

"Again, sir!" he chortled.

"I don't think so, Freddy," Rafe grunted, then closed his eyes and waited to die.

He felt a weight like that of his spirit lifting from his chest. He hesitantly opened one eye and saw a heavenly visage. "Go away, Grace," he moaned, "and let me expire in peace."

He grunted again as she began prodding at his chest. "Does that hurt?" he heard her ask.

119

"I imagine it would if I could feel anything."

"Oh, Rafe!" He opened both eyes fully to see her hovering over him, terror written across her face. "Have you . . . are you . . . ?"

"I will be just fine, once you stop poking at me." To prove his point, he pushed himself up onto his elbows. Every bone in his body protested. She promptly grasped his arm, whether to help him up or send him prostrate, he could not tell. It hurt. "Damnit, Grace, leave off! I have yet to fully survive this experience, and you are not helping."

He ignored the wounded look she gave him as she obeyed and instead studied the marble bust resting several feet away. It was lying facedown in a rather impressive crater. "I never was particularly fond of Bach," he muttered. He thought he heard Phoebe giggle.

Michaela bent down and surveyed the damaged parquet floor. "I am certain Aunt Aurelie will not mind so much when she hears how you rescued Freddy."

"Thank you, Michaela, I feel ever so much—"

"But Mama says that when women are expecting, they are not always in full control of their faculties. She says Aunt Aurelie has been doing quite the oddest things. Still, I do not believe she will be too harsh with you."

Rafe had no idea what to say to that. He was ultimately spared the necessity of saying anything by Phoebe's loud pronouncement. "We found Freddy, Aunt Grace. It is time for our broom!"

Grace, her face still a shade past pale, nodded. "Yes, cake and lemonade for all. Rafe, would you like . . . ? No, I do not suppose you would." She took another lingering glance at his torso. "Are you quite certain you are all right?"

"Splendid. And refreshment sounds like a very good idea." He tested his limbs, which seemed sound enough to support him. "I must say, Gracie," he drawled, "I am prodigiously glad I came. What more could a simple man ask for? A holiday spent trapped inside a house with one of you, two pregnant ladies, and three children!" With that, he pushed himself to his feet. "I will say one thing for Havensgate, though . . . there is always the liquor."

Then, pausing only long enough to pat each child on the head, he limped toward the door.

Grace watched him go. Rafe. That had been the Rafe she had known. A slow smile spread across her face. More food and less drink was what he needed. And to be reminded that he was still very much alive. That life was as much a blessing as death was a curse. It was, of course, up to her to do it. The beginnings of a plan formed in her mind.

She nearly laughed aloud. Rafe was very likely going to kill her.

"Aurelie has planned the most delightful evening," Vivian announced that evening when all of the guests had assembled in the drawing room. "So we may all forget that we have been snowed in all day."

"Tell us what you have planned, dear," Jane, the Dowager Countess of St. Helier, urged.

As Aurelie complied, Grace glanced about the room. Her whole family was there, of course, and the St. Heliers. Lord and Lady Warren, neighbors and longtime friends of her parents, had arrived the day before, as had Aurelie's grandmother. Myrtle had spent the day knitting and was even now surveying her vastly expanded woolly masterpiece as if measuring it for Freddy. Grace could not see Rafe, as he was somewhere behind her, but she heard him groan at the mention of charades. Rafe loathed charades.

And of course, there was Chloe and her older brother, Dunstan.

All things considered, Aurelie had put together quite a party. The high sticklers of the ton could not complain. Older gentlemen, matrons, the young married couples, the younger unmarried—properly chaperoned by the matrons, of course—and even several children thrown in for spice. And Catherine's children certainly made things lively, on those occasions when they were allowed out of the nursery. After the events of the afternoon, Grace wondered if young Freddy would be seen again during their stay. He would certainly resist being kept upstairs. All bets, she decided, would best be placed on his resourcefulness.

Charades after supper, was it? Grace had never been much for charades, but it was better than everyone sitting about, staring at each other. That got very tedious very quickly.

"Drink, anyone?" Rickey asked from his post across the room. As the requests began, Dunstan moved over to help him. After several minutes, Rickey cleared his throat. "I say, Jason, could you come here for a moment?"

Jason did, and his younger brother spoke briefly to him in hushed tones. A silence followed, broken only by an occasional grunt. "Aurelie," Jason called. She joined the three.

"I haven't the foggiest idea, dear," she said after listening to whatever he was saying. "You may send for more, of course, but supper will be served soon."

Jason coughed. "I am afraid we are having a bit of a problem with some of the bottles. . . ."

"Problem?" Lord Heathfield barked.

"Yes, sir. We cannot seem to get them open." Grace saw her brother give a faint smile. "Sherry, anyone? Or lemonade."

"Not amusing, Tare," Rafe grunted. "Ring for something else."

"Yes, I could, but as Aurelie has pointed out, we will all be going in to supper soon. May I offer you a glass of sherry?"

"I detest sherry. Always have."

Jason shrugged. "Lemonade, then?"

Rafe groaned.

The party accepted their drinks. Grace caught more than one curious glance aimed at her over sherry and lemonade glasses. She merely smiled back, her gaze all innocence.

Goodness, she thought with wry humor, *it is almost as if you all think I did it.*

"I will not do it," Rafe muttered some time later that evening. "I will not."

"Dash it all, Avemar, you must! Won't work otherwise."

Rafe glowered at Dunstan Somersham. He had never had an ill opinion of Chloe's older brother, but the clod now rated just above Napoleon on his list of least favorite persons. "Not if hell freezes over and swine fly," he growled. "I had my misgivings from the onset, but after listening to the lot of you for the past quarter hour, I am now firmly convinced that I should rather participate in the Apocalypse."

The young marquess, to his credit, sat back and shut his mouth. His sister, unfortunately, was not cowed. "Oh, do not be such a curmudgeon, Rafe! We are doing it, so you must do it, too."

"My response to that, my dear, is to inquire as to whether, if you were all leaping from London Bridge, you would expect me to do the same."

Dunstan chuckled. "Very good, Avemar! Got you there, Chlo."

Chloe merely tossed her red curls. "You really must stop toadeating, brother dear. It does not suit you above half." Then, to Rafe, "Give me your slip." Before he could comply, she snatched the paper from his hand. "All right, then, since you are so averse to this role, we shall give it to Dunstan."

"But I already have one," her brother protested.

"Expendable," Chloe retorted.

"I would offer my role," the elder Lady St. Helier announced dryly, "but I cringe to think of how he would play it. Yes, Dunstan, you must take Avemar's."

"And what of Avemar?"

Chloe's hazel eyes gleamed, and Rafe found himself highly apprehensive of whatever would drop from the full, expressive lips. "Avemar," she said tartly, "will be scenery."

Rafe sighed. He wished with every ounce of his being that he could stalk off to Tarrant's library with nothing more than a decanter and glass for company. But he knew full well that Chloe would come bouncing after him and, despite her paltry size, would herd him right back into the salon. She was rather like Grace in her sheer determination. No wonder they had always seemed to get along famously.

"Scenery," he echoed grimly.

"Yes," Chloe announced firmly, "scenery. I have decided, Rafael, that everything will go so much better for us if you simply stand and be decorative. You are rather nice to look at, but wearying on the ears and soul of late."

He could not help himself; he grinned. "Yet you still wished to be paired with me."

She rolled her eyes. "As if I have a choice. Now, come along. We must prepare."

Grace heard the end of their exchange as she took her seat. Rather than feeling heartened by Chloe's assertion, she felt decidedly worse. It seemed Chloe did not really want to marry Rafe at all, or at least had not wanted the match initially. It was bad enough thinking of the two being wed, immeasurably worse to think it would be a *mariage de convenance*. The question, of course, was precisely whose convenience was being addressed. Neither family needed money. All the better, she supposed. No one lost anything.

Except the potentially unhappy couple. And Grace herself.

Aurelie's clap brought her out of her miserable thoughts. "All right, we are ready to begin!" She gestured toward the makeshift stage. Two footmen held a sheet taut between them. "Our first group is about to open."

There was a muffled grunt from the far side of the "curtain" and some part of someone's anatomy leaned momentarily into the linen before withdrawing. Rafe's curse rang out loudly, the sheet giving no disguise to his voice. Then, to the assembled party's collective surprise, Chloe's head appeared a good seven feet in the air. The flaming curls wavered for a moment, Rafe cursed again, and Chloe's eyes—just visible above the sheet—widened comically. After a tense second, she seemed to steady herself. Lady St. Helier whispered something and the curtain dropped.

Chloe's vastly increased height was soon explained. She was perched, quite comfortably, it seemed, on Rafe's right shoulder. It could not have been much of a chore, holding her, for she was quite petite, and Rafe did not appear taxed in the least. He did appear thoroughly bored. He even yawned.

"Hold still," Grace heard Chloe hiss at him. "You are scenery!"

He yawned again.

Dunstan appeared then, a folded damask tablecloth tossed over his shoulders like a cape. He raised his hand level with his brow and pantomimed scanning the area. His gaze came to rest on Chloe, and with a dramatic sweep of his tablecloth-cum-cape, he cast himself to his knees below her.

"Rapunzel!" Lady Warren cried out. Aurelie shook her head.

Chloe, ostensibly on spying Dunstan, flashed a glorious smile and thrust her arms toward him. Broad as Rafe's shoulders were, they did not prevent her from nearly tumbling down upon the wildly gesticulating Dunstan. Rafe's hands flew upward at the same time as Chloe tangled one fist in his overlong hair. She succeeded in preventing a fall, but Rafe's pained epithet quite ruined the silent drama of the scene.

"Beauty and the Beast!" Lord Heathfield barked.

His elder daughter, Catherine, seated by his side, gave a plaintive "Really, Papa."

"What, you don't think it a demmed good guess?" the earl demanded. "Well, Aurelie?"

"A truly inspired guess, sir," his daughter-in-law managed, "but incorrect, I am afraid."

"See there?" Heathfield muttered to Catherine. "Inspired, she said."

"Really, Papa."

Lady St. Helier entered the scene then, her lovely face set in uncustomarily stern lines. She gestured forcefully toward the prostrate Dunstan, who proceeded to clap his hands over his heart beseechingly.

"I have it!" Noel proclaimed. "Romeo and Juliet!"

Aurelie tilted her head. "You are close."

"You mean I am wrong?" Noel seemed to find the concept a bit beyond him.

His wife grinned. "What a shame." Then she guessed, "Tristan and Isolde?"

"Noel was closer, Vivian," Aurelie teased.

"Tragedy," Jason drawled.

"Disobedient children," was his mother's terse offering.

There was a long silence. All the while, Lady St. Helier remonstrated, Dunstan emoted, and Chloe clung to Rafe's hair.

"No one else has a guess?" Aurelie asked, disappointment clear on her lovely face.

"Ah!"

Everyone turned to look at Myrtle.

"Lady Hammond?" Aurelie coaxed.

"Oh, I am sorry. Did I startle you?" The older woman beamed apologetically. "I missed a stitch." She held up the now truly voluminous wool object. "Were you waiting for me to guess as to the charade? How sweet of you." She poked at her knitting.

"Well," Aurelie sighed, "I suppose I must tell—"

"Clandestine lovers." Myrtle's eyes were fastened on her hands. "One, two . . . ah, yes, there it is!"

Aurelie laughed aloud. "Lady Hammond got it! The answer was 'Lovers.' Now, if the next group would like to take the stage . . ."

Lovers. Grace sighed as she rose to her feet. Her group, comprised of Vivian, Lord Warren, Catherine's husband Stephen, and Rickey, had been assigned "Surprise." They

126

had decided to enact a battle scene, complete with Wellington routing a complacent Napoleon. Grace had thought it a rather convoluted scenario, but Rickey and Stephen had been adamant.

She sighed again. With her luck, one of the next groups would have "Wedding," and all of the scenes, when put together, would lead to the answer of "The Worthington-Dillard Union."

Thomasina Worthington, daughter of one of the country's wealthiest and most powerful MPs, had been married to Lord Robert Dillard, military hero, the June before in the Society Wedding to End All Weddings. The bride had looked a bit smug. The groom had looked drunk. The rumor, of course, was that the betrothal had followed a night in a Weybridge inn. It had been quite the talk of the town.

Aurelie, Grace remembered, had found the entire circus vastly amusing.

It was not a heartening thought.

10

HIS SHOULDER HURT like the very devil. At first Rafe had thought it was due to having hefted Chloe about the night before. Now he remembered the dramatic descent of Herr Johann Sebastian Bach. Being coshed with a marble statue was enough to make anyone's body ache.

Three days. He had been in the house three days and it seemed an eternity. A quick glance out the window showed that the snow had stopped sometime during the night. The grounds of the manor were heavily cloaked in white, however, putting an effective end to his thoughts of escape. He cared more for his horse than to put the beast through the strain of making the ride, and even if he were to convince Tarrant to lend him a coach, they would very likely end up in a ditch somewhere within an hour.

He winced as he shrugged into his coat. He had not looked at his shoulder as he had dressed, but he imagined there was a colorful bruise. He had gotten a good view of his chin after Tarrant's valet had shaved him, and had seen red. And blue. And yellow. Courtesy of his close encounter with the top of the harpsichord. He could not, in all good conscience, blame Phoebe. She had been trying to help. And Freddy had merely been being Freddy.

He had spent enough time with Catherine Granville Seymour's children to know them well. And he rather liked them, when they were not under his feet. No, he amended, he simply liked them. They were *always* under one's feet.

Grace. Burnished curls and wicked eyes flashed into his

mind. Yes, he would blame Grace. Logic bedamned, it was convenient to do so. He was fairly certain she had had a hand in the liquor bottles refusing to open. In fact, he was more than a bit curious as to how she had managed it.

There had been wine at supper and port after. But by the time it had occurred to him that *someone* had best ring for a bottle of brandy, the god-awful game of charades had commenced. Charades. He loathed charades. Even more so when he was forced to participate fully sober.

Somewhere in the hall, a clock chimed. He had overslept, and he had not even been inebriated. His shoulder hurt like the very devil, but his head was clear. Food seemed like a very good idea. Breakfast should still be laid out. One thing he could say for Aurelie was that she knew how to feed a party.

One glance into the dining room and he nearly crept right back out. Lady Heathfield sat at the head of the table, as if she were still chatelaine of Havensgate. At various points below her were several Granvilles, his own aunt, and one St. Helier. He returned their greetings, filled his plate at the sideboard, and took a seat beside the dowager countess.

"Good morning, Rafael," she said pleasantly.

"Madam." He had always liked Noel's mother. Everyone liked Noel's mother. Lovely and delicate as a porcelain doll, the woman had the fortitude of an army general and the stunning wit of a king's mistress.

"Have you been sparring with my son?"

Both Rafe and Noel were members of Gentleman Jackson's boxing club. Noel was by far the better pugilist. Rafe always left the club feeling as if he had had his clock cleaned—and the springs and cogs put back in the wrong places.

He fingered his discolored jaw and smiled ruefully. "Not at all, madam. It was a harpsichord. I was having a difficult time with a Bach piece."

"Well, I expect the instrument is sporting a few bruises of its own," Lady St. Helier quipped. Apparently the tale of

Freddy-in-the-conservatory had not reached the guests. "If it were your eye, I would recommend a beefsteak. . . ."

"I have sausages, madam." Rafe indicated his loaded plate. "Will they do?"

"As long as you do not mind grease stains on your cravat, dear."

Myrtle looked up a short time later. "You look rested, dearest. Did you sleep well?"

"Perfectly well, Aunt, thank you."

"Good. I hesitate to bring the matter up, Rafael dear, but you can be somewhat of a beastie when you have . . . not slept well."

Rafe bared his teeth. "I was under the impression that I am somewhat of a beast in general."

His aunt fluttered her napkin at him. "Nonsense! You are a delightful creature at heart when you are feeling quite yourself. Always have been. You know, this snow reminds me of the time you and your father had shut yourselves up in that charming hunting box near Lewes—"

"Really, Aunt, I hardly think—"

"A week without women, I believe Alexander said it was meant to be, though I am certain he missed your mother terribly. The Marlowe men have always been such very devoted husbands."

"Aunt," Rafe growled.

"I did not intend to interrupt your sojourn, of course, but with all the snow, and my carriage wheel not quite turning properly . . ." She tilted her head, clearly reliving the memory. Then she smiled gently. "Well, no matter. I was simply thinking that you have always been so very sweet to the chilled and troubled among us."

Rafe sighed. His aunt's memory, even when it had nothing whatsoever to do with anything, was a dangerous thing. He had more than once speculated that, had Wellington had Myrtle's sievelike mind at his disposal, he would have routed Napoleon a good deal sooner.

He speared a last sausage and rose to his feet. "If you

will excuse me, I believe I will ... go ..." He hadn't the foggiest idea where.

"Grouse!" Lord Heathfield barked from the other end of the table.

"I beg your pardon, sir?"

"Ought to be demmed good hunting," the earl grunted. "Very large grouse."

The concept of trudging across the estate, hip-deep in snow, made Rafe's bones ache anew. "Most definitely, sir," he replied vaguely, and crept from the room.

There was no doubt that Aurelie had planned some marvelous entertainment for the day, snow or no snow. Rafe thought that if he was very quiet—and very clever—he could avoid participating.

With that in mind, he wandered down the hall toward the library. Ordinarily it would have been the first place he would have gone to find Aurelie or Tarrant, and the last place he would have gone if trying to avoid them. But with the house party going in full swing, he expected both were well and fully occupied elsewhere. If anyone was to be among the comfortable leather furniture and countless books, it would be St. Helier. He could stomach a bit of time with Noel. The man had gone a bit cork-brained since his marriage, to be sure, but he still showed remnants of his careless bachelor days. They could crack a bottle of brandy, assuming a crackable bottle could be found, and, if Rafe had his druthers, sit in companionable silence.

There was a fire burning in the grate, but the room was empty. With a smile, he closed the door behind him and surveyed the scene before him. There was a bottle of something in a corner nook, and one of the high-backed chairs would do splendidly. Tall as he was, he would not be visible from the doorway. His grin broadened as he stalked toward the liquor.

"Hullo, Rafe."

He nearly leapt out of his skin. Grace, small as she was, and with her legs tucked up beneath her, had not been visible in the high-backed chair. "Good God, Grace, you just frightened me out of ten years of my life!"

She was garbed in a pale blue, long-sleeved gown. Wrapped in a fluffy white shawl, with her hair curling in a golden cloud, she looked utterly angelic. Except, of course, for the snapping eyes.

"I am sorry. You may have ten of mine."

"I beg your pardon?"

"Years. Of my life. You may have ten of them."

He had thought to spin on his heel and depart for more solitary climes. Curiosity got the better of him. "You do not need your allotment?"

She sighed and blew a stray curl from her forehead. "At this rate, Rafe, I shall be old and gray at twenty."

"Really, Grace . . ."

She waved a hand to silence him. "I am rambling. Pay me no heed." Her glossy head dropped back to the book she held. "Go ahead, avail yourself of the brandy."

To her surprise, he did not. Instead, he settled himself in the second chair. He did not speak, and she took the opportunity to study him. Oh, but he was beautiful. There was a visible bruise on his jaw, courtesy of Phoebe and the harpsichord, she assumed. But he had shaved, his clothes were neat, and he even seemed to be filling them out a bit better. It was probably her imagination, but the thought that three days of Havensgate's food and company had helped him warmed her heart.

Her heart. It was feeling as bruised as his chin looked, but it was still functioning. Or at least it thumped, and was still as full of him as ever. Her fingers clenched on the book in her lap. For the briefest of moments, she wished him away. Her heart was having a very difficult time recently being near him. Knowing he was somehow connected to another woman. Knowing, as perhaps she had always known but refused to accept, that he did not want—would never want—*her.*

"Do you suppose," she asked, not really having meant to

speak, "that we are truly doomed to have reality fall far short of expectation?"

"Hmm?" Rafe looked up from his contemplation of the fire.

She repeated her question, adding, "It seems terribly unfair to think that we go along day to day with our grand expectations, only to find that we're to have turbot again for supper and the same miserable weather the following morning."

"Good Lord, Grace. What are you reading?"

She held up the book. *"Childe Harold's Pilgrimage."*

To her chagrin, he chuckled. "Ah, Byron. He makes the matrons sigh and the maidens weep."

"Really, Rafe, I am being quite serious."

"As am I. The man is far too romantic for his own good. Makes the rest of us poor fellows appear witless oafs." He rested his elbows on his knees and tented his fingers at his lips. "And to think I knew him well when the reviewers called *him* a witless oaf."

"You know Byron well?"

"I know Prinny, too. Though that association fails to bring stars to women's eyes."

To himself, he thought that Byron was, in truth, a far more worthy acquaintance. The man had a way of reducing life to its corporeal elements while elevating the soul. He was a satyric bounder at times, certainly, but had from the beginning inspired in Rafe a sort of grand, primal admiration.

In the spirit of his current, almost tranquil mood, however, he was not going to admit as much to Grace. "If you believe that Childe Harold is really Byron himself . . ." he began.

"How could you not?"

"Then you must consider the fact that when he wrote the piece, he was nothing more than an erstwhile bard with an impoverished title. Why, he could scarce afford a hand at Watier's."

She scowled at him, a perfect study in impatience. "What does that degenerate club have to do with expectations?"

"I feel compelled to remind you that I am a member of that degenerate club. I have even managed to drag your brother—"

"Rafe."

He chuckled. "What I am getting at is that it is all well and good to speak of disillusionment when one is destitute and unknown. Things are, I imagine, vastly different for Byron since he woke up famous."

"I cannot accept that!" She thumped the book against her knee for emphasis. "He speaks from the soul, not the pocket."

He could not banish the thought that she really did look thoroughly angelic at the moment—an avenging angel, perhaps, with her determined little chin and flashing topaz eyes. "All right," he said, giving in a bit. "I will grant that the man speaks from the soul, and extremely cleverly." He paused. "So what was your question again?"

He managed to catch the book when it came flying at his head. "Shame on you, treating an ode of the soul like that." He stared thoughtfully at the embossed leather cover. "Expectations are tricky things, Grace. Sometimes those that are met are far more disturbing than those that are not."

After all, he had fully expected to attain the Avemar dukedom at some point in his life. And he would gladly have handed it right back now that he had.

"What about you?" he queried finally. "Have there been so many turbot suppers that your appetite has waned?" He was startled to notice that her pursed lips would be, in another man's eyes, of course, lush enough to whet a very different sort of appetite. He cleared his throat. "I mean, is your reality so very disappointing when compared to your expectations?"

Grace thought for a time, debating glibness, before replying honestly, "I suppose I would have to spend a good amount of time considering my expectations before I could answer that. When I ponder the matter, I tend to wonder how much is desire, how much honest expectation, and how they coincide."

"Ah, you became philosophical. Perhaps I ought to have your family restrict your exposure to Byron."

"According to you," she shot back, "Byron is far more likely to give me romantical thoughts than philosophical."

"True, perhaps, though my experience had led me to the conclusion that, with young ladies, the two are basically one and the same. Present to me one girl whose deepest, most soulful thoughts are not irrevocably attached to the realm of romance and I will present to you a mistress of self-delusion."

"I think that perhaps I have just been insulted," she muttered dryly.

Now Rafe propped his chin on his intertwined fingers. "Can you honestly tell me that you do not spend a great deal of time dreaming of your one true love?"

No, of course I cannot, she thought sadly. *How could I when it is you I think of nearly every waking moment?*

The words very nearly slipped from her tongue. She bit them back, saying instead, "I think of a great many things."

Like you and Chloe—and whether, should I cry at the wedding, it would merely appear a silly young woman's emotional response to the sheer romantical nature of it all.

"Hmm. Let us go back to your philosophical moment, shall we?" Rafe suggested. "You say that there is an inevitable connection between desire and expectation."

"Did I say that?"

"Semantics. So what are your expectations, Grace, really? To marry, I would imagine. That is certainly what your family has planned. And what are your desires? Much the same, probably. Now the connection between desire and expectation: Your family will want you to marry an acceptable man—wealthy, titled, secure in his position in Society. You will want to marry a dream prince—some adoring, blond Adonis who will write odes to your earlobes and sonnets to your toes. . . . Why on earth are you scowling at me?"

"You are being very hard on me."

"Not at all. I am being hard on the Adonis. Am I wrong, then? About your desires?"

"Yes," she said emphatically, "you are very wrong." If only she could tell him just how wrong he was. "Do you really believe I could love someone who wrote odes to my earlobes?"

A strange smile spread across his face. "You do happen to have very nice earlobes. Though you probably know that as you've chosen a hairstyle which displays them to full advantage."

"Now you are mocking me." Gone was the easy complacency, replaced by a sort of vague desperation. "What if I were to tell you that my desires are far different than what you have suggested?"

Rafe watched as two spots of angry color appeared on her cheeks and wondered what he could possibly have said to inspire them. "It appears I have touched a nerve here. Care to talk about it?"

"No," she snapped, "I would not."

"Pique does not suit you. Come now, tell Uncle Rafe what he has done to displease you."

"You, Uncle Rafe, may take yourself off to the nether regions! My God, you are treating me like a child!"

He was, and it had become deliberate. She was rather splendid in her pique, not at all childlike, and it made him more determined to treat her so. There was something about the image of some fair fop caressing her earlobes that irked him greatly. And he was irked by the fact that he was irked.

Years of seeing her grow up—yes, that was it. Brotherly protectiveness, no more. On her better days, or rather, his better days, he was very fond of Grace. He had, after all, gone to great pains to make certain she had been returned to the bosom of her loving family safe and sound, reputation unsullied.

Her utter lack of gratitude rankled suddenly, dispelling the placid mood.

"I believe I have changed my mind," he muttered. "I have no desire to hear what is causing this tantrum. Here." He tossed the book in her direction. "Go back to Byron. Indulge your romantical philosophies."

She caught the book deftly. "You do not want to hear? Well, too bad. You could not possibly understand my desires. Nor do you have any reason to think me so vapid as to mindlessly accept the absurd dictates of Society."

"Really, Grace," he began with a dismissive wave, but she cut him off.

"There, you see? You are beginning to sound like my mother." Grace watched him lever himself forward in the chair, his gaze straying to the crystal nook. "Don't you dare go for that bottle now, Rafael Marlowe. I will not be dismissed like that. I mean it—one more inch and I will be forced to take it myself and cosh you with it!"

She nodded in satisfaction as he stopped scooting. "Now, in answer to your offensive discourse, I have no desire for any witless blond Adonis, though I cannot say that my own brain rules my heart. No, they seem entirely separated from each other. The man my heart ... imagines ... would never write insipid sonnets. He is ... would be far too intelligent, with beautiful, shadowed eyes to which *I* would be inspired to write poetry. I would not want to love him, but I would have no choice. He would be a devil, damn it, not a god, and he would need my love, desperately! And once he had figured that out, he would understand that he had never been so blessed in his life!"

She had run out of breath, and refilled her lungs in preparation to continue only to find herself too shocked at the words she had spoken to continue. What had she done?

Terrified, mortified, she darted a frantic look at Rafe. To her relief, he did not look particularly illuminated. Nor did

137

he look chastised. Instead, he was merely staring at her. In the ensuing silence, she was certain that she could hear each beat of her heart. Thinking that her only hope for speedy redemption was a dignified exit, she plunked Byron onto the low table, rose gracefully to her feet, and, chin raised, headed at a brisk pace for the door.

She nearly ran over the butler. Considering the speed with which she was moving and the solidity of the obstacle, she literally bounced off his shirtfront. He managed to catch her before she hit the floor, but it was only after a rather dramatic flailing of limbs that she regained her equilibrium. He kept his grip on her elbows as if to ensure that she not tumble spontaneously off her feet. Had he not rescued her from countless falls throughout her childhood, the situation would have been humiliating.

"Thank you, Quinby," she managed.

His hair was now steel gray and there were creases beside his eyes. But the gaze was the same, loyal and kind, and she could all but see him resisting the urge to pat her consolingly on the head. She almost wished he would.

"Her ladyship asked that I find you, m'lady. She requests your presence in the salon."

"Which ladyship?" Grace asked with a sigh. Images of being called onto the carpet by her mother were enough to make her scream and run for cover.

"Ah, I beg your pardon. There are many ladies here at present. It is Lady Tarrant who wishes to see you."

Aurelie was by far a more appealing image. "Thank you, Quinby," she said again, and turned to leave. She stopped at the sound of Rafe's voice.

"Tell me, Quinby, what are we having for luncheon? Lady Grace and I have been discussing turbot."

The butler's impressive brows rose. "Turbot, m'lord? I should be most surprised. With nothing but ice fishing on the lake to be done today, I believe Cook is preparing stuffed carp."

"There, you see, Gracie?" Rafe called as she headed for the salon. "You are to have carp!"

Yes, she thought as she crossed the hall, carp. A natural optimist, Grace found the change heartening. The problem, of course, she decided with wry humor, was that it was still fish.

11

"WAX," JASON MUTTERED. "You expect us to be impressed by the use of wax."

"Really, my love," his wife scolded, "I find it quite commendable. It is truly amazing what one can achieve with the most basic of materials."

"I think it a splendid idea," Vivian chimed in. "I have been wanting to see Madame Tussaud's exhibit for the longest time. I hear she has an absolutely remarkable likeness of Marie Antoinette, dressed in one of the queen's own gowns."

"Is she wearing her head or holding it?" her husband asked dryly. Vivian swatted him.

The conversation had been going on for quite some time, and Grace had long since despaired of a consensus ever being reached. Aurelie had planned an excursion to Brighton, where Madame Tussaud's collection was making a brief appearance. The traveling museum had caused quite a stir among the ton. Grace had seen it in London and had found it impressive, if a bit macabre. It was one thing to view dead persons fashioned in marble, quite another to see them standing about with rosy cheeks and glassy eyes. Even more disconcerting was viewing wax reproductions of persons still alive. An elderly matron in her party had actually commenced a conversation with the king. Deaf as the woman was, she had not seemed overly concerned with the fact that there was no response.

"I cannot think a jaunt to Brighton the best of plans," Jason remarked.

"It is only ten miles," Aurelie argued.

"Ten miles through the snow. We would not arrive until late afternoon, if we arrived at all."

Jason had ever been the voice of common sense. It was a bit dampening at times. There was no questioning his statement, however. While there was no snow falling at present, that which had fallen during the past day was quite evident on the ground. Grace suspected they would be hard put to find the road, let alone travel it.

Aurelie frowned. "But I had it all planned."

"Well, sweetheart, you should have compared schedules with Mother Nature," her husband teased. "She took precedence."

"As always." Aurelie had the grace to laugh. "I just do so hate to be trumped in my entertaining. We shall have to go to Plan Number Two, then. Oh, don't scowl, Jason. It does not involve traveling any great distance."

"I am more concerned that it involves grouse."

"No, although I suppose you will have to organize a hunt of sorts for tomorrow. Your father has been lurking about the guns, and I am afraid he will start shooting sconces from the walls unless we provide him with another target."

Grace winced. The word "target" when paired with either of her parents made her uneasy. It was almost as if she had spent her life with a bull's-eye sewn to her bodice. "What is your second plan, Aurelie?"

"A skating party. The river is frozen solid and I am certain we have enough skates about for all who wish to participate." She looked thoughtful. "I suppose we could furnish your father with a gun and let him loose, provided he promises only to shoot *away* from the party."

"Bad idea," Jason said with a wry grin.

"Yes, I suppose it is. Well then, we shall simply put him in a pair of skates and hope he does not slide off into the Channel."

So skating it was.

Within an hour, Aurelie had a tent set up beside the river with braziers and urns of hot chocolate. A search of the

141

winter storage room had produced enough skates to serve a small regiment. Even Myrtle found a pair to fit. She was, at present, clinging to Noel's arm at the edge of the ice. With her bright eyes and pinkened cheeks, she resembled nothing as much as a gnome on runners.

"Really, St. Helier," she chirped, "it is very simple. Just keep your ankles straight and do not look down." With that, she stepped onto the ice, dragging a wobbling Noel behind her. Grace found herself holding her breath. Myrtle looked steady enough, but should Noel go down, she would go with him, and at her age, a fall could be a serious matter.

Several minutes later, Grace was grinning. Noel, despite his weaving, was clearly a sound skater. He was giving a great show of ineptitude, however, and Myrtle was loving every moment.

"Look, Aunt Grace, I'm a swan!" Phoebe flashed by on one leg, arms extended. Unfortunately, with her neck stretched into a dramatic arc, she could not quite see where she was going. Where she went was straight into Rickey, and they both went downward in a tangle of limbs. Grace started toward them, but Phoebe's laughter, soon followed by Rickey's, drifted upward. She left them to untangle themselves and glided toward the center of the river.

She had always loved the ice, even before she could skate. In fact, she had been so insistent on learning that, at the ripe age of four, she had purloined a pair of Catherine's old skates and followed Jason and Rafe to the river. Knowing they would not welcome her presence, she had stayed out of sight until they reached their destination. Then, convinced that she could do spins and sprints every bit as well as they, she had rushed onto the ice.

Skating, she had learned then, was not as simple as it looked. One minute she had been skidding along on her feet, the next she was sliding toward them on her bottom, her speed undiminished by the fall. She had upended Rafe first. He, in turn, had taken Jason down, and the three made it all the way to the far bank before Jason's encounter with a low-hanging branch stopped their slide.

In retrospect, Grace had to give them credit for taking the whole thing as they had. After all, they had been fifteen, an age not naturally conducive to entertaining a small child. Jason had threatened to wallop her soundly; Rafe had vowed to give her such a push that she would not stop sliding until she hit France. Then they had each taken one of her hands in theirs and given her her first lesson.

It was, she realized, a truly cherished memory. While they had never precisely invited her along in subsequent winters, she had spent countless hours skating in their wake, happy to the point of bursting.

A silvery laugh reached her ears, and she watched Aurelie float gracefully by. Jason, trying his best to effect a stern expression, was firmly attached to her coat. He had been more than vocal in his objection to his pregnant wife donning skates, and it was obvious that he was taking no chances with her falling. It was also clear that they were both having a glorious time. Grace smiled as Jason released Aurelie just long enough to execute a perfect spin. Under the facade of the serious, slightly stodgy viscount had always lurked the soul of the showman.

Rafe, of course, was nowhere to be seen. Aurelie, Vivian, and Chloe had all taken turns at bullying and cajoling. He had merely drawn deeper into his chair and clasped a bottle of brandy as a drowning man would a lifeline. Eventually they had given up and left without him. Grace could picture him now, happy as a stoat with his silence, his fireside, and his liquor.

"Graaaaace!"

She spun about just in time to see Dunstan heading in her direction, arms flailing and eyes wide with terror. She deftly reached out and caught his arm as he sailed by. Now, Dunstan, unlike his sister, was not a petite creature, and Grace found herself being dragged alongside him. Going was far easier than stopping when on skates except, of course, when one stopped by going in a downward direction. It appeared the young marquess was about to do just that, so she reluctantly released him.

His feet went out from under him seconds later and he landed hard, bouncing once before coming to rest several yards away. Grace skated over to make certain he was all right, and to help him back to his feet. He grinned at her from beneath a shock of disheveled, tawny curls. "Splendid rescue, Gracie. And to think I was concerned I might fall."

She shrugged. "Well, now you know you would survive." She offered her hand. "And do not even think of pulling me down with you."

He laughed, proving he had been thinking along the same lines. Once back on his feet, he wrapped a friendly arm about her shoulders. "You are a cheeky little baggage."

Her elbow to his ribs sent him prone again. She grinned down at him. "And you are a clumsy oaf!"

He gave her a look of such wounded dignity that she laughed aloud. His glinting hazel eyes quite ruined the picture. "In the presence of such grace and glory, what man could possibly maintain his equilibrium?" he intoned, mittened hand clasped to his heart.

"Doing it up too brown, Dunny, but you do it so very well."

Michaela skated up then, every bit as adept as her sister, but a good deal more sedate. "Why are you not helping Lord Aubert up, Aunt Grace?" she queried. "It cannot be good for him to sit on the ice."

She sent the marquess an adoring look. Grace grinned. Women were always tripping over themselves to assist Dunstan. She half believed he cultivated his appealingly bumbling mien just for that purpose. "His lordship cannot seem to keep his feet under him, sweetheart. Perhaps you could help."

Now the girl's eyes glowed. "Oh, yes. I could!"

Dunstan, bless his heart, played right along. "You know, Miss Michaela," he said solemnly, "I think you are just the young lady to rescue me. If you would be so kind as to agree, perhaps we could take a few slow turns about the ice."

With Michaela's eager assistance, he rose and, tucking

her hand into the crook of his arm, set off again. The girl glanced back once, her face aglow. Grace shook her head. She had never been precisely certain how Dunstan managed it.

There had been a bit of clucking between their parents several years before, a futile attempt to make a match of it. Grace, on hearing of their machinations, had laughed. Dunstan, his sister had later informed her, promptly slid off his chair. Grace imagined a maid had hurried forward to help him up.

They liked each other, to be sure, but it would have been a match made in Bedlam.

Now she watched as he paid court to the melting Michaela. Even young girls still in the schoolroom were not immune to his peculiar charm. Chloe flitted past the pair then, affectionately thumbing her nose at her brother. She, too, was possessed of a truly singular appeal. She was pretty, of course, with her elfin face and brilliantly red hair, but her own charm was in her utterly unique spirit. There seemed to be nothing that daunted her, nor any act beyond her. In fact, Grace mused, Chloe was the only woman she knew who got into more scrapes than she did.

Perhaps that was why her family had pressed a suit with Rafe. It was no secret that the duke was consistently baffled by his youngest child. In moments of apoplectic befuddlement, he even went so far as to loudly and publicly despair of ever being rid of her. In the end, it appeared Chloe had not done so badly for herself. True, she might not appreciate Rafe for the glorious gift he was, but she would have a lifetime to learn.

Either that, Grace thought, or a lifetime of misery. As deeply as she loved Rafe and as devastated as she was by the concept of their union, she would never wish Chloe ill. They were friends, and no matter how hard she tried, she could neither blame the other girl for accepting the suit nor begrudge her any happiness she might find in it.

As far as Rafe was concerned, Grace was less generous. She could not possibly wish him to be miserable, but she could not truly wish him happy without her. It seemed entirely Christian to be magnanimous, but just not fair.

"Whoever said life was fair, Disgrace?" she muttered, paraphrasing one of her father's favorite maxims: *I never said life was fair, but demmed if it ain't worse for the fox!* How nice it would be, she thought, not to find it easier to relate to the fox.

She had been standing still for some minutes and realized she was thoroughly chilled. It seemed as good a time as any to take advantage of Aurelie's hostessing skills. Her stiff fingers made unlacing her skates a trial, but she managed eventually. Tying her own boots seemed a waste of time, so she thrust her feet into them and tromped up to the tent.

Quinby, looking mildly put upon, was presiding over the refreshments. Freddy and Phoebe were there, squabbling over ownership of a particularly large tart. Grace solved the matter by breaking the thing in half, then accepted a cup of chocolate. From the muddy appearance of her niece and nephew's faces, she surmised they had indulged to their hearts' content. She pitied the still-ailing Miss Thurston. Sugar had the predictable but distressing effect of turning two already lively children into veritable whirlwinds.

"More chocolate," Phoebe demanded, and Grace and Quinby exchanged knowing glances over the top of her head. The poor, beleaguered governess was in for a wild evening.

Grace was just lifting her own cup to her lips when the shot rang out. It was followed by a loud cry. Startled, she nearly doused herself with chocolate. Her father's familiar bellow reached her ears then, and she felt her heart lodge in her throat. All but dropping the cup, she rushed outside.

Her first thought was that she was seeing the perfect winter tableau. The skaters all stood stock-still on the ice, Chloe with her arms still outstretched. Only Jason was moving, tearing at his skate laces and cursing. The earl bellowed again.

Grace rushed in the direction of the noise. Her progress

was slowed by the snow and her own flapping boot laces. She found her father at last, standing under an ice-covered tree, his usually ruddy face pale as the shrouded ground.

"Papa?" she cried breathlessly.

He looked up from the hunting rifle in his hands to stare toward a nearby copse of oaks. "Think I might've shot someone," he mumbled.

"Oh, Papa . . ."

"Think it might've been young Avemar."

"Oh, God!"

"Well, blast it all, he looked like a . . ."

"Like what, Papa? A very large grouse?" Grace was already running toward the trees. She heard shouting behind her, and figured Jason and the others had heard. "Rafe!" she cried as she plowed through the drifts. "Rafe!"

Nothing.

A sob caught in her throat as she went. *No, please!* Then she saw the stain. Dark and ominous, the size of a plate, it was already being lost to the snow. *No!* She kept running.

The earth dropped away just as one of her boots landed on the laces of the other. With a startled cry, she pitched forward, going headfirst down the embankment. Head over heels she tumbled, her mouth and eyes filling with snow, until she came to a sudden and jarring stop. Thinking she had hit a tree, and certain every bone in her body was broken, she lay facedown in the snow and tried not to move.

"Hullo, Grace. Marvelous entrance."

Her head snapped up. Or snapped as far as it could. Rafe's elbow blocked further motion. Her nose was pressed firmly into his side and one of her hands was wedged into his coat pocket. It took a bit of scrambling, but she freed herself and promptly threw her arms about his neck.

It occurred to Rafe that he ought to disengage her, but he was feeling rather sluggish, and she was rather warm. Or at least warmer than the snow that was coating both of them. Then he decided he really ought to do something. She had quite literally landed herself across his thighs.

He cleared his throat. "Grace?"

"Hmm?" Her face was buried in his neck.

"Remove yourself from my lap, if you would."

To his surprise, she did so immediately. She had never been one for following commands, and it took him a moment to realize that he had not had to repeat himself. Then, suddenly, she was pawing at him, her hands running fast and firm over parts of him she damn well should not be touching.

"Where is it?"

He nearly choked. "Where is what?"

"The wound, for God's sake! Where is it?"

Knowing he had to still her hands, he caught them in one of his. "What wound?"

"Papa shot you! Oh, God, you have not gone numb, have you?"

Not a chance. "Your father did not shoot me, Grace."

The gold eyes that met his flashed with hope. "Are you certain?"

"Quite."

"But you yelled . . . and there was blood. . . ."

"Wine."

"What?" she gasped.

He lifted his other hand. In it was clasped the neck of the shattered bottle. "Your father," he muttered, "has always been an appalling shot."

"Oh, Rafe." Her glossy head dropped to rest against his chest.

He knew exactly how she felt. He had lost a perfectly spectacular bottle of French burgundy. "Nasty business," he sighed, "almost being shot here. I can just see the notice: *Avemar, while passing the holidays with friends, was unfortunately shot near the banks of the Ouse.* Terrible word, Ouse. Now, the Welland . . ."

"What are you babbling about?"

Grace was back to prodding at him again, this time around his head. "Leave off, Gracie, I am perfectly fine." She did not desist, and he was forced to admit that the touch of her fingers at his temples was rather pleasant.

Shouts came from above then, and he looked up to see Tarrant sliding awkwardly down the hill. "My God, man," his friend gasped, "are you all right?"

"Splendid, other than the fact that your sister almost flattened me. Unlike you, she decided to roll her way down."

He had seen Tarrant look pale on precisely two previous occasions. The first had been when they were both nearly killed during a battle on the Peninsula. The second had been when, before the marriage, a dreadful misunderstanding had caused Aurelie to leave him. This made a third.

"Can you stand?" Tarrant asked, his voice hoarse with concern.

"I imagine so, as soon as Grace gets off me." She immediately scrambled to her feet. Rafe tried to follow. His legs did not seem to be working, however, and he ended up sliding right back down onto his rump.

"Oh, God, he *was* shot!" Grace moaned, reaching toward him.

He blocked her hands. "Told you, it was the wine." He tried his legs again. "Appears this is the wine, too. Damned fine stuff, Tare. Too bad I only got through half the bottle." He sighed and lifted one arm. "If you would be so kind . . ."

It took some doing, but with Tarrant half dragging and half carrying him, he made it up the embankment. It was not an unfamiliar experience, really. They had taken turns playing crutch to each other many times over the years. At the top, Rafe grinned and patted his friend on the top of the head. "Rather reminds one of Oxford, doesn't it?"

Tarrant muttered something rude and hefted him along.

"You frightened me half out of my wits, Rafe!" Grace scolded some time later when a dry, warmly wrapped Rafe had been settled by the fire.

"That so?" he drawled. "That leaves you with . . . how many? Two?" He turned to Chloe. "How many wits is a normal person born with, my lady? Twenty or so, I should imagine."

Chloe rolled her eyes. "Sometimes you really can be a beast, Rafael."

"So I have been told," he replied, but he did not comment that she was no Beauty.

Grace thought that perhaps she should creep off somewhere and leave the two alone. But she was loath to be away from Rafe, and besides, the rest of the party was in the drawing room with them.

"Thought you were a deer, boy," Lord Heathfield muttered. Most of the color had returned to his face, but he was still looking a bit white about the lips. Grace thought it would be some time before he would pick up another gun.

"Better that than a grouse, sir," was Rafe's cheerful reply.

"What on earth were you doing out there?" Lady Heathfield asked. "Skulking about in the snow with a bottle, no less."

"I was not aware I was skulking, madam. In fact, I have never been much good at skulking. My approach, I have heard, puts one in mind of a pack of howler monkeys."

Grace suppressed a smile. If there was one thing her mother truly deplored, it was being roasted, even charmingly.

"I was outside," Rafe continued, "because it had suddenly become damnably quiet in here. Bad for a man's nerves, all that silence."

More wonderful than those words, Grace decided seconds later, was the fact that he was clearly unaware he had said them. Silence had bothered him. To the point that he had come outside in search of company. She nearly laughed aloud with the sheer glory of it.

"So true, dear boy," Myrtle offered. She was seated next to him, her copious knitting adding to the covers already draped over his form. "Silence and solitude can be so very difficult on a body. Of course, when one is used to being alone, it does not seem so bad . . . until one has had companionship and lost it." She clucked her tongue. "Terrible."

"Being alone, Lady Hammond?" Vivian asked sympathetically.

"Hmm?" Myrtle looked up. "Oh, no, dear. I missed a stitch."

"Like a sieve without the holes," Rafe muttered under his breath.

"What was that, dearest?"

"Nothing, Aunt."

Myrtle's words seemed to have had an effect on the gathering. "How lovely it must have been," Chloe offered, "for you to have Grace with you, Lady Hammond, even if only for a short time. I myself am often quite terribly lonely."

"What rot!" her brother snorted. "Father scarcely ever allows you out without a veritable army in tow."

Chloe regarded him seriously. "True."

"So what are you moaning about? You are never alone."

It was one of those moments when Grace realized how very much alike she and Chloe were. "I do not believe alone and lonely are at all the same thing," she said softly.

Dunstan rolled his eyes. "The wonders of the female mind!"

Chloe reached over and patted Grace's hand. "The limits of my brother's mind. But you and I understand each other here."

"Yes," Grace replied. "We do."

"Understanding is such a blessing," Myrtle offered cheerfully. "Though I fear it is often underestimated, at least in females. My dear Horatio was ever so fond of saying, 'Myrtle, my love, if the young girls today had your brains, the world would be a truly frightening place.' "

Rafe managed to keep a straight face. "Uncle Horatio certainly had a way with words."

"Yes, he did, did he not?" His aunt gave a misty smile. "How I miss him! But then, I have always believed that a moment with the right person is better than a lifetime with the wrong one."

Not particularly caring for the direction her quirky mind seemed to be taking, Rafe cleared his throat. "I say, Tare,

151

if there is a bottle about which will not defeat you, I should very much appreciate a glass of brandy." Several others added their own drink requests.

"Make yourself useful, Grace," her mother commanded, "and help your brother." Rafe heard Grace sigh, but she obeyed.

"Make yourself useful, Rafael, dear," his aunt commanded. The giggle spoiled the effect. "Hold this up for me."

He grasped the fuzzy corner she thrust at him and held it out. Even with his arm fully extended, a large section remained folded in his lap. "Good God, Aunt, what *is* this thing?"

"Just a little throw, of course."

"For whom—Goliath?"

"Oh, you do tease. Now, lift that part in the middle."

Rafe did, nearly knocking over the brandy glass that had been placed on the long table beside him. "This would cover Hannibal, with room to spare."

Myrtle peered intently at the woolly mass. "Higher, please," she said. "Really, Rafe, you would think I was asking you to perform feats of acrobatics. Just lift that end. . . . Ah, yes, I thought so," she murmured, and hauled it back into her own lap.

Rafe gingerly removed a bit of fuzz from his jaw. Inexplicably, there seemed to be some in his mouth as well. He debated unraveling the whole thing. It would not do at all for someone to be asphyxiated by his aunt's little throw. He rubbed his tongue against his teeth, but could not dispel the woolly feeling. It would simply have to be washed away.

He thrust his hand out for the glass. And watched as it skittered out from between his fingers to shoot down the table. It teetered on the edge for a moment before tipping onto the rug below.

"Beautiful shot, Rafe," Tarrant muttered. "That rug is an Aubusson and the brandy was Napoleon's finest."

Rafe blinked and flexed his fingers. They seemed to be working well enough. "I do not understand. . . ." he began.

"Obviously the dear boy's coordination was affected by his unfortunate accident this afternoon." Myrtle patted his perfectly mobile fingers. "Perhaps a cup with a handle would be best, with something warm in it, of course. Tea, I think."

Rafe jerked his head about, searching for Grace. She was seated across the room, her head bowed as she studied Lady St. Helier's embroidery square. With her golden curls and celestial blue gown, she looked positively angelic.

12

GRACE WAS READING Byron again. She wished she had remembered to bring *Tom Jones* with her from Dickerdean or, even better, the *Canterbury Tales* from Rafe's hunting box. She was certain Jason must possess a copy of both, but the library shelves still bore the distinctive stamp of her father's tenure as viscount: extensive but boring. She rather thought Byron had been Aurelie's addition. All things considered, she could not complain. She was feeling just melancholy enough that the mirthless cantos suited her fine. Suffering loved company.

She set *Childe Harold* aside for a moment to scratch at itchy arms. She had always loved decking the halls with boughs of holly and fir, but could not help but wonder why every piece of vegetation used during the holidays seemed to be of the prickly variety.

Aurelie drifted into the room then, arms laden with more fir branches. "I really ought to have seen to this days ago," she announced, "but with the party . . ." She arranged the greenery across the mantel. "What do you think?"

Grace smiled. "It smells lovely."

"But looks as if it ought to be in the fireplace rather than atop it. Perhaps with a few candles . . ." Aurelie left the room, still chattering to herself.

Vivian poked her head in moments later. "It needs candles," she remarked, wandering in to study the mantel.

"Aurelie has gone for some."

"May I join you?" Without waiting for a response,

154

Vivian lowered herself onto the divan. "Noel will just have to find me here. I have sent him on a quest."

"For . . . ?"

"Pickled onions."

Grace shuddered. "Whatever for?"

"For me to eat, of course." Vivian laughed at her grimace. "I have been craving the oddest things of late. Last week it was jellied snipe. Noel's mother says it is only to be expected. Before Noel was born, she found herself going into the gardens herself at night to find unripe radishes."

"I wonder she did not suffer terrible bellyaches."

"Not at all, although she does blame her cravings for Noel's character. His humor can be beyond earthy at times." Vivian peered at Grace's book. "Byron, hmm? Only appropriate, I suppose."

"Because of the assembled company?" In truth, it was appropriate. Vivian had, upon her arrival in England, forged a friendship of sorts with the charismatic poet. Chloe, too, had ties to Byron. He was married, not particularly happily, to her cousin Annabella.

"No, I did not mean the company. I meant the state of affairs."

With her raven hair and brilliant green eyes, Vivian often jokingly called herself a witch. Lately, Grace was more than happy to concur. She made a truly beautiful witch, certainly, but there was something otherworldly about her perceptiveness.

"You know, Vivvy, you are frightening sometimes."

Her friend laughed. "You should see me when I wake up in the morning!"

"If I asked, would you let the . . . matter rest?"

"Yes, I would, but I think you need to talk about it. Being in love can be the most horrid experience known to woman."

"And to think all the bards call it the most glorious," Grace returned dryly. "Someone really ought to set them straight on the matter."

Vivian leaned forward, concern etched on her face. "Oh, Gracie," she murmured. "This is all so very hard on you. I can tell."

"Can you? I thought I was hiding it rather well. Perhaps, should I ever be allowed to return to London, I shall plead with Mr. Kean to instruct me in my thespian skills."

"This jesting is below you, you know." Vivian shook her head at Grace's undignified snort. "But that aside, you are a lovely shade of pale and have circles beneath your eyes which would do a raccoon proud."

"I suppose I should be offended if only I knew what a raccoon was."

"Suffice it to say that they have black rings about their eyes, wander about at night, and my grandfather used to take great pleasure in shooting them."

"Marvelous." Grace sighed, then yawned—widely. "As a matter of fact, I have good reason for my raccoon circles. I was up very late last night."

"Yes, well, that is one of the symptoms of love."

Grace stifled another yawn. "It had nothing to do with love." *Not true.* "Well, a bit perhaps. . . . Really, Vivvy, I appreciate your concern. Truly I do."

"But you wish me to take it elsewhere." Vivian's eyes narrowed. "I really ought to give *him* a piece of my mind. He has about as much sense as a moose, and rather less charm of late."

"A moose?"

"Imagine a great, hulking cow with a pea-size brain and enormous antlers."

Grace chuckled. "Now I know what Papa was shooting at yesterday."

She really did not feel like discussing Rafe's mooselike sensibilities, although she would have very much liked to know whether raccoons were intelligent creatures. She did not have the chance to ask, for Aurelie returned then with her candles. Noel was right behind her. He was carrying a laden platter, which, Grace noticed, he was holding as far away from his person as possible.

"I certainly hope you appreciate this, Viv," he muttered as he approached. "These onions are making my eyes water from here, and my gut positively roils at the thought of eating one."

"I do not intend to share them with you," his wife shot back, "so your gut may cease its roiling. How marvelous—Cook provided mustard as well. I wonder how she knew." She promptly seized an onion, dunked it in the thick, brown mustard, and popped it into her mouth.

Several feet away, Grace felt her own eyes watering. Vivian took another onion and sighed with pleasure. Noel groaned quietly. Grace knew exactly how he felt. Her own stomach was beginning to turn.

Aurelie, having arranged the candles to her satisfaction, settled herself on the divan beside her friend. "May I have one?" she asked. Vivian gestured to the platter.

Noel and Grace left them to it.

No, Rafe did not wish to play whist.

"Thank you all the same, madam," he said to Lady Warren. "I am afraid my lack of skill makes me a poor partner."

He was certain the lady was of an age with his aunt, but apparently she was not aware of the fact. She shook her dubiously blond sausage curls and peered up at him from under darkened lashes. "La, sir, I would delight in teaching you! I am vastly experienced."

Rafe managed to keep a straight face as he bowed over her hand. "And I am certain you are a great proficient. Sadly, I really must decline."

Her pout would have been well suited to young Phoebe. "Oh, well, if you are sure I cannot convince you otherwise . . ."

He beat a hasty path from the salon, lest she decide to try. He had no destination in mind and paused in the hall. A distressing wail drifted from the conservatory. Either Chloe was having a go at the harp, or his aunt was singing.

He had heard both at various times and was loath to repeat the experience.

Dunstan, Lord Warren, and the Granville men, minus Tarrant, were out hunting whatever birds should have the misfortune of leaving their coveys. Lord Heathfield had shouldered his gun with a bit less enthusiasm than usual, but had been whistling by the time he reached the door. Trying to keep the man from the hunt would be like trying to keep Prinny away from courtesans.

Rafe decided with some humor that, had the earl actually shot him the day before, he might have quit his hobby. For a sennight at most.

Tarrant and St. Helier were about somewhere. He thought he might seek them out and have a game of billiards. He found them both in the estate room and paused in the doorway. From the sound of it, they were discussing schools. All three had attended Oxford, and Rafe thought a chat about their wild days would not be such a bad thing. He would unquestionably win any contest comparing rowdy escapades.

"Christ Church, of course," Tarrant said.

"You cannot be serious, man," St. Helier protested with a grimace. "All those scholarly types rushing about with their noses in Socrates. Deadly dull. Magdalen is the only way to go it."

"Rogues and rascals, all," was the dry rejoinder.

"Here, here! Always a good game and drink to be found."

Rafe agreed wholeheartedly with St. Helier. It had been during their days together at Magdalen College that Noel Windram had been dubbed Hel. The sobriquet had been well deserved, and had precious little to do with his title.

He stepped into the room just as Tarrant said, "At least we agree on Eton."

Eton? That was diving a bit deep into the memory pool. St. Helier chuckled. "I would delight in disagreeing with you, Tare, but I cannot come up with another school which equals Eton." He looked up then and grinned. "Hullo, Rafe. I was wondering what had happened to you. Thought you might have been wheedled into turning pages for Lady Chloe."

"God forbid. No, I came to challenge the two of you to a game of billiards."

"Ah, a challenge." Tarrant rose from his chair. "We accept."

As the three headed for the game room, St. Helier queried, "So what do you say, old man—Eton or Rugby?"

"Eton," Rafe replied promptly, "though it is a moot point as we all cut our wolf teeth in those hallowed halls."

"As will our sons. I fear they shall have to forge their comradeship there, for Tare and I will never see eye to eye on the matter of colleges."

Rafe blinked. "You are arguing over which colleges your sons will attend?"

"Arguing?" Tarrant shook his head. "I would not call it that. The young Windrams will have the unfortunate experience of Magdalen while the Granvilles will flourish at Christ Church."

They encountered the butler in the hall. "Quinby, send a bottle of brandy into the game room, if you would." Rafe turned to his companions. "And for you gentlemen?"

Tarrant grinned. "Best make that two bottles, Quinby."

"Of course, my lord."

The butler returned as Rafe was preparing to take his first shot. The game had been delayed a good fifteen minutes by a heated argument over which clubs the young Granvilles and Windrams would join. Tarrant insisted on White's; St. Helier refused to dismiss Watier's.

Curiously, Quinby's hands were empty. "I beg your pardon, my lord. . . ." He approached Tarrant and spoke softly for a moment.

Tarrant's black brows rose, then snapped together. "What do you mean you cannot unlock them?"

159

Quinby shot the other men an apologetic look. "The cellars have not been locked as far back as I can remember, my lord. If a key exists, it is nowhere to be found."

"Well, of course a key exists," Tarrant replied. "Someone must have used it. Question the kitchen staff."

"I did so immediately, my lord." The butler was clearly affronted that the matter was even in question. "And other members of the downstairs staff as well. No one had any reason to lock the wine cellar."

Rafe was beginning to catch on. He was not in the least pleased by his conclusions. "The key . . ." he growled.

"I assure you, Your Grace, I have a footman trying every key on the house rings."

Rafe deliberately kept his voice even. "May I suggest you question Lady Grace?"

He was the recipient of two curious gazes. Tarrant, he noticed, was studying his cue tip with great interest. "Why on earth would he do that?" St. Helier asked. "Grace is hardly likely to have been tippling in the cellars."

"Ask her about the key," Rafe repeated.

Quinby, quite the master of impassivity, almost managed to hide the fact that he clearly thought Rafe to be nicked in the nob. "I would, Your Grace," he said solemnly, "but her ladyship has gone out with the children for a stroll about the grounds."

"In three feet of snow?"

"Her ladyship is fond of the crisp air," Quinby replied with all the dignity of an archbishop pronouncing an edict. "She would not be deterred by a bit of snow."

"Perhaps you could locate another bottle elsewhere, Quinby," Tarrant suggested mildly.

Again the butler was clearly insulted. "I have looked, my lord." Now all three pairs of eyes swung toward Rafe. He shrugged. There had not been more than a third left in the bottle in the library. He had polished it off the night before. "Then I took the liberty of seeking out a bottle of port as an alternative."

"Let me guess," Rafe said dryly. "No port."

"No, Your Grace."

Rafe turned to Tarrant. "I am very much afraid I am going to have to murder your sister."

This pronouncement finally succeeded in cracking the butler's stolid countenance. He hastened to say, "I do not believe such an extreme course will be necessary, Your Grace."

"You have an alternative? I was under the assumption that all of the liquor was locked in the cellar."

"All but what was removed for Christmas, Your Grace: cider and some fine Jamaican rum for the eggnog."

Rafe nodded. "The rum will do quite nicely. Bring us a bottle."

Quinby cleared his throat. "I am afraid I cannot do that, Your Grace."

"You cannot? You said there was rum for eggnog."

"Yes, Your Grace, I did say that." The man gave another apologetic, slightly nervous smile. "But you see, the rum is already *in* the eggnog." He flinched when Rafe snarled, but quickly regained his composure. "May I suggest mulled cider? It is Cook's special recipe."

"I loathe cider."

"Perhaps some sherry, then? I believe there is still a bottle in—"

This time, when Rafe thrust his hands into his hair with a wild groan, the butler actually moved away. Tarrant stepped forward, the corners of his mouth twitching in ill-suppressed amusement. "Why don't you do this, Quinby: continue searching for the key. In the meantime, have some eggnog sent in."

"Yes, my lord." The man hurried from the room.

"Really, Rafe," Tarrant chided, not bothering to hide his smile now, "it is not necessary to threaten my staff."

"Not to put too fine a point on it," Rafe retorted, "but I was not threatening your staff. I was threatening your sister. And I fully intend to follow up on it. The chit needs a good paddling and a no-return passage to the Colonies!"

To his annoyance, his friend merely chuckled and turned back to the table. "I believe it was your shot, Hel."

But St. Helier was not paying attention to the game. He was staring bemusedly into space. "I have just had the most staggering thought," he announced.

"Batten down the hatches," Rafe muttered.

St. Helier ignored him. "We have missed a terribly important consideration, Tare."

"And that is?"

Noel's eyes were wide in his face. "Our children might be female!"

As it turned out, Rafe could not get within ten feet of Grace for the remainder of the day. Every time he tried, someone got in the way. Before supper, he stalked her twice around the perimeter of the drawing room, only to be brought up short when Aurelie blocked his path, demanding that he escort her into the dining room. He thought then to claim the seat next to his prey, but was efficiently herded to the far end of the table.

The evening's entertainment consisted of an impromptu concert. Catherine played the pianoforte. Vivian sang. Chloe dragged away at the harp strings. Rafe took advantage of a break in the performances to go after Grace. He was very nearly upon her when his aunt chirped, "Now Grace must play!"

He knew Grace would rather hang by her toes from the Tower parapets, but she sprang to her feet and all but ran to the instrument. She would need someone to turn the pages for her. He stepped forward and was thwarted as both Tarrant and St. Helier moved in to do the honors.

"Grace, dear?"

"Yes, Lady Hammond?"

"If I might make a suggestion, perhaps you should avoid Scottish reels. It is a bit chilly in the room."

He saw Grace smile. "I quite agree, madam."

She played Bach.

Rafe drank tea. And tried not to grind his molars into dust. In the end, he went to bed completely sober and cranky as a hen with wet feathers. He rather regretted having snarled at his aunt when she wished him a good night. It was hardly her fault that Grace delighted in tormenting him.

He amended that thought seconds later. It was more than likely the girl had gotten the idea to lock the cellars from Myrtle. Mention of the dearly departed Percival regularly peppered his aunt's conversation of late.

Had he not been so provoked by her machinations, he would have applauded Grace's ingenuity. She had always been a smart creature, and used her impressive mind in countless creative manners. He had to admit that he was damned curious how she had sealed the bottles and greased his glass. Perhaps, should he ever overcome the desire to throttle her senseless when they were in the same room, he would ask.

Grace, with her devilish mind and angelic countenance. Angelic. If he really paused to consider the matter, he had to admit that she did not set out to be a pox. Rather, she had always appeared to want nothing more than to be of use and appeal to those around her. She simply had the misfortune to have been born into a family and Society that resisted any form of kindness.

A guardian angel.

Rafe was so startled by the following realization that he gave a choked laugh. Grace actually thought to save him. From what? His solitude, he supposed, and from drowning himself in the ooze of liquor casks. Well, she had done a damned good job thus far. She had managed to force him into attending Aurelie's blasted house party and had made his drinking a difficult, if not downright impossible, task.

The chit deserved a halo. Or a thrashing she would feel for years to come. He could not quite make up his mind which was the more appropriate concept. Perhaps she ought to be thrashed *with* a halo.

He gave a muffled groan. Obviously his time in her presence had rattled his brains. He must be truly mad to even be thinking of her with any degree of warmth. She had, angelic aspirations aside, made his life an utter hell of late. Well, his life had been hell for nearly a year, and he had felt better in the past two weeks than at any time in recent memory, but that did not signify in the least. She vexed him like a creeping rash, and he wanted nothing more than to see her—or himself—sent off to some distant clime.

You would miss her, you buffle-headed clod.

"About as much as a case of the pox," he grumbled into the darkness.

Admit it; she has grown on you.

"Like plague lesions."

You need a bit of warmth and vitality in your sorry life.

"What I need," Rafe snapped, "is a drink." But the cellars, courtesy of Grace and the ghost of Percival, remained locked.

Cursing recalcitrant young women and drooling, tippling mastiffs, he rolled onto his stomach and buried his face in the pillows.

Grace tiptoed quietly down the stairs. It was well past midnight, but she did not want to take the chance of encountering anyone on her way. The kitchens were dark, and she took the time to light a candle. Then, digging into her dressing gown pocket, she withdrew the key ring. It had been easy enough to spirit out of the butler's pantry. Seldom-used keys had always been stored there.

She was loath to unlock the wine cellar, but it seemed the best thing to do. The next day was Christmas Eve, and the party deserved to imbibe whatever it chose. Besides, her father had been notably subdued throughout the evening. Routine was of paramount importance to the earl, and he had been forced to forgo his after-supper port.

She had not meant to inconvenience anyone but Rafe,

164

really. Coating the stoppers of the drawing room decanters with hot wax had been a temporary solution. She had known replacements would be found soon enough. Coating his brandy glass with the medicinal unguent Aurelie had provided for his chest had been a spontaneous act. Locking the wine cellars had, at the time, seemed a brilliant idea.

It had not seemed quite so brilliant when he had stalked her all evening, murder in his eyes. She had been ready to scuttle for cover on more than one occasion, but each time he had gotten close, someone had thwarted him. She rather suspected the interventions were unintended, but she blessed her unwitting saviors nonetheless.

It had occurred to her that she was really hurting herself in her efforts to keep Rafe sober. He was hardly likely to fall madly in love with the one person who consistently got in the way of his single pleasure. But then, she had reasoned, it was absurd to think that he would want her no matter what she did. In his eyes she would forever be the awkward, fractious, unappealing little sister of his oldest friend.

All things considered, her own life would be far easier if she simply let him waste his away. How unfortunate that she could not seem to overcome the monumental need to see him well.

She would have very much liked to leave the cellars locked. But her father needed his port, and Rafe would likely go at the door with an axe eventually. So, holding her candle aloft, she descended the stone stairs. As a child, she had been terrified of the dark, lower recesses of the house. Catherine had often bullied her into submission by threatening to lock her there.

Even now, the place seemed ominous and oppressively cold. She hurried to unlock the correct door, wanting nothing more than to regain the warm safety of her bed. Task completed, she made her way back toward the stairs.

She was nearly there when the shadow loomed before her. Her terrified shriek promptly died in her throat, and the only thing that kept her on her feet when a heavy hand descended onto her shoulder was the fact that she was a Granville. Granville women, after all, never fainted.

13

"YOU SHALL SUFFER for your acts of trickery," a sepulchral voice intoned. "The time of retribution is near!"

Grace's candle slipped from her nerveless fingers and the cellar was plunged into merciless darkness. "I suppose I deserved that," she muttered, "but you have just taken ten years off my life."

"That would make twenty, then."

"Because of the ten I offered you? I take them back." She scrabbled about on the floor for the candle. "Really, Rafe, that was unkind."

"Locking the cellars was not?" His hand closed over hers and she gasped at the warm contact. He jerked away immediately. "Damnit, Grace, could you not have held on to the candle?"

"Could you not have brought one?" she shot back, carefully reaching about the floor. Searching for the candle seemed a very good excuse to hold his hand, even if only for a second.

"I had other things on my mind. Have you a tinderbox with you?"

"Yes. What were the other things? Scaring me out of my wits?"

"Ah, so it is your wits now, is it? You must be seriously depleted by this point." She could hear the smile in his voice and resisted first the urge to smack him, then to hurl herself into his arms. "Here it is. . . ."

His fingers drifted over hers for the second time. She

caught her breath. Her heart was thundering in her chest and she knew it had little to do with her momentary terror. Instead of pulling away, this time he tightened his grip. "Rafe," she whispered, reveling in the tiny shivers that raced up her arm.

"This seems the only way to keep your hands out of the way of mine," he grumbled. Then, "Good Lord, Grace, your skin is like ice!"

It felt rather flushed and heated to her. The chills she was experiencing had less to do with cold than her racing pulse did with fear. "Rafe," she began again, but was cut off as he grunted, this time as his free hand encountered her slippered toes.

"Well, hell. I needed that candle."

"There are more upstairs. I do not need light to find my way out."

He sighed as he hauled her to her feet. "Perhaps, but I need it to find my way back in after I send you back upstairs." He shoved her in front of him, and she suppressed a sigh as he untangled his fingers from her. "Lead on," he commanded, and dropped a heavy hand on her shoulder.

She debated taking him into the vegetable cellar and leaving him there, but it was a fleeting impulse. She would have wanted to stay right there with him in the dark, and she imagined he would throttle her should she get too close. Hoping that she was, in fact, going in the right direction, she headed for the stairs.

"What are you doing down here?"

He grunted. "Perhaps I should ask you the same."

"Perhaps, but I think you have a very good idea."

"Yes, I do. What was it, Grace—guilt or wisdom? I cannot see you unlocking the cellars out of the goodness of your heart."

"I cannot see it as wisdom," was her retort.

"Really, my dear? It has saved you something very important."

"My life?" she queried dryly.

"There, you see. You *are* a wise woman."

She had no intention of telling him precisely how stupid she thought herself. Instead, she repeated, "Why are you down here?"

"I was hungry and thought I would raid the kitchens. I saw your light descending the stairs."

"How fortuitous," Grace muttered as she began to ascend the stairs. Then concern took over. "You could not sleep?" She hated to think of him lying in the dark, tormented by whichever demons lived in his mind. Not paying attention to her steps, she stumbled.

"Damnit, Grace!" Rafe snapped as she nearly took them both down. The last thing he needed was more bruises. He reached for her waist and instead grasped the soft curve of her hip. His fingers began to tighten of their own volition and he cursed under his breath. "Watch where you are going!"

"Interesting advice to be given in the dark."

Despite himself, he smiled. "Feel where you are going, then." He promptly dropped his own hands.

They reached the top of the stairs and he groped about on the central table for a candle. "Give me the tinderbox." Seconds later, the faint light illuminated the room. He lit a second candle. "You may go to bed now."

It would, he realized, be a perfectly angelic face if not for the bold eyes. Right now they were fixed squarely on his face. "What of you? I thought you came to eat."

"Now I believe I will drink instead."

"I will prepare food for you."

Her stubborn determination amused him only slightly less than the concept of her cooking. "I think not. I wish to enjoy your ten years."

"I took them back. Now you have only your own life to live, and drinking it away . . ." She broke off and flushed.

"What, Grace? Do not turn missish on me now."

Ordinarily he would have been irked by her puritanical interference, but he was finding himself thoroughly distracted by the faint blush that stained her cheeks. Not roses, he thought, but the delicate pink of first light. He shook his head, astounded by the workings of his mind. "Come now, you have held your tongue, if not your meddling impulses, up to now. I am giving you the opportunity to tell me precisely what a reprobate I have become."

"Is that what you wish to hear from me, Rafe?"

In truth, he did not wish to hear it at all. He had called himself every vile name imaginable over the past ten months. Once, just once, it would be pleasant to hear something else. He steeled himself against the hated self-pity. "What I should really like to hear is that you are taking yourself off to bed."

"And I should like to hear the same from you," she shot back.

He sighed. "You are clever, Grace. Be careful that you do not amuse me too much. I might just have to—"

"Do what?" she cut in. "Throttle me? I do not think Jason would appreciate you murdering his sister in his home. Believe it or not, there are members of my family who prefer me alive." She paused, eyes snapping. "Growl at me like a wounded bear? Mock me? Good heavens, Rafe, you must certainly have run out of insults by now."

"Grace," he warned.

"You did not come down to eat. You came down to have another go at the cellar doors." She plunked a ring of keys onto the table and threw up her hands. "There! Lock yourself in!"

He stared at her, bemused. "You are an odd creature."

"Why? Because I, like a good person should, care about you? Or because I, like any sane person would, know when to give up?" Her shoulders slumped then and she left the table to wander toward the door. "I cannot do it anymore, Rafe. I cannot be responsible for you."

"You were never responsible for me."

He did not hear all of her grumbled response, but it sounded something like "Tell that to buy harp." Grace never made much sense when she was upset.

"Grace." She stopped, but did not turn back. He had no

idea what he had meant to say. "You have a spider on your shoulder."

"Brilliant sally," she muttered.

"I am quite serious."

She turned her head then, let out a startled yelp, and promptly ran back to him. "Get it off!"

He leaned forward and gave a low whistle. "Impressive. I should think anything that big should be kept on a lead."

"Oh, for pity's sake!" She swatted blindly at her shoulder, sending the spider to the floor. It scuttled off into the shadows. When she looked up, Rafe was grinning. Her pique waned as she gazed into the azure eyes. "You are a beast, Rafe."

"And you look rather splendid with insects on your back."

"Spiders are not insects," she countered, but there was no bite to the words. His crooked smile dispelled the last of the irritation. "You have dust in your hair."

"What a pair we are," he quipped.

No, what a pair we could be. She suppressed a sigh. "I suppose I will go to bed, then."

To her astonishment, he shook his head and said, "Join me."

Her heart leapt, then dived. "While you drink?"

"While I eat. I find myself with an appetite after all."

"Truly?"

"Truly." He headed for the pantry. "This is Havensgate; there must be some ambrosia about somewhere."

Ten minutes later, they were back at the table, the impromptu repast spread between them. Grace bit into a strawberry tart and mused that she really should not be sitting about in the middle of the night with Rafe, garbed in her nightclothes. Especially not with her parents a mere floor above. But as far as she was concerned, they were as distant as they had been the last time she had sat up with Rafe, and should the whole of His Majesty's army descend upon them, she would merely thumb her nose and fling a tart.

Rafe, too, was less than decently attired. His dressing gown was tied loosely, and she spied a wedge of hair-dusted skin whenever he moved. She found her eyes slewing to his torso each time he so much as twitched.

They sat in companionable silence for a time. Grace's heart swelled with the sight of him tucking into a pigeon pie. He had always loved food to the extent that Jason had once suggested that Rafe's frequent visits were not to see him, but to raid his kitchens. It would take a long time to fill in the distressing hollows under his cheekbones, but at least he seemed to be making a start.

He looked up, catching her staring. "What, did I just consume the spider?" he asked with his mouth full.

"I have missed you!" she blurted, then dropped her head in mortification.

He gave a choked laugh. "I cannot think why." When she did not respond, he flicked a bit of crust at her. "Your heart, Gracie, is surpassed in softness only by your head."

"Yes," she agreed miserably, wondering why she had so little control over either, "I seem destined to play the fool."

"No, you are not a fool. You merely do foolish things." He took a sip of the cider she had poured. "Care to tell me about it now? What you did to get yourself banished?"

No, she did not care to tell him, but somehow she needed to. Perhaps it was nothing more than the comfort of their present accord, or perhaps it was the cider she herself had consumed. Perhaps she thought he might understand.

She took a deep breath. "I tried to fight a duel."

He swallowed his drink with an audible gulp. "I beg your pardon?"

"I challenged Lord Fremont to a duel."

"You are not serious."

"Yes, I am." She winced at the memory. "He declined, of course, which made it all the worse."

"Good God, Grace, you wished him to accept?"

She thought for a moment, then shook her head. "No, I do not suppose I did, but he merely laughed. He insulted me, and then compounded it by laughing when I demanded

172

satisfaction." Now she dropped her head into her hands. "Then he had me thrown out."

"Out of where?"

"White's."

She looked up when Rafe made a strangled sound, concerned he was choking. "You challenged him at his club? You actually walked into *White's*?" When she nodded, he gaped at her, jaw slack. Obviously it was a galling concept.

It had been galling to Fremont, too, and those members and staff who had been astounded to witness her slightly drunken invasion of the exclusively male, thoroughly exclusive domain. The large amount of champagne she had drunk at the Jarmyn ball had bolstered her courage. The pistol, purloined from her father's library, had held the club's denizens at bay while she tracked her prey down in the cardroom.

"I suppose I had better tell you all of it."

"Yes," he agreed. "You had better."

"He was telling people that I . . . that I . . ." She flushed. "Well, that I had allowed him certain liberties. It was most distressing." Remembering the humiliation of hearing the sordid tales, she instinctively lifted her chin. "I did what any self-respecting person would have done if insulted so."

"You tried to call him out."

"Of course."

Rafe shook his head. Grace did not think it was in admiration. "It was a damned harebrained thing to do. You should know that no one believes anything Fremont says. For God's sake, Grace, to storm a men's club . . ."

She sighed. She had heard every word he had just spoken dozens of times after the incident. "What would you have done if he had been spreading scandalous lies about you?"

"That is an entirely different—"

"No," she cut in sharply, "it is not! He insulted my honor, and I had every right to respond as you—or any man—would have."

This argument had carried no weight whatsoever with

173

her parents or the ton, but she could see Rafe pondering her words. "It was your father's job to see to the matter," he said eventually, "or your brothers'."

She gave him a sad smile. "Perhaps. But neither my father nor Rickey seemed in the least inclined to act, and Jason was in Scotland. I had only myself to defend my honor."

"Well, hell," Rafe muttered. He had no trouble imagining Grace, eyes flashing and chin high, storming right up to the dissolute baron's ornate waistcoat and demanding he meet her with pistols at dawn. He also had no trouble imagining the man's response. "You really crossed the line, Gracie."

"You think I was in the wrong then?"

"In the wrong? Damn right . . ." He broke off as she planted her hands on the table and slowly rose to her feet.

"I have allowed everyone to mock me for my want of sense," she said slowly. "It is true enough. But I cannot allow *anyone* to question my honor. I have every bit as much as most men—" her chin went up another notch "—and a good deal more than some." She lifted her hands from the table. "Good night, Rafe."

Her hair glowed gold in the candlelight, her eyes a brilliant amber. She looked like an angel—an avenging angel, proud and determined. Rafe's hands worked faster than his mind, shooting out to grasp her arm before she could step away. Slowly, firmly, he drew her forward until she leaned across the table.

"Had I been there," he said softly, "I would have challenged him for you. I would have defended your honor."

He was dismayed to see her eyes well with tears. One slipped down her cheek, leaving a faint, silvery trail. "You were not there for me, Rafe. No one was there."

He knew she had just described most of her life. True, she had a staggering propensity for getting herself into scrapes, but for the most part, she had always been the one to get herself out of them. And she had usually suffered the consequences quite alone. Right then, he was almost glad he had been at that inn. Saving Grace. It had a tolerable ring to it.

He never meant to kiss her. Even in his deepest drunken state, he would never have thought to kiss her. But he did.

The touch of his mouth to hers, which started as nothing more than a comforting caress, became something utterly different when she parted her lips with the faintest whimper. He tasted her, cider and warmth, felt her gentle giving, and suddenly his free hand was tangled in her curls.

"Grace," he whispered into her mouth. "Good God, Grace!"

He pulled away, stunned. When she leaned forward as if to follow, he tightened his fingers in her hair and held her still. Her eyes fluttered open and he saw her struggling to focus. She lifted a hand to touch her full lips. His gaze followed the motion and he stifled a groan.

"Rafe . . ."

He released her and leaned back. "Go to bed, Grace."

"But—"

"Go!"

She jerked back as if burned. There was a moment of complete silence while shadowed gold eyes searched his. Then, with a small, lost sound, she spun on her heel and all but ran to the door. To his surprise, she paused there, one delicate hand pressed to the frame.

"Good night, Rafe. I hope you will be able to sleep now."

A hundred words flitted through his mind. He could say none of them. He could not tell her that he had been sleeping just fine until the dream had come. He had awakened, chilled, with the image of his parents' beseeching eyes, lit by flames, burned into his brain. He had fled the chamber and the dream to seek even a vestige of solace downstairs.

Nor could he tell her that, should he try to sleep now, it would be her eyes that would haunt him.

So he said nothing. She waited for a moment, still not facing him. Then she was gone. Rafe watched the place where she had been for several minutes. A snatch of a poem Vivian had been reading aloud earlier flashed into his mind. A new book, he thought it was, by Thomas Campbell. He had not really been listening, but he recalled a fragment. Something about brief hours of bliss like angels' visits, few and far between.

It seemed so apt suddenly that he could almost believe Vivian had done it on purpose. But she could not have.

He had known fleeting bliss in the company of an angel. Grace, with her impossibly soft heart, had all but flown into his life. She had amused him, infuriated him, driven him unwillingly from the safety of his self-imposed hell. And she had given him solace.

He could not allow it to happen again.

Burying his face in his hands, he allowed himself one low moan. Then he straightened and reached for the candle. Yes, Grace had given him solace; she had unlocked the cellars.

He was at Havensgate, and if he could not have heaven, he would simply go in the opposite direction. Holding the candle aloft, he descended into the cellar's black depths.

Grace peered through the confectioner's shop window at the Christmas display. Papier-mâché animals, shepherds, and Magi vied for space around the Nativity scene. It looked decidedly crowded, and she thought the painted smile of the angel suspended above was one of relief.

"Come along!" Chloe tugged at her arm. "We haven't much time and I know precisely what I wish to buy."

Aurelie, knowing there were far too many people for exchanging gifts, had come up with the clever idea of putting all the names in a basket and having each person draw one. That way, everyone got a present and had only one to purchase. The entire party had driven into Newhaven to shop and were presently darting about, casting furtive glances at each other and trying to make their purchases in privacy.

"Yes, Aunt Grace, come along!" Phoebe added her plea to Chloe's. Grace had drawn Rickey for herself and was in charge of purchasing something for Lady St. Helier, who had been Phoebe's draw, as well.

She sighed as she tried to keep up with Chloe. The other girl seemed to have two speeds: full tilt and complete stop. She bounced into another shop, her enthusiasm almost but not quite infectious. She had drawn Rafe's name, and Grace tried not to hate her for it.

He had kissed her.

She had dreamed of his kiss for years, in every possible manner, every possible setting. Her favorite had been imagining him drawing her into his arms in a shadowed bower somewhere, the scent of roses around them and stars above. In her dreams she had gone weak with pleasure and answered yearning.

Reality had been inconceivably better. For that fleeting, blissful moment when his lips had been on hers, she had thought herself in heaven. Then he had pulled away, cold and remote, and she had fallen back to earth with a jarring thump.

Why had he done it? Why had he kissed her and then stopped so suddenly? She did not like the answers that came to mind. He had merely thought to comfort her in her distress, no more. The Rafe of old had always teased her out of the blue devils. Kissing her must have seemed more appropriate, she assumed, than his usual act of ruffling her hair or poking her in the ribs.

She had been too forward, all but crawling across the table and into his lap. That was why he had stopped. A wave of mortification swept over her and she felt her face heating. Her behavior had been disgraceful.

"... disgrace?"

She spun about to face Chloe. "What?"

"I asked what you thought of this, Grace." Her friend was bouncing with excitement. "Is it not perfect?"

She dutifully moved to look. "Perfect."

"I wish to buy one for Lady St. Hillier," Phoebe announced. "It's pretty."

"Yes, it is, minx, but I am afraid Lady St. Helier would

have no use for it. We shall go next door next and find something pretty for a lady."

She could not imagine what Rafe would do with an enameled snuffbox, either, as he did not take snuff, but she was not in the mood to propose an alternative. As Chloe made her purchase, she wandered through the shop, Phoebe in tow. She decided on an ornate silver quizzing glass for her brother. It was a truly ghastly image—Rickey tripping about peering at people through the lens—but he had long prattled about getting one, and she might as well oblige him.

They found a lovely bottle of French perfume for Lady St. Helier. Phoebe was still in favor of a snuffbox, but she gave in at the sight of the roses painted on the bottle. Feeling extremely proud of herself, she skipped from the store, clasping the parcel as if it contained the crown jewels.

They encountered Aurelie, Jason, and Michaela in the street. Aurelie was grinning broadly. Jason looked rather grim, his arms filled with gaily wrapped parcels. "Well, I believe I am finished!" his wife announced brightly. "I have purchased our gifts and Freddy's."

"I chose my own," Michaela said with quiet pride.

"So did I!" her sister informed her. "I wanted to buy Lady St. Hillier a snuffbox, but I got her a bottle instead."

This earned her a smile from her uncle. "A snuffbottle? How unique."

Phoebe rolled her eyes. "Not a snuffbottle, Uncle Jason. A *perfume* bottle."

"Ah, even better."

Aurelie suggested tea while they waited for the others to complete their shopping. On their way to the inn, they passed the haberdasher's, which had been Grace's first stop that morning. She had seen a truly beautiful pair of oxblood leather gloves. They had been sinfully lush and supple, and she had given in to the urge to lift them to her face. For a scant instant she had considered purchasing them for her brother. An instant later, she was setting them down. Rickey would have lost them within a week.

Her steps slowed as they passed the shop. "Go ahead," she told her companions. "I shall join you in a moment."

She entered the private salon Jason had hired minutes later, the parcel containing the gloves tucked under her arm. Had anyone asked about it, she would have been hard put to answer. She would never be able to give them to Rafe. He had always had his gloves custom made in London, and she really had no excuse to present him with any gift.

No, he would never wear the gloves. But she would keep them, a souvenir of sorts. He would never wear them, but they were *his*.

No one asked. Aurelie merely poured her a cup of tea and offered, "I think this was a rather splendid idea, if I do say so myself. We all needed to get away from the house."

Her companions' responses were forestalled by the appearance of several more members of the party. Noel and Vivian entered first, both carrying parcels and grinning. Rickey was behind them, his face flushed with cold and pleasure. And on his heels was Rafe. He, too, had been smiling. Upon meeting Grace's eyes, however, he froze, his face tightening into an unreadable mask.

"For God's sake, man," Dunstan's voice came from behind him, "move your feet! If I don't get something in my gut soon, I shall collapse." Rafe silently stepped into the room. Dunstan bounded in and promptly reached for the tray. "Dashed exhausting, this shopping rot. Can't see why you women think it all the thing."

His sister swatted his hand away from the cakes. "Really, Dunny, your manners!" She waved him into a chair. "I cannot see why women think *you* all the thing."

He grinned, unabashed. "I can't either. Women's minds are an utter mystery to me. No rhyme nor reason to the way they work. Ain't that right, Rafe?"

Grace watched as Rafe's mouth curved into a humorless smile. "Oh, I don't know," he mused. "I would say our brains work even more haphazardly at times."

"Rubbish." Dunstan seized a cake. "A man always

knows precisely what he is doing. Can't go about making silly blunders, you know."

Rafe snorted, then called to the landlord for a bottle of brandy.

14

RICKEY NEARLY TRIPPED over his feet for the third time in as many minutes. Rafe could not fathom Grace's reasoning in giving her brother a quizzing glass. She was an intelligent creature and must have known what the result would be. They would now be subjected to a squinting, stumbling fop for at least the remainder of the party, if not the following year.

But then, he mused, he was hardly qualified to question Grace's sense, when his own had taken such ignominious flight. He had kissed her. The thought made him groan inwardly. He had actually kissed *Grace*. He was certain there was a special section in Bedlam set aside for corkbrained idiots just like him. She had looked at him with those proud, desolate eyes, and his brain had promptly emptied of anything useful.

True, he had regained his senses quickly enough. No, he amended, *not* quickly enough. Quickly, but not enough. By the time his wits had returned, mere moments after their flight, the deed was done. He had kissed *Grace*. Of all the truly imbecilic things he had done over the past thirty years, this one took the prize. In retrospect, the only thing he could say with utter certainty was that trying to plant rosebushes in his mother's parlor had been an act of pure rationality in comparison.

Capping the matter was the fact that, bad as it had been for him to allow the impulse to overrule intellect, it was far, far worse for him to have liked the result. And he had liked it.

It was, he decided, time for him to leave Havensgate. He had no idea why he had stayed as long as he had, but that hardly mattered at this point. He had to leave before he went completely out of control and started kissing every lady there. He allowed himself a small smile at the prospect. Kissing Aurelie and Vivian would be no hardship, but he valued their friendship and was rather certain their husbands would be somewhat less than understanding. Chloe was not such an unpleasant image, either, although he supposed she would bounce all the while, and he did not fancy biting his tongue during the process.

The terror, of course, was that he was so far gone that he would end up grabbing either Lady Heathfield or Lady Warren. The former would freeze him like an icicle, and the latter . . . He shuddered. Lady Warren would probably cosh him over the head with the Yule log and drag him off to her bed.

"Avemar?" A voice cut into his distressing reverie. *"Avemar!"*

"Hmm?" He turned, found himself looking into Lady Warren's kohl-rimmed eyes, and gave a startled yelp. He would have launched himself right off the settee, but he was trapped between the padded arm and the lady's padded bosom.

"Lost in pleasurable thoughts, Your Grace?" She winked at him. "The holidays always bring to mind the jolliest . . . activities."

"To be sure, madam," he replied, thinking a fast gallop toward Lewes would be a jolly activity indeed.

"What a cunning little box Lady Chloe chose for you. I did not know you took snuff." When he did not respond immediately, Lady Warren continued. "Of course, I imagine there are a great many things I do not know about you. I have always said there is nothing quite so romantic as a man of mystery. . . ."

He could take no more. "Excuse me, madam. I must thank Lady Chloe for this cunning little box."

"Of course you must. And you might want to suggest

that you have your initials engraved inside. Entwined with hers, perhaps."

Rafe paused in the act of wriggling his way from his seat. "I beg your pardon?"

"Is that not how it is done? I had always thought such personal gifts between betrotheds should be given with an intimate touch. Of course, arranged matches do not always—"

"Madam, excuse me." The carved wooden arm of the settee dug into his side as he struggled to his feet.

In all honesty, he had no idea where he was going. He had already thanked Chloe for the gift. She had blushed to the roots of her brilliant hair and murmured that she had just *known* it was the right gift for him. Far more distressing than the knowledge that she did not know him at all was the question of whether she was perhaps confusing him with her father, who snorted snuff with a vengeance. The thought did not merit contemplation.

He decided to avail himself of the brandy. Due to the celebration, the men had been forced to forgo their after-supper port, and it was high time for a drink.

He was waylaid halfway across the room by a beaming Aurelie. "Would it be too much for me to thank you again?" she asked warmly. "You chose the perfect gift."

He could not help but return her smile. "I am afraid your husband does not agree."

"Oh, pish! Jason is merely miffed because he did not think of it first."

"Yes, well, it is a very good thing that I did not buy you diamonds," he teased. "Then I would have been the miffed one."

She reached up to caress the sparkling gems at her throat. "He did rather splendidly with his gift, did he not?" Then she reached out to grasp his hand. "But I shall have countless hours of fun with the rune stones. Thank you, Rafe."

"It was my pleasure," he replied, and meant it.

He knew Tarrant was something less than pleased with the gift he had given Aurelie. The man tended to be a bit high in the instep regarding such things as mysticism and fortune-telling. But the moment Rafe had seen the Gypsy woman's wares in Newhaven, he had known Aurelie must have the stones. As Celtic as the gift of blarney, she would find great amusement in learning the ancient soothsaying ritual.

Fortunately for him, she had not offered to test her prowess on him. He could only imagine what the stones would have said. *You have a great future among illustrious minds* was a distinct possibility. He rather imagined Bedlam was full of incomparably memorable thinkers.

The brandy was well in his sights when a tug at his ankle stopped him. He looked down to find Freddy gripping his trousers. "Look," the boy commanded, "it's Napoleen! Lady Sillier gave him to me."

Rafe obediently crouched down to examine the tin soldier the boy was holding. It looked more like a hussar than Bonaparte, but he was not about to say so. There was an entire regiment, some on horseback, and there was even a tiny cannon. Freddy was clearly entranced. Rafe wondered which Lady St. Helier had purchased the set. Odds were even. Both Vivian and her mother-in-law would somehow know precisely what gift would make the child giddy with delight.

"This is Uncle Jason," Freddy announced, holding one figure aloft. "And you can be this one. . . ." He then proceeded to name each figure. Rafe took a last, longing look at the brandy, then settled himself on the floor. He could not very well leave when the boy had graciously put him in colonel's gear.

Grace watched him with her heart in her throat. He was leaning down to hear what her nephew said, his dark hair blending with the boy's fair. She could give him a golden-haired son, she mused, although she would rather have had one with mahogany curls and tilted cobalt eyes. It was hardly a proper thought, she knew, but at least her thoughts were her own.

"Another moment and he will begin to smolder."

184

She spun around to face Vivian. "I beg your pardon?"

"Your gaze, Gracie, could melt a snowman. A flesh-and-blood creature stands no chance whatsoever."

Grace sighed. "Should my mother hear you saying such things, she would freeze us both into snowmen."

"Snow-women, dear. And should your mother see you devouring Rafael with your eyes, she would send you right off to Siberia."

"Yes, I suppose you are right. Silly of me to worry about the Americas."

"Hmm?"

"Oh, merely a flash of the future." Grace glanced at Rafe again, drinking in the familiar planes of his face, softened now by the firelight and his easy smile. She reluctantly dragged her eyes away. "Tell me about Boston, Vivvy. Would I like it? And please feel free to lie should you think I would not."

Sometime later, she found herself seated next to Myrtle on the settee. The ever-present woolly mass flowed from the woman's lap to the floor. Grace had been rather relieved to see it. She had been concerned that it might have become someone else's possession during the exchange of gifts. But Myrtle had given Lord Heathfield a pair of hunting glasses, much like those one would take to the opera, and he had been delighted. Grace silently speculated that, as Myrtle had attached herself to Lady Heathfield during the shopping expedition, it had been her mother who had really made the choice.

Her own gift, a rose-colored kashmir shawl, had been a gift from Aurelie. Rather, it had been from Freddy, but she knew Aurelie had chosen it. It was a beautiful thing, and she clasped it about her arms now, warmed as much by the affection behind its purchase as its soft mass.

"I do so adore Christmas," Myrtle sighed happily. "To be among loved ones during the holidays is to be truly blessed."

"To be sure," was Grace's dutiful reply. To be around one particular loved one was proving excessively painful.

Rickey wandered over and promptly trod upon her toes. "Oh, I say, Gracie, so sorry!"

She did not have the heart to scold him. He was too happy with his glass. And she really had no one to blame but herself for his present clumsiness. She supposed he would get the hang of using it soon enough. At the moment, he did not quite seem to grasp the concept that he had to be aware of more than whatever single object he was quizzing.

"I do so adore your family!" Myrtle beamed as she watched her ball of yarn skitter across the floor. Rickey had tangled himself in the slack. "There is never a dull moment."

Grace retrieved the yarn, wincing as her brother's elbow connected with her ear. "I would venture to agree, madam." She regained her seat and held the ball safely in her lap. "The Granvilles are not renowned for dullness."

Freddy whooped in delight, apparently having executed some brilliant strategic maneuver with his tin army. Phoebe swept past, regal in the tin and paste-jewel crown that had been her gift from her uncle Jason. She prodded Rickey with the matching scepter and he obligingly moved out of the way. Lord Heathfield chuckled as he peered about the room through his glasses, pausing as his younger son bumped into a side table and nearly sent a trio of porcelain shepherdesses to the floor.

"No," Grace said, "Granvilles are never dull."

Rickey, having managed to leave the table intact, chose that moment to launch into a rousing rendition of a wassail song. Apparently his vision had been unimpaired enough earlier to lead him to the brandy. One by one, other members of the party joined in until the room was filled with swelling voices. After a time, Grace even picked her father's booming baritone out of the chorus. It seemed Christmas really did bring a change of spirit.

She looked at Rafe. He was still sitting on the floor, a lustily bellowing Freddy in his lap. He was not singing, but he looked entirely genial. She did not particularly care if it was music that had soothed the savage beast, or liquor. He appeared soothed.

"He always was a handsome devil."

"Madam?" Grace tried her best to direct a bland smile in Myrtle's direction. Whatever the lady said next was lost in the hearty wassailing. "I am afraid I did not hear you."

"I said, dear, that I do not believe an agreement has been reached between my nephew and Lady Chloe."

Grace tried to maintain the bland smile. It was not easy. "Is that so?"

"Such things can be so very complicated, you know." Again her words were lost to the singing. ". . . serendipity."

"I beg your pardon?"

Myrtle raised her voice. "I said, I believe with all my heart in serendipity."

Very little good had happened in Grace's life by accident. "I should like very much to believe in serendipity."

"But you do not? You should, dearest."

"Why is that, madam?"

"Well, I should not think . . ." Myrtle paused as Rickey's tenor crescendo all but rattled the paintings on the walls. "I should not think—" she smiled patiently and raised her voice "—that you and I would have had our delightful little visit had Rafael not sent you. And I hardly think your time alone with him at the hunting box was planned!"

The clock chimed the hour, its bells echoing through the completely silent room. The song was over.

It seemed like a very long silence indeed. Then, *"Grace!"* Lady Heathfield's shriek was loud and shrill enough to be heard in London.

"Now, Mama," Grace began, but closed her mouth when she saw her mother's prone form. The countess, draped elegantly but precariously over the arm of her chair, had fainted dead away.

"Fetch her vinaigrette," Vivian suggested vaguely.

"Best of luck finding one." Grace sighed. "She has never fainted before."

No one bothered to check the condition of the supine countess. All eyes were riveted on her daughter.

It was Aurelie who broke the even longer silence that followed. She cleared her throat. "Surely, Lady Hammond, you are mistaken. Grace went straight to you from Crowborough."

"Nonsense," Myrtle announced with a sniff. "I knew the moment she arrived on my doorstep. She was wearing Rafael's coat and what I can only assume were his breeches, and sniffling into his handkerchief. I embroidered his crest on it myself. 'Twas a birthday gift." Her brow furrowed. "Was it last year? No, last year I gave him a watch fob . . . or perhaps it was a snuffbox. No matter. The handkerchiefs were this past June."

Everyone turned to look at Grace. She was not supposed to have seen Rafe since February. "I do not believe Lady Hammond means to imply . . ." Her voice trailed off. Lady Hammond had meant precisely what she had said. Odd, she thought dazedly, that the woman's words, usually taken as no more than sweet nonsense, seemed to carry the weight of a royal decree now.

Myrtle aside, it would do no good to lie to her family. She was utterly dismal at it, and suffered no illusions on the matter. "You do not understand," she began again, then turned pleading eyes to Rafe. He was staring up at the ceiling. She knew better than to think he was praying.

"Are you telling us," Jason said slowly, as if weighing the words, "that you went to Rafe and he escorted you to Lady Hammond?"

"Precisely! You see, there was so much snow, and then in the pub at the Lewes inn—"

"Pub?" Lady Heathfield's eyes fluttered closed again.

"Well, yes, but that was not deliberate. You see, I meant to come straight here, but the snow stopped us at Lewes. Rafe just happened to be there, which was very fortunate because of the thugs—"

"Grace," Rafe cut in, his voice toneless and heavy. "Perhaps you ought to let me tell the tale."

188

"Oh, by all means!"

He should have left when he had the chance. Hindsight, he decided as he tried to find the right words to counter his aunt's, was usually a matter of perfect vision. "Grace ran into a bit of trouble while waiting for her coach at Lewes," he said to no one in particular. "Luckily, I happened to be there. It was a simple enough matter to get her to Dickerdean." True enough. "I knew my aunt would be coming here." Not so true, but it hardly mattered.

"There," Myrtle said triumphantly, "you see?" She waved her knitting needles in Aurelie's direction. "I knew dearest Rafael had sent her." Rafe tried not to snarl as she turned back to him and asked, "Why did you not come in, dear boy? I know you have not been yourself lately, but it was beyond rude to drop Grace off like some unwanted parcel. I imagine she was ever so wounded. What *were* you thinking?"

"Yes, Rafe, what *were* you thinking?"

Rafe did not like Tarrant's expression. He did not like it at all. "Really, man, you cannot think . . ."

"What in God's name am I supposed to think? That you promptly shoved my sister into your coat and transported her through the snow to Dickerdean? What sort of fool do you take me for?" He took a menacing stride forward.

"Jason, please." Aurelie stepped in with a weak smile. "I think it has all been explained quite satisfactorily. Grace had the good fortune to meet up with Rafe, and he promptly escorted her to Dickerdean."

"Quite right!" Myrtle chimed in. "Well, perhaps not quite . . ."

"Aunt."

She might have been stone-deaf for all the heed she paid Rafe's warning. "Do not scowl at me, dearest. I will not be told my powers of recognition are faulty here. She was wearing your coat. It was the one you were wearing the last time I dropped in to see you. . . ."

"How long?" Tarrant's voice had the sting of a cracked whip.

"Oh, I suppose it was last month sometime," Myrtle offered helpfully.

Tarrant ignored her. "Rafe?"

"Really, Tare, it was an insignificant amount of time."

"How long?" When Rafe hesitated, Tarrant spun on his sister. "Well, Grace?"

Grace, her face devoid of color, cast beseeching eyes in Rafe's direction. He did not know what to say. He had just gotten a very good look at Lady Warren's face, and her ill-disguised glee had caused his gut to tighten. Any hope that the matter would stay within the room vanished with her expression. The old biddy would have the tale to London in days even if she had to carry it there herself.

His stomach wrenched, but the following sensation was even worse. It felt unmistakably like a noose being tightened about his neck.

He wondered vaguely if Grace was not feeling the same. She seemed to be having a very difficult time speaking. "I . . . well, I suppose . . . two . . . three . . ." Perhaps she was going to say *hours*, but she never had the chance to complete the statement.

Lady Heathfield's moan swelled over the stammering. "Disgrace," she wailed, hand clasped to her breast. "The ultimate disgrace!"

"Mama, please," Grace implored, her hands up as if to ward off a blow—or a curse.

The curse came. "Foolish, ungrateful girl! For years I have struggled against your willfulness. Now it will be the downfall of the family, and you shall suffer most for it!"

"Oh, Mama!"

"Do not talk to me, you wretched creature!"

For a time, the only sound was Grace's ragged breathing. Then a crash, loud as a gun blast, rang out. The entire room spun to regard Lord Heathfield. He raised the mahogany-cased hunting glasses as if to bang them against the marquetry table again. Instead, he gave an alarming growl and slammed them down on the settee beside him.

"Madam," he addressed his wife, "you will cease with

the caterwauling! No—not another bloody word!" She gasped, then closed her mouth with a snap. "This is not a matter to be discussed here. Daughter, you will await me in the blue salon."

"But, Papa—"

"Damme, girl, do as you are told! For once, do as you are told!"

With a muffled sob, Grace rose to her feet and rushed from the room. Aurelie began to follow, but her father-in-law's bark stopped her in her tracks.

Rafe had a very good idea what was coming next. He was correct. The man rounded on him with the narrowed eyes of a hunter bearing down for the kill. "On your feet, young man!" he snapped. "The library!"

Refusal was a possibility, but Rafe had never believed in public displays of gutlessness. Better, too, for their conversation to be had in private. He did pause long enough to pat Freddy on the head. "Remind me sometime to tell you about Waterloo, soldier."

He had not been there, but he had a very good idea how the principals had felt.

Grace huddled miserably in the chair, feeling chilled to the bone despite the fire burning in the grate. She did not know how long she had been sitting there, but eternity seemed a reasonable guess.

There was no question in her mind of what was going on elsewhere. The children would have been sent upstairs, and those persons remaining in the drawing room would be scattered about in various states of shock. No doubt Myrtle would be inclined to prattle about dearest Grace and Rafael, and Lady Warren would be all but bursting with the salacious joy of an inveterate gossipmonger. Lady Heathfield would still be moaning. There was some comfort in knowing Aurelie and Vivian would not allow anything too terrible to be said, but it was fleeting.

She was certain that truly awful words were being exchanged wherever her father and Rafe were.

It did not matter that very little was known of her time at the hunting box. Scandals had been made of far less. An unchaperoned girl found in the presence of a man not in her immediate family was, at the very least, an unseemly blight on the name of propriety. A girl already in disgrace found to have been in an isolated house with a dissolute rake was something far worse.

No, she had no doubt what the results would be. The earl would demand marriage. The duke would refuse. If neither ended up dead on a dueling field—or even if one did—the girl would soon find herself in the wilds of some distant land.

As far as Grace was concerned, there was no hope of a happy ending.

She did not even bother to rise when the door slammed open and Rafe stalked in. She knew her legs would not support her. He crossed the room to stand before the mantel. His cobalt eyes were nearly black with an emotion she could only assume was fury.

"I will not marry you."

The words were only to be expected, but she tried not to flinch at the cutting, utterly cold tone. "I am so terribly sorry, Rafe. I never meant for this to happen."

It was all she could think of to say.

"Fine. You are sorry."

"You do not believe me?"

His laugh was more wounding than any words. "That you are sorry? Your remorse, or lack thereof, is no concern of mine. Save it for your father."

"He challenged you." It was not a question. She could see it in his face.

"Amusing, isn't it? He couldn't be bothered to deal with Fremont, but he thinks to put a bullet in me." He laughed again, a sound devoid of any humor. "Why is that, do you suppose?" he queried bitterly, then rolled his eyes and slapped a palm to his forehead. "Of course! How foolish of me to ask. Fremont, we know, cheats."

"Rafe, please . . ."

"What do you think, Grace? Would your esteemed papa expect me to be different? I imagine having known my family as long as he has, he would have reason to assume I would show some vestige of honor on the dueling field." He seemed to ponder the matter. "I have not fired a pistol in years, but I think I remember the way of it."

She felt the blood draining from her face as she imagined Rafe lying on the cold earth somewhere, his own blood seeping away. "Dear God," she whispered. Then, desperately, "Please, Rafe, no! I will do anything. I will beg him not to do this, I will leave—"

His hand hit the mantel with bone-jarring force. "Silence! This is not Beauty and the Beast, Grace! Nobly offering yourself in your father's stead is not an option. I want nothing you could give."

She felt the tears welling and fought for control. It seemed of paramount importance suddenly to keep from showing how deeply and irrevocably he was wounding her. "I will not allow him to meet you," she managed with far more strength than she felt.

There was a heavy, agonizing moment while he did nothing but stare at her with his cold, angry eyes. "You really are a fool. There will be no duel."

"But what . . . ?" She felt her jaw dropping. He could not mean . . . could not possibly mean . . .

"I have said it before and I mean it, Grace. I will not marry you!"

15

THE ROOM GREW no warmer after his departure. In fact, Grace decided, he had left behind a distinct chill. His parting words still echoed dully in her ears. *You might look like an angel, but you are a devil to the core. . . . Nothing to do with the matter? Do not delude yourself, Grace. You are damn well responsible for every wretched bit of it.*

She wondered if perhaps he were correct. Not about the angel and devil bit, but about her culpability. He probably was. Intent had nothing to do with it, but that hardly seemed important. She had put them both in an appalling position. She could only imagine how he had felt in her father's presence. Cornered, furious, and sickened came to mind.

A good half hour had passed after his departure when the soft tap came at the door. Grace answered it more out of instinct than politeness. Company, at the moment, was hardly welcome. She glanced up to see her sister-in-law entering, a tray in her hands.

"I thought you might be in need of a bit of refreshment."

"Thank you," she said mechanically.

Aurelie set the tray on the table and poured two cups of tea. She pressed one into Grace's numb fingers. "How are you? Or is that a terrible question?"

"I have been asked worse. I suppose you could say I am giddy with anticipation." She almost smiled at her sister-in-law's befuddled expression. "I fear my nerves will not be able to stand the strain of waiting for Papa to appear."

"Oh, Grace, he will not . . ." Either the list of awful

194

things the earl would not do was too long for Aurelie to mention, or she realized he might just do anything.

"I have no idea what he will do," Grace said honestly. "But I should not count on anything pleasant."

As a child, she had always believed the waiting to be worse than the punishment. Now she knew better. In fact, she would be more than content to wait until the final Judgment Day to hear her father's decree.

"Grace, I hate to ask this of you, but it might make a very great difference in how everything proceeds." Aurelie leaned forward, her gray eyes filled with compassion. "Oh dear, this is awkward. . . . Did you and Rafe . . . Did he . . . ?"

The urge to laugh was nearly overpowering. "No," Grace replied, wondering if perhaps a little bit of her amusement was hysteria-tinged, "we did not. He did not. The entire time we were together, he did not so much as touch me."

What a terrible shame. She did not even bother trying to suppress the improper thought. Rafe had not touched her, and now, knowing how utterly wondrous his touch felt, she regretted the loss with every fiber of her being.

"Well, I certainly expected that to be the case, but it is comforting to hear. Perhaps your parents will be more inclined to be lenient."

Offhand, Grace did not agree, but perhaps there was a chance. She wondered idly what her parents would say if she were to openly lament her still-unsullied virtue. She rather thought they would not be surprised. They seemed to think only the worst of her as it was.

She sighed. "It does not signify, really. There will be no marriage, of course, and Lady Warren will be certain to spread the tale as far and wide as possible. I broke the rules, Aurelie. I shall have to bear the consequences."

She was grateful when her sister-in-law did not offer banal platitudes. "Jason and I will do what we can, of course." Aurelie reached for her hand and squeezed it reassuringly. "I know things look grim right now, but we will support you."

Well, Grace thought, she would certainly look forward to receiving their letters—wherever she ended up being banished. "Thank you. I could not ask for more."

Now Aurelie's mouth tightened. "You could ask for a good deal more! You deserve more!"

Grace could not reply. She knew if she so much as opened her mouth, she would burst into uncontrollable sobbing. So she grasped Aurelie's fingers tightly and tried to remember the wonderful things Vivian had told her of Boston.

The door opened again minutes later. This time she did rise to her feet. "Papa," she managed.

Lord Heathfield did not look angry, precisely. But he did look stern, and very tired. His eyes swung to Aurelie, who hesitated, but removed herself. The glance she cast over her shoulder was full of the compassion and support that had made Grace love her in the first place. Strengthened slightly, she was able to raise her eyes to her father's.

He strode to the hearth and stood in the very spot Rafe had occupied what seemed aeons earlier. "I find I have no idea what to say to you, Grace."

"I understand—"

He cut her off with an impatient wave. "Had my words all planned. Now I can't seem to say them." He fixed her with a familiar topaz gaze. "What did we not give you?"

"I . . . I beg your pardon, sir?"

"What was it? Discipline? A sense of honor?" If he saw her stiffen at that, he gave no indication. "You have brains, girl, which makes it all the more difficult for me to understand why you have behaved as you have." He sighed then, a bone-weary sound. "I can come to only one conclusion."

She could tell he expected her to say something. Anything. "Yes, sir?"

"You want him."

"I . . . I beg—"

His fist hit the mantel. "Don't beg my pardon, Grace! It is galling in this situation."

"Yes, sir." Like a figure receding into the distance, she felt as if she were growing smaller with every second.

"You want him, and you thought to get him with this absurd scene!"

Some paltry vestige of pride rose within her. She drew herself up stiffly and, despite the fact that she felt as tiny in his presence as she had as a very small child, faced him squarely. "You cannot believe that. You cannot believe I deliberately cast myself in Rafe's path—in a snowstorm in a strange inn, no less—in hopes that I might be so compromised that he would be forced to offer for me!" She was gasping now, with rage and a sort of sick helplessness. "No matter what you think of me, you cannot believe that!"

There was a moment of torturous silence before he replied, "No, Grace, I confess I cannot." He looked older suddenly, and more human than she had ever seen him. "Whatever *you* think of me, I have never thought ill of you. Damme, girl, you are my flesh and blood, and I care for you!"

It was the closest he had ever come to showing any emotion other than exasperation in her presence. In that moment, Grace wanted nothing more than to fling herself into his arms and beg forgiveness for every transgression she had ever committed. His stiff shoulders held her back. "Thank you, Papa."

He grunted. "You do want him."

"I . . ." She found she could not lie. "Yes, I do . . . I did."

"Well, damme." The curse lacked its customary vehemence. "I would've done what I could. I would've tried to . . ." He broke off and shrugged. "I would have tried before."

"Oh, Papa!" The dam burst. With a sob, she hurtled herself at his chest.

His arms came around her and, for countless minutes, he held her as she cried, awkwardly stroking her hair. When at last he held her away from him, his eyes held a profound and wrenching sadness.

"He does not want you, Gracie."

The words should not have hurt as much as they did. She shuddered. "I know."

"And I don't know what I'm to do with you."

Love me! she cried silently. *Tell me that, no matter what I have done, you forgive me.*

"Your mother wants me to pack you off to the Colonies," he continued. Grace could do no more than nod miserably. "I . . . I told her I would have to give the matter careful thought."

Something like faint hope flared within her. "Papa, I will stay here. I will promise never to disgrace you. . . ."

He shook her slightly. "I can't hear this from you now." She bit her lip, but remained silent. "You will stay out of your mother's sight until I come to a decision. Is that clear?"

"Yes, Papa."

He nodded and turned to leave the room. Then he paused. "Suppose I can't put all the blame on you, girl. You're a Granville, after all, and Granvilles have never been ruled by their brains."

He was at the door when she stopped him. "Papa?"

"Hmm?"

A wise woman would undoubtedly have kept her mouth shut. But Grace was a Granville, and wisdom had never been a Granville strength. "What about Rafe?"

"What about him?"

"You will not . . . you will not try to avenge something I have not lost?"

His gaze was unreadable when he turned back. "If I put a bullet through his black heart, it will be for hurting you now, not before."

Rafe had ridden down the lane, half expecting to feel a bullet in his back as he went. But there had been no shot. He had been neither quiet nor clandestine in his departure, yet, he decided, it was still entirely possible that no one knew he had left. For the first time since his arrival, he had not tripped over a St. Helier, Granville, or Somersham as he had navigated the hall.

There had been an eerie stillness to the house, an almost funereal pall. He wondered if Lady Heathfield would insist on draping everything that did not move in black. Very probably. The woman's flair for the dramatic was bested only by her devotion to tragedy.

Havensgate was not a pleasant place to be at present. Even the dark and icy road back to Lewes was preferable. If he were fortunate, he would be back at his lodge before midnight. If his luck were as expected considering the past week, he would end up in a ditch somewhere along the way, frozen into a snowman. At present, he was not tremendously concerned with which it would be. He was too vexed to care much one way or another.

He did not question that he was doing the right thing. Staying at Havensgate would have smacked of idiocy, not to mention martyrdom. And he detested martyrs. He had no intention of waking up one morning to find himself legshackled to Grace, and was fairly convinced that, should he have continued refusing marriage, he would have woken up one morning quite dead, one of Lord Heathfield's bullets lodged somewhere vital in his anatomy.

Marriage to Grace. Even as the thought flashed through his head, he prepared himself for the shudder that would follow. But his body did not react as expected. He thought again, *tied for life to Grace*, and practiced a satisfactory shudder. Instead, he got no more than a faint twitch in his left shoulder.

"Absolutely not!" he muttered, and twitched again.

He allowed himself a brief moment to speculate just how bad it would be for her in the wake of his defection. Not that he planned to spend much time worrying about the matter, of course. The feckless, harrying chit deserved whatever she got this go-around. It was high time she learned that every action had a consequence. She simply could not go blithely through life acting on every impulse. Nor could she continue to drag others into the fray with her.

You live by impulse.

He ignored the voice, which, of course, was not his own.

It was altogether too easy to be deceived by an angelic countenance; he had seen it happen to too many good men. A pretty face and demure mien could snare a man like a noose. It seemed likely that acting teachers were as frequently to be found in the employ of debutantes' papas as the ubiquitous dancing masters. Such rampant innocence could only be the work of master thespians. He pitied the poor sods who had offered for angels and found themselves married to thorny harridans. Far better to avoid the lure entirely.

You were certainly allured, you poor sod.

Yes, it was a very good thing he had gotten out while he had. Grace was likely to take it into her head to make a break for parts unknown, and he could only imagine what the result would be. If the chit had only learned to behave herself with a modicum of restraint, or at least to stay where she was supposed to, everyone's life would be much simpler.

You were not where you were supposed to be.

He cursed aloud, startling his horse. Hard as he tried, and he did try—hard and determined—he could only escape his blasted conscience for so long. No, he had not been where he was supposed to be. Instead of being at Margrave with his parents, he had been in Suffolk with a collection of the ton's best and brightest. He knew it was not fair to blame the merry widow who had ultimately proven herself to be among the best of bedmates, if not the brightest companion. The fault was his alone.

He should have been at Margrave.

As Hannibal plodded stolidly along, Rafe considered the tearing guilt that had plagued him since the fire. He did not particularly want to ponder the subject, but there was little else to do. Besides, it effectively kept him from thinking about Grace.

Culpability, he mused, was all well and good. Redemption was quite another matter. How did a dissolute duke go about redeeming himself? The answers were not pleasant, even as they were predictable. He could marry, of course, and set about producing new Marlowes to replace those who had been lost. It was certainly what was expected of him. Fill a nursery with noise and posterity.

The problem, of course, was that he felt neither like marrying nor reproducing himself. The former brought to mind images of simpering debutantes with wide, doelike eyes, fringed by constantly batting lashes and unerringly fixed on his title and his mother's jewels. The latter implied an heir, and perhaps a spare, who would have every potential of growing up to be just like him. He wondered if utter want of wits could be passed through bloodlines and decided it was entirely likely.

He had not felt so depressed in days.

If propagating the line was one option, avoiding propagation was another. Of course, avoiding the fairer sex was a different matter, but there were always women who would expect nothing more than a bit of money. It should be no problem to keep away from the other kind, the ones with aspirations forged of a combination of romantic notions and practical avarice. He would simply stay away from London. And Sussex, Essex, Derbyshire, and anywhere else one was likely to find rusticating young ladies.

His hunting box was calling, loudly. It was entirely possible that Heathfield would take it into his muddled mind to come after him, but not probable. The man had never lifted as much as an avenging finger for his daughter in the past. Pitiful as it was, it was hardly likely he would do so now. Nor was young Rickey much of a threat. The man was too busy quizzing furniture to take up any sort of heroic quest.

Tarrant was the real concern. Not that he was likely to storm up with pistols blazing. Aurelie would staunch that notion quickly should it ever enter her habitually stodgy husband's head. No, it was just that Rafe would be sorry to lose the friendship. Tare, and later his wife, had become something as close to family as one not related could be.

Well, at least he still had Myrtle.

He supposed he had every right to be furious with his aunt. She had, after all, let the cat out of the bag. And he was far too intelligent to blindly assume it had been an accident. Myrtle's mind was a puzzle suited only to the world's great scientists. He had a strong conviction that she had spoken with utter forethought and clarity.

The old hen had recognized his coat. In truth, he should not have been surprised. Myrtle often could not remember what she had eaten for breakfast, but flashes of the past seemed as bright in her mind as lightning. Of course, much of that lightning was a complete mirage, but this time she had gotten it right.

Perhaps he ought to have paid more attention to her blathering about grandnieces and nephews. Not that he would have done anything about it, but he might have been able to divert her thought processes before they took a dangerous turn into matchmaking. The references to an arrangement with Chloe had been of minimal concern. The matter with Grace was something else entirely.

And he did not want to think about Grace.

Yes, he had every right to be furious. His aunt had done everything in her power to see him trapped into marriage. But he could not maintain any degree of anger. Myrtle was the only close family he had left, and he was fond of her. In time, he would even be able to forget that she had, for some unfathomable reason, created a plan for his future that included marriage to Grace.

Grace. Grace was, quite simply, a persistent and immutable pox on the very hide of his existence. With her angel's countenance and devil's obstinance, she had weaseled her way into his . . . home. He, like the gentleman he had been raised to be, had snatched her from the jaws of danger, taken her in, and even gone so far as to see that she ended up safely back in the bosom of her loving family. Marriage, he thought with utter certainty, would have been taking the whole dismal affair an unnecessary step too far.

"Damned if I didn't do all that was bloody proper," he muttered aloud. Hannibal bobbed his head.

And what had been the reward? A thunderous row with her father, a slightly more genial one with his own aunt, and a long ride through the bitterly cold night toward the blasted place where it all had started.

It mattered not in the least that she had an impossibly soft heart. Nor that she had a fathomless, gold, completely unfluttering gaze and a lush, tart mouth. No, Grace was no simpering, cow-eyed chit. She possessed none of the qualities he found so distasteful in women. In fact, she had the wit, mettle, and honor that made for a damn good friend in a man. The difference, of course, was that his friends' parents had never made insane demands of marriage.

The truth, of course, was that he had never had the overwhelming desire to kiss any of his friends breathless.

He cursed again, long and eloquently. This time it appeared Hannibal was too tired to nod. Instead, the beast merely snorted his agreement and slogged on. There were still miles to go, and Rafe was beginning to feel both the cold and a new, hotter flash of temper. He had passed an inn a quarter hour before. It would be perfectly easy to turn the horse about and go back. Hannibal could have a warm stall and a pail of oats, and he could have a bottle of brandy.

Yes, that would do quite well. He would drink and think of simpler days while, miles away, the party at Havensgate could slink about in furtive chaos. Or funereal gloom. Whichever they chose, he would only give it as much thought as to thank his stars that he would not have to be among the blighted group for the remainder of their party.

His actions, he finally acknowledged, were cowardly to an extreme. And something worse. The worse was something he did not care to think of at all. Better a free coward than a wretched hero. Anything, he decided firmly, was better than being wretched.

He tugged on the reins. Moments later, despite Hannibal's stubborn protests, they were heading back the way they had come.

* * *

The guests began departing Havensgate the following morning. Such had not been the plan, of course, but the festive atmosphere was quite gone. Chloe and Dunstan were among the first to go. Grace, taking her father's advice, had remained in her chamber through breakfast, not wanting to encounter her mother. When the tap came at her door, she assumed it was Aurelie or Vivian, come to keep her company. Instead, it was Chloe who bounced into the chamber.

"We are off," the girl announced, her mouth drawn into a disappointed frown. "I do not wish to leave, but Dunny feels it is best." She sighed. "I was rather hoping to avoid my parents for another sennight."

"I am sorry," Grace sighed.

"Whatever for?"

"Well, it is my fault that you feel compelled to go."

"Not at all." Chloe reached forward to pat her hand, grinning now. "You will forgive me for saying so, but it is your mother's fault entirely."

"My mother?"

"Of course. With all her moaning, she has made it quite impossible to have a polite conversation with anyone."

Grace was not certain what she had expected from Chloe, but it was certainly not this warmth and humor. She had, after all, been exposed for having spent several days alone with the other girl's intended. At the very least, some righteous indignation would have been called for. The cut direct would not have been inappropriate. But Chloe was smiling at her with the ease of long friendship, all the while bouncing cheerfully on the counterpane.

Needless to say, Grace was confused. "Chloe," she said eventually, "I do not understand. . . ."

"What? About your mother. I daresay that was rather rude of me and I do apologize, but one can only be expected to listen to so much moaning."

Grace could not help but smile. "No, I quite understand about my mother, and heartily agree. What confuses me is . . ." She broke off and stared at the other girl helplessly, hoping for a bit of assistance. Chloe merely regarded her

204

pleasantly. "I mean . . . Well, blast! I am in disgrace for being alone with Rafe!"

"Unfair, I say," Chloe retorted. Grace blinked at her. "Why is it that women always seem to be blamed for the most inconsequential matters, while men are allowed to trip blithely through life, uncensored as long as they do not commit murder, treason, or bad business investments?" Red curls bounced with emphasis. "Answer that for me, if you can!"

Grace was speechless.

"See? 'Tis impossible! I, for one, think *he* ought to be tarred and feathered!"

"For . . . ruining me?"

Chloe gave an impressive snort. "Do you truly feel ruined?"

Grace did not even have to ponder the matter. "Not in the least. I have all my limbs, most of my wits, and a firm conviction that I am quite as capable of wreaking havoc on my own life as I ever was!" She even laughed. "Ruined. Compromised. It rather makes one feel like a piece of turbot left out in the sun."

"Turbot! Precisely!"

"So do tell me why you think Rafe ought to be . . ."

"Tarred? Turboted?" Chloe grimaced. "Really, Grace, the man is the worst sort of idiot. He had every opportunity to attach himself to you for the rest of his life, and he declined!"

Grace felt her jaw go slack. "Are you quite mad?"

"Mad?" Chloe looked genuinely surprised. "Good heavens, of course I am mad. It runs in my family. But I am also of the firm conviction that you are the very best thing for our Rafael, and I suspect he knows it as well. Of course, he knew you would refuse him, and there is nothing so absurd as the power of the male ego. Makes them utterly insensible at times. . . ."

"Chloe! Have you any idea what you are saying?"

"What a silly question. I am the one saying it, after all."

"But . . . you . . . Rafe . . ." Grace choked back a helpless giggle. "You are telling me that your future husband ought to be marrying me!"

This time it was Chloe who went slack-jawed. "My future husband? Good Lord, Gracie, wherever did you get that crackbrained notion?"

"Lady Hammond said . . . Rafe said . . ." She broke off when the other girl gave a peal of laughter.

"And you took it in all seriousness! Really now, you ought to know that what one's family wishes and connives and what one intends are seldom the same. My mother made a complete cake of herself last year, trying to make a match of it. Rafael and I nearly laughed ourselves ill."

"Then there never was an . . . arrangement?"

"Gracious, no! 'Tis bad enough that we should be paired together in a game of charades. We would be an utter disaster in marriage!" Chloe rolled her eyes. "The very thought!"

Grace, already feeling decidedly battered by recent events, was having a very hard time processing this information. "It seemed to make so much sense," she mumbled.

"Rubbish. What makes sense is the two of you. If you were any better suited to each other, you would *be* each other!" A shout came from the hall and Chloe sighed. "Dunstan's manners really are appalling at times." She rose to her feet and shook her hopelessly creased skirts. "Just let Rafael imagine you marrying someone else. He would burst something, and it would serve him right." Her brother shouted again. "Now, do not allow your parents to send you off anywhere too distant. You must be easily findable."

"Findable?" Grace repeated vaguely.

"Of course. I feel a bit guilty speaking of your perfect mate so, but Rafe is a bit dense. We must be certain he knows precisely where to look."

Then, giving Grace a brief but hearty hug, Chloe bounced off.

Aurelie narrowly avoided a collision in the doorway. "Your brother . . ." she began.

"Yes, I know. And I do apologize." Chloe embraced her

hostess. "Thank you so much for having us! You really must visit soon, but I expect you to leave Grace behind."

Aurelie frowned. "I beg your pardon?"

"Well, it would simply be too confusing, you see. She must be findable!"

Aurelie stared bemusedly at Chloe's departing back until the girl had bounced out of sight. Then she turned back to Grace. "What on earth was she talking about?"

Torn between the urge to laugh and cry, Grace gave a stifled groan. "How can I possibly be findable," she asked poignantly, "when I have allowed myself to be lost?"

16

THE TURBOT WAS growing quite cold. The first several removes had been consumed in near silence, but no one at the table was paying the least attention to the food now.

"What did you say, girl?" Lord Heathfield barked. "You have *found* yourself?"

Grace nodded. She had, after three days, finally been allowed out of her chamber and was not about to let what she had accomplished during that time go to waste. "I have found myself."

"What in the devil does that mean?"

"It means that I will not be going to Boston, Papa." Grace lifted her chin and met his eyes, so like her own. "Nor will I box with kangaroos."

"Kangaroos? What in God's name . . . ?"

"Yes, I know you chose Boston over Australia, but I am merely eliminating the possibility. I do not wish to leave England, you see, and do not believe you truly wish me to go."

There was a moment of silence while the earl studied her, his expression troubled. "I wasn't aware the matter was up for discussion," he muttered finally, "but nothing's final about Boston."

"Heathfield!" his wife gasped. "We had agreed—"

"Apparently not, Mama," Grace cut in. "I do suppose you will believe me when I say I do not mean to be impudent, but I will not allow my future to be planned out as if

I have no say in the matter. And I will certainly not be sent off like some unwanted parcel."

An angry flush appeared on the countess's pale cheeks. "Need I remind you, daughter, that you are quite ruined?"

"Like a *mangled* parcel, then," Grace amended, smiling with a recent memory. "But I assure you, I am not ruined in the least. I am precisely what I was three months ago. Well, no—" she gave a rueful laugh "—perhaps not precisely. I am rather wiser than I was then. In fact, I am wiser than I was three *days* ago."

She glanced about the table. The rest of the guests had long since departed, leaving only the Granvilles at Havensgate. Both Aurelie and Jason were regarding her now, clearly bemused, but just as clearly in support of her. "I will not be accompanying you to Staffordshire, either, Papa."

The earl's brows snapped together. "You will not? And where, may I ask, do you plan to stay?"

"Here in East Sussex," was her firm reply.

"You've been busy these last three days, girl. Care to share more of these plans of yours with your father?"

"Of course, Papa." She took a fortifying breath. "At first I thought simply to stay where I could be found—"

"Thought you'd already found yourself," Rickey cut in genially, his unglassed eye winking. "Lost again already?"

Grace sighed. "Eat your turbot, Rickey. It is getting cold." Then, to her father, "You see, I had lost more than I thought, which was quite upsetting—until, of course, I saved a goodly portion from utter loss." She noted her father's slack jaw. "I am not explaining myself well, but I am very much afraid I cannot do better at present. I can simply repeat that I will not be leaving East Sussex just yet."

A quick glance between her father's face and her mother's told her that things were not going as well as she had hoped. In fact, if her sire's deepening scowl was any indication, she was in for a full-force gale. She could only hope it would not be on the Atlantic Ocean.

209

Taking a deep breath, she went on. "I have been abysmally hen-witted about a good many things, not the least of which is Lord Avemar." She flinched when her mother gave a strangled moan and debated calling for some smelling salts. Of course, it would not be worth the effort. "As I said, I have been somewhat of a fool—"

"Somewhat?" Lady Heathfield gasped. "You allowed yourself to be seduced by the perfidious fiend, and then you allowed him to escape his duty as a gentleman!"

"I was not seduced, Mama," Grace said on a sigh. "And I cannot imagine, no matter how poor an opinion you have of me at present, that you would wish me to be married to . . . how did you phrase it? A pernicious fiend?"

"It was perfidious, Gracie," Rickey corrected her.

"So it was. Thank you, Rickey. A perfidious fiend. You see, forcing a union would not have done at all. How wise of you to see that, Mama."

The countess turned quite white. Grace did not think she was contemplating her wisdom, but at least she was silent.

"Damme, girl, you cannot expect us to simply brush the matter under the carpet!"

She smiled sadly at her father. "I would like you to do just that, but no, I do not expect it. I expect nothing. I do ask, however, that you allow me to stay here. It is very important, you see, for the finding."

"Don't see anything," was the mumbled retort.

It was Aurelie who ultimately broke the charged silence that followed. "I, for one, would be ever so grateful if you would allow Grace to remain here with us, sir. I could certainly use her help in preparing for the arrival of the babe."

The earl grunted. "Don't know . . ."

"Really, sir, it would greatly lessen the tedium of my confinement if I could have the company of another lady. Awaiting the birth of an heir—" Aurelie let the words hang for a moment "—cannot help but be a significant matter. I should very much appreciate having your daughter with me through the momentous occasion."

To herself, Grace thought her sister-in-law was doing it

up a bit too brown, but she should have known that Aurelie would find the perfect words to reach the earl.

"An heir," he mused. "Yes, very significant." A faint smile played around his mouth. Then he sobered. "Have *you* any idea what all this finding rot she's spouting is about?"

It was becoming rather tiresome, being spoken about as if she were not present, and Grace opened her mouth to protest. A flash from her sister-in-law's silver eyes stalled her.

"I believe Grace has been doing some soul-searching, sir," Aurelie said gently. "Surely that is an admirable pursuit."

The earl grunted again, but did not disagree. "Don't see how it could hurt for now. . . ."

In a perfect world, Grace mused, the matter would have been settled then. Any world containing her family, of course, could hardly boast of perfection. Not that she had any intention of meekly closeting herself at Havensgate, but her father seemed well on his way to being swayed. Now she could but hope that her mother would accept an aura of martyred resignation. The countess, after all, could not wholly object to martyrdom.

She really should have known better.

"I will not have it, Heathfield!" Lady Heathfield announced stridently. "I will not be forced to hide my head in Staffordshire while she resides here as if nothing untoward has happened. I will not have it!"

"Mama, please . . ." Grace began, then fell silent. Her mother would not even look at her.

It was Rickey who came to her aid again, clumsily, but with the best of intentions. "As we're off to Staffordshire anyway, Mother, I can't see that it makes much of a difference where Grace is. You can hide your head as well without her there."

"Richard!" Lady Heathfield snapped. "Your impertinence is galling!"

"Sorry, Mother, but it's true. What's done is done. Nothing to do but live with it."

"Nothing to do?" Their mother's eyes flashed with enough fire, Grace thought, to set even wet wood aflame. "What any self-respecting person would do would be to send the ungrateful creature off to distant relatives somewhere." She shot her husband an icy glare. To his credit, he glared back.

"Seems to me you tried that already," Rickey muttered. "Didn't work." He peered at the turbot through his glass and gave it an experimental poke.

"But the scandal!"

"I do not believe there will be a scandal, Mother," Jason said, apparently deciding it was high time to step in— somehow. "No one who was here wishes Grace ill. The fault, after all, is Avemar's." Grace did not particularly care for the red glint that appeared in his eye as he spoke Rafe's name, but at least he was trying to help. "I daresay Grace has been through quite enough."

The countess sniffed. "Men simply do not comprehend. Your sister has shredded her own reputation. Whether or not she was aided makes no difference. Mary Warren will not have a peaceful night's sleep until she has the whole sordid tale spread from Brighton to Edinburgh."

Grace flinched. Her mother might have a definite flair for the dramatic, but she was unquestionably savvy when it came to the ways of Society. An image of Lady Warren came to mind, madly scribbling out letters and posting them to reach every corner of the kingdom before falling into an exhausted slumber across her desk.

A soft cough from across the table brought her head up. Aurelie was aiming a decidedly catlike smile in the direction of her turbot. "We need not concern ourselves with Lady Warren," she announced.

Then, rather than elaborating, she reached for the bell beside her plate. The butler appeared in the doorway. "I think we are finished with the fish, Quinby. Yes, we have had quite enough turbot." As the footmen cleared the table, she caught Grace's gaze. *"Kangaroo?"* she mouthed, and rolled her eyes. Grace shrugged.

Whatever story Aurelie was about to impart might be important, but she had weightier matters on her mind. Her father seemed well on his way to granting her wishes, but there was no guarantee he would not change his mind. The countess could be extremely obdurate when her position in Society was involved. No, it appeared that more drastic measures were called for.

She glanced up when Quinby returned moments later, followed by a footman bearing the final remove. "Apple *tourteau*, my lady."

Aurelie turned back to face the table. She took one look at the assembled faces and gave a wicked grin. "How appropriate," she said airily. "A country tart."

Rafe felt awful. It served him right, he supposed, but he had never been one to take severe physical discomfort with an overabundance of grace. He was mildly nauseous, chilled to the bone, and was startled every time he listened to himself breathe. He sounded just like a pug dog that had belonged to a former mistress. It had been the dog who had ultimately caused the end of the affair. Not only had the woman insisted on having the creature sleep at the foot of the bed, where its snorting and wheezing had been impossible to ignore, but she had also taken no measures to keep the miserable little cretin from piddling on Rafe's boots.

"Romeo," the lady had insisted, was merely expressing his own undying love by leaving his generous mark. Rafe, an erstwhile reader of the Stratford bard, had considered hurrying Romeo to an untimely, but thoroughly literary, end. In the end, he had left both woman and dog as they were, not out of kindness, but out of an inability to remember if Shakespeare's Romeo had dispatched himself with poison or a stiletto.

Now he wondered what actions would be necessary to put himself out of his own misery. Unfortunately, the swollen, achy sphere that used to be his head was in no shape to think at all. Cursing and snorting, he burrowed more deeply under the covers.

He had never honestly considered the fact that he might slide from his horse into a ditch somewhere between Havensgate and his lodge. Nor had he ever considered that he might have an inordinately hard time extricating himself from said ditch. Well, he mused, it only served him right. Crackbrained behavior often led to distressing results.

There was some comfort in blaming his current state on Grace. He had become very adept at blaming things on Grace. Well, why not? Everyone else did. Besides, the girl was utterly responsible for every bit of torment he had endured during the past several days. He only wished he could get his hands on her to express his discomfiture in a more forceful and personal manner.

He thought of the brandy downstairs. It seemed a very long way to go on his aching limbs, but it also seemed a reasonably good idea. Then again, staying in bed for the rest of his natural life seemed like a good idea, too.

Deciding not to make any earth-shattering decisions right at that moment, he stared up at the canopy. The bed, designed a good century past, was really an atrocious piece. Its maker had either been blind or blind drunk when he had taken up his tools. Appallingly plump cherubs cavorted about the posts and across the canopy struts on tiny wings far too delicate to support their rotund bodies. He peered at one particularly capricious-looking Cupid and was startled to see its bowstring hanging loose and wafting in a draft. No, he saw on closer inspection, it was a cobweb.

He grunted at the sight, then snorted. The snort had not been intentional, but it seemed utterly appropriate to his sentiments. Love, he mused grumpily, was rather like a cobweb, fashioned by small, pesty creatures and destined to get in one's eyes and fill one's attics. A man was far better off without it.

He closed his eyes, having had more than enough of the cavorting cherubs. It was a good deal more difficult to close his mind, and he found himself wondering just who was responsible for the myth of Cupid. Whoever it was must have been a bitter, misanthropic chap. What placid mind could possibly have come up with the concept of conveying love through an arrow? Nasty business, getting a loaded dart in one's backside. Now, face-on was another matter entirely, but from all he knew of Cupid, the little blighter did not have a gentlemanly bone in his adipose body.

Cupids, cherubs, angels. Rafe cursed the entire bunch. Then snorted. Again, the snort was not deliberate, but it was fitting. To be honest, he had to admit that it had been far less forceful than in the past four days. By all accounts, he was improving, or at least his body was on the mend. His mind was still wretchedly muddled.

There was no way around it; the only thing to be done was to drag his mending body out of bed, into some clothing, and down the stairs. Of course, that was all well and good while he was still prostrate. The moment one bare foot hit the floor, he decided that his brain was indeed thoroughly rattled and ought to be rested until such time as it could be relied upon to make rational choices.

It took several minutes, but he finally managed to get the rest of himself upright. If he were fortunate, he would be able to stay that way until he had seen to the matters at hand. It would not do at all for his strength to fall short of his determination.

After a bit of a struggle, he got himself dressed. His boots presented a challenge, as he had to fight the urge to fall backwards onto the bed each time he lifted a leg. But he vanquished, and made his way over to the cheval glass. It was not a pretty sight. Three days' growth of beard shadowed his jaw, and the unwhiskered skin bore a dull, decidedly gray cast. Only the eyes showed much life, burning with a blue fire he sincerely hoped was fever of soul and not body.

He splashed some cold water on his face and, feeling slightly better for it, ventured into the hallway. By the time he reached the stairs, he was reasonably confident he would be able to manage matters, after all. The floor did seem to be sloping a bit, but he credited that to warped wood.

Once downstairs, he paused. He had only the haziest recollection of arriving at the inn days earlier and was not certain which way he ought to go. Had he not been nearly frozen from his unfortunate tumble into the ditch, he would have been far more alert. As it was, when the horse had stumbled, he had gone head over heels and struck his head on something only slightly softened by the mantle of snow, the same snow that had made climbing *out* of the ditch a laborious process.

He thought it had been the innkeeper himself who had seen him carried up the stairs and into a chamber. Seeking the man out now seemed the most reasonable thing to do. Readying Hannibal and settling the bill could not take more than a few minutes.

The inn seemed unnaturally quiet for midafternoon, and Rafe surmised that the weather had taken another turn for the worse. He seemed to remember a good deal of snow falling past his window during the past days. Blasted snow. Made it damned hard for a man to see to the important things in life.

He took a right at the base of the stairs and followed the faint hum of voices to a closed door. He was about to knock when the carpet beneath his feet seemed to reach out and seize his ankle. As he stumbled forward, he reached for the knob and managed to half step, half tumble into the room. The piercing scream that followed did nothing to help his balance and he nearly went down on one knee.

"Damn and rot!" he snapped, and tried to keep from meeting the worn rug face-on.

The woman shrieked again. "Help! Murder! *Brigand!*"

Rafe regained his feet in time to see a portly matron, dressed from head to toe in brilliant chartreuse, rise from the table and come at him, brandishing a pewter candlestick. He flinched and recoiled from the overwhelming wool. "I beg your pardon, madam, I—"

"Fiend!" the woman bellowed, and advanced with amazing speed for her bulk.

"My mistake," Rafe stammered, raising his hands. "I am sorry. . . ." He tried to step out of her way and barked his hip soundly against the sideboard. "Ouch, damnit!" he grunted, then, "Oww!" as the candlestick connected with his shoulder.

He threw up his arm, more by instinct than design, a fortunate move as the pewter merely glanced off his temple. All the while, the matron was squawking at the top of her formidable lungs. Spurred by desperation, Rafe lunged for the doorway and succeeded in launching himself into the hall. He pulled the door shut behind him and leaned against it, holding the knob tightly and trying to keep his knees from buckling.

At that moment, a half dozen figures appeared around the corner. He thought he saw the landlord's ruddy face among the group. "Bit of a mix-up," Rafe muttered, grimacing as the knob rattled in his hand. "No harm done."

The group scuttled to a halt before him. The landlord was there, as was his wife, a frying pan gripped in her fist. Rafe sincerely hoped he would be allowed to explain before she applied it to his skull. Everyone seemed to be talking at once, and the noise was compounded by the racket behind him. Apparently Madam Goliath did not appreciate her present safety, and was hammering at the door with the candlestick. Rafe grinned weakly at the assembled crowd and debated the wisdom of releasing his hold on the doorknob. A dozen or so eyes widened as the creature behind the portal gave an enraged bellow and all but rattled the hinges.

Then, suddenly, a small form began pushing its way through the knot of bodies. Rafe got the impression of a small, compact body and a tousle of short blond curls. He shook his head in hopes of clearing his vision. By this time, the person was close enough that he could see the heart-shaped face and gold eyes.

"Good heavens, Rafe!"

"Bloody hell. Hullo, Grace," he said. And promptly released the doorknob, hauled her to him, and captured her mouth in a long, deep, searing kiss. That accomplished, he groaned and, letting the inviting blackness take over, crumpled to the stone floor.

17

HE WAS TAKING far too long to wake up. Grace, having spent the better part of the last four days confined to her chamber, was not feeling especially patient. Sighing, she dampened a fresh cloth and applied it to Rafe's forehead. He did not appear to have a fever. In fact, the only warmth in his face was in the color of his nose and the fast-rising lump on his forehead. Both were a lovely red.

After what seemed an eternity, his eyelids fluttered and he let out a faint groan. Then he snorted.

"Rafe?" she whispered, bending over him. "Rafe, you must wake up."

She gave a startled cry when his hands flashed upward to grasp her shoulders. She managed no more than a whimper when he dragged her face down to his and kissed her with enough warmth to turn her red from head to toe. His lips, firm and insistent, fitted to hers with an ease that quite took her breath away. Not that she was overly concerned with breathing. Being kissed was, at the moment, far more important.

When he had finished, she collapsed against his chest. He chuckled. Then snorted. "Always wanted to kiss an angel," he mumbled.

When she looked up, his eyes were closed again.

She took a few deep breaths to calm her racing heart, then clapped her palm over his forehead. He *must* have a fever. But no, the skin beneath her hand was perfectly cool. Grace promptly placed her free hand to her own head. Yes, she was feeling decidedly warm. Perhaps it was she who was suffering fevered delusions. More than a bit rattled, she rose from the bed and wandered over to the window. She pressed her cheek to the cold pane and wondered if, once Rafe woke up, he would remember kissing her at all. Sadly, it did not seem at all likely.

"I would suggest the door."

She spun around to find him very much awake, or at least doing a very good imitation of it. "Wh-what?"

"The door. If you are leaving, I would suggest the door. Far simpler than the window."

She managed a faint smile. "I shall keep that in mind. Do you want me to leave?"

"Not especially." He patted the place beside his hip that she had so recently vacated. "Come sit down."

Still not certain of his lucidity, Grace eyed him warily. If she sat down so close to him, he might very well kiss her again. That would make three times, and that would be highly unusual, not to mention highly improper.

She scurried across the room and settled herself beside him.

"Thank you. Now, would you care to tell me how you found me?"

She sighed. It appeared he was truly awake after all. "Serendipity."

"I beg your pardon?"

"Serendipity. You know, when good things happen by acciden—"

"Yes, Grace, I am aware of the meaning of the word."

"Oh." She looked into his eyes and tried not to get lost. "Yes, I rather thought you would be. If I were to say that I was doing the finding, would it make any sense to you?"

"Not a bit."

She sighed again. "I was afraid not." She caught him eyeing the carafe on the bedside table. "Would you like some water?" She waited for him to say that no, he did not care for water, but that brandy would be perfectly lovely, thank you.

He did not. "Yes, please." He accepted the glass and

220

peered at her over the rim. "So you were not looking for me."

"No. Well, yes, I was. But not here." Every word she had so carefully planned vanished without a trace. "I thought you might find me. . . . Well, Chloe said . . . Oh, bother!" She tried to get up, but one of his hands snaked out to circle her waist.

"It appears I must ask you specific questions, then. Shall I start simply?" She nodded. "When did you get here?"

"Just before you . . . collapsed. Rafe, do you know the woman in the yellow gown? She was saying the most interesting things about you while the landlord was removing you from the floor."

He gave a choked laugh. "I am well acquainted with her right hook. Other than that . . ."

"She does not like you at all." In truth, Grace had been rather offended by the woman's comments on Rafe's character and had ended up pulling the door shut in her face again. "I have the candlestick."

His hand tightened. "I am prodigiously glad to hear that. But you will not change the subject, if you please. How did you get here?"

"Mail coach. The weather, you see. And it was forced to stop here. . . ."

"Does your family know you've gone missing again?"

"I am fairly certain they do by now. And I left a note this time."

"I am afraid to ask what it said."

She was surprised to see that he was smiling, and could not help but smile back. "I am not about to tell you, so you may abandon your fear." With the utmost casualness, she moved her elbow so it held his hand captive. One of his black brows raised a fraction, but he did not move his hand. "May I ask you a question now?"

"Do I have to answer?"

"What are *you* doing here? It is hardly your style, Rafe."

He gave a choked laugh. "Why, because its denizens are

of the moneyed variety? I assure you, Gracie, they serve whiskey here."

"Are you foxed?" Somehow, she did not think he was. There was no liquor on his breath, and his gaze, while decidedly languid, was clear.

"No, I am not. In fact, I have not had a drink since leaving Havensgate."

"Truly?"

"Truly. My current state is due in full to a devilish head cold which I found in a ditch about a mile away. And, I suppose, a pewter candlestick."

He decided it was far better to fix his gaze on her wide eyes than her wide, now open mouth.

"A ditch? You mean you fell into a ditch on your way from Havensgate?"

A number of blithe retorts came to mind. He settled instead on the truth. "No. I fell into a ditch on my way *to* Havensgate. I was coming back."

"Back?"

"I am so glad you are hearing me. It will make the rest of the conversation ever so much easier."

"You were coming back to Havensgate?"

He tried not to laugh. Then he tried not to think of how very sweet she tasted. "Brava, Grace. You have now proven your grasp of the English language."

"Have you gone quite mad?"

By the time he realized she was moving, she was halfway across the room. He flexed his empty fingers. "Mad? Yes, I rather think so, and you have driven me to it. No sane man would face your father when he was both angry and within a hundred feet of a gun." He reached out. "Yes, I have gone quite mad for you."

"Do not mock me, Rafe. Not now."

"I was not. Now come back here."

She shook her head, setting blond curls into motion. "I do not think so. You are behaving very oddly."

He dropped his hand against the counterpane. "Of *course* I am behaving oddly! My present state does that to a man."

"Fine. I will secure a room for myself, and when you are feeling more the thing, we shall talk."

The words lacked Grace's customary conviction, but he was not taking any chances on her walking out the door. He felt reasonably human, but the welt on his head ached, and he did not think he would be able to catch her in a hurry should she decide to bolt.

"I do not think I will ever be rid of this affliction, Gracie," he said gruffly, "but I would feel ever so much better if you would come back here."

"Why?"

"I should think that would be perfectly obvious. I want to kiss you again."

"Why?" she repeated. He noticed that she was twisting pleats into the hem of a coat that might, in younger and better days, have been a Weston.

"Whose clothes are you wearing now?"

"Rickey's. I could not very well travel in my own."

She had come no closer, but at least she was not edging—or running—toward the door. "You know what I would like to hear you say, Grace?" She shook her head again. "I would like to hear you say that you were coming to find me."

Her brows promptly drew together in a frown. "Well, of course I was coming to find you! Did I not say so?"

"Did you?"

Now she was beginning to wonder if the fall he had mentioned had not perhaps rattled his brains. No matter what Chloe said, Grace could not begin to believe he had undergone such a complete change of heart. In fact, she had embarked for his hunting lodge fully prepared to have him growl, howl, and rage at her. She had also been prepared to go at his resistance with every fiber of her being. And a few small lies.

"I was coming to you," she said, trying her best lost look, "because I did not know where else to go."

"Ah," was all he said.

223

"They were going to send me to Boxing, you know . . . kangaroos."

"Boxing? Is that so?"

She felt herself flushing. "I mean Boston, of course. Or Australia."

"Come here, Grace."

"China," she tried, then gave it up and rolled her eyes. "I have made a royal hash of it, haven't I? How predictable." She let her shoulders slump, defeated. "I simply wanted to be with you, Rafe. I am not very happy, you see, when you are not in the vicinity."

When she dared look up, he was smiling at her—a slow, languorous smile that registered somewhere deep inside her. "I am prodigiously glad to hear that. Now come here, or I will be forced to come get you. I do not recommend that, because I suspect I will be none too steady on my feet and I shall undoubtedly go down like a load of bricks, with you in tow. Please, Grace. I need you here."

She waited only a second. Then she was beside him again. He clasped her face between his palms, and she thought he was going to kiss her. She even closed her eyes in preparation.

"Open your eyes." She did, and he let out a low groan. "God, you really are beautiful." When she merely gaped at him, he continued, "I have been a beast, and all I can hope is that you will let me make it up to you."

She felt the tears welling in her eyes. "Why now? Why are you saying all these things now?"

He gently stroked the dampness from her cheeks. "Why? Because I have had far too much time to reminisce recently. And, as I realized you have been the very best part of my past, and must be the center of my future, I thought to tell you so as soon as possible. A wise man does what he can to begin a happy future posthaste."

Now, Grace, as the carriage had lumbered its way toward Lewes, had created a good many scenarios just like this one. She could not, however, quite believe her ears. Affecting her best stern gaze, which was, she feared, not helped

224

by her tears, she asked, "What changed, Rafe? I assure you, I have not."

"Oh, Gracie, do you not see? You saved me. When I was at my very worst, you stayed by me. And when I was unable to come for you, you came for me."

"You called me a pox!"

She watched him fight, unsuccessfully, against a smile. "It is not a comfortable thing, sweetheart, to be jerked back to life. Falling in love, it seems, is not the most pleasant experience known to man."

She could not help but smile back. "You know, Vivian said much the same thing about women."

"Vivian is very wise. Did she by chance complete the sentiment?"

"What do you mean?"

Grace's heart did a mighty flip when his thumbs caressed her cheeks with almost torturous tenderness. "Falling in love is hell," he said, his voice rough, "but *being* in love is as close to heaven as a man could get."

"Oh," she gasped. "Oh, Rafe!" And this time she kissed him. With all the years of hope and passion she had held within.

She might have gone on kissing him for years to come if an ungodly racket had not sounded outside the door. Over the banging, a familiar voice rang out.

"Open the damn door, Avemar! I know you are in there!"

"My father!" Grace gasped, and tried to disengage herself from Rafe's arms. He refused to let her go.

"How did he come to be here?"

She shrugged. "Tracked the mail coach, I suppose."

The landlady's voice carried just as well as the earl's. "Here now, you have no call to disturb his lordship and his wife while they are resting!"

Rafe's brows shot up. "My wife?"

"Well, I had to tell them something. The way you kissed me downstairs was rather . . . familiar."

"Yes, we're rather natural at it, aren't we?" He chuckled

when her gaze centered unerringly on his lips. "A duchess in breeches, traveling alone. I'm certain they believed every word of it."

Grace lifted both her eyes and her chin. "I am a very good liar when it is necessary."

"Sweetheart, you are an appalling liar. Especially when it is necessary." He looked up as Heathfield began banging anew. "I suppose we had best let him in."

He levered his body off the bed and frowned when she promptly attached herself to his chest. "He might have a gun," she announced matter-of-factly, protesting when he lifted her away and tucked her behind him. "Really, Rafe, I do not want him shooting you!"

"That, too, is welcome news, I assure you. But I have been cowardly enough for one lifetime. It is high time that I faced my future father-in-law. Now, stay there."

Never one to obey officious commands, Grace slipped under his arm as he reached for the door. In the scuffle that ensued, she tugged his shirt from his breeches, and he sent her already tousled hair into greater disarray. But she was standing beside him when he swung open the door to reveal not only an extremely red-faced Lord Heathfield, but also an equally irate-looking Jason and a clearly befuddled Rickey.

The earl took one look at his daughter's rumpled appearance, bellowed, and raised the pistol he was carrying. Jason, however, moved faster. His fist flashed out, connecting solidly with Rafe's jaw. As he had earlier predicted, Rafe went down like a load of bricks. Grace, clinging to his arm, went with him.

He stayed down. She did not. Before her father and brothers could take more than one step into the room, she was on her feet. In a second, she had grabbed the candlestick taken from the irate woman in yellow and was brandishing it like a sword. When her father stepped toward her, she gave a quick sweep and knocked a button from his waistcoat. As he gaped down at the dangling thread, she

226

gave a quick thrust and poked him soundly in the chest. He stumbled backward, right into his sons.

Knowing an advantage when she had it, Grace poked again. And again, until all three were back in the hallway. Then, with a victorious cry, she slammed the door in their stunned faces and slammed the bolt home.

Then she spun around to check on Rafe. He was sitting up, fingering his jaw, and grinning from ear to ear. "Remind me never to anger you once we are wed," he announced. "You wield a fierce candlestick."

She dropped to her knees and surveyed the damage. His jaw was red as the lump above his eyes, and would undoubtedly swell just as much. "No doubt you will anger me on a regular basis," she retorted. "You always have."

"Yet you love me anyway?"

She gave an exasperated sigh. "I have *always* loved you, you dolt! You just never saw it."

Whatever Rafe said in response was lost to a renewed banging at the door. "You will let me in at once!" the earl bellowed. "Do you hear me, Grace?"

"Of course I hear you, Papa. All of East Sussex can hear you."

Heathfield bellowed again, and Rafe, deciding impoliteness would not serve them best, cleared his throat. "Just a moment, sir, and I will let you in."

"You will do nothing of the sort," Grace hissed.

"I will not?"

"You will not. Jason would only hit you again. No, I suspect he has broken his hand. Rickey would hit you, and as he is probably sporting his glass, he might very well miss and hit *me*!"

Rafe laughed. "I do love you, Gracie."

"I am prodigiously glad to hear that." She kissed him once, hard. He managed not to wince as his jaw protested. Then she turned back to face the door. "Are you listening, Papa?" There was a reasonably affirmative grunt. "You will not shoot Rafe. Is that clear?"

"Give me one good reason!"

"I will give you one very good reason. I am going to marry him and do not care to be a widow just yet!"

"Just *yet?*" Rafe muttered. She grinned at him.

"Marry, you say?"

"Yes, Papa, marry. It is all the rage, or so I understand."

"Grace!" Rafe chided. She grinned at him. Damned if the minx wasn't having the time of her life.

"Avemar, can you hear me?"

"Yes, sir. All of East Sussex can hear you, or so I understand."

"Damme, boy, I will have none of your cheek! You really intend to marry the girl?"

"As soon as possible, sir."

Grace elbowed him. "That is not at all necessary, Rafe. There will be no scandal. Aurelie dealt with Lady Warren quite splendidly."

"I was not overly concerned with scandal. But since we have little else to do, you might as well regale me with the tale."

"Well, I do not know all of it, of course. Aurelie was most evasive on the matter. But I believe it had something to do with a duke, a footman, and several grooms."

Rafe's brows went up. "You don't say!" Grace nodded and he let out a low whistle. "Who'd have thought it? Lady Warren bedding a duke!" He laughed. Then snorted. "Damnit, I'd thought I was rid of this cursed thing!"

"What was that, Avemar?" the earl bellowed.

"Nothing, sir." Rafe cleared his throat. "Now, if you gentlemen would be so kind as to take yourselves downstairs, I am certain our landlord could come up with a bottle of Napoleon's finest. Grace and I will be down in a moment."

There was a bit of noise from the other side of the door, but Heathfield eventually grunted his agreement. Heavy footsteps receded down the hallway. Rafe turned back to Grace, who was still grinning like a mischievous child. "I do not suppose you brought any more appropriate clothing with you."

228

"Of course I did not. Pink muslin is hardly suitable for your hunting box."

He sighed. "I would feel ever so much better if we did not have to face your irate male relatives with you dressed as you are."

As he watched, her eyes took on a decidedly evil glow. "We do not really have to face them at all, you know." She leaned toward him.

"They will come back," he murmured against her lips. "And if we keep this up, you will undoubtedly catch my cold."

"Interesting thought," she answered. "I suppose that means a honeymoon in bed."

"Grace!" he gasped, stunned, but not in the least displeased.

She grinned. "Everyone has been calling me Disgrace for years. Now I finally have the opportunity to earn the sobriquet." She sighed happily as his hand tangled in her hair. "Unless you save me from it, of course."

"Not a chance," was Rafe's husky reply. "I want you just as you are."

"I think," she said, wrapping her arms around his neck, "that might be the sweetest thing you have ever said to me. Do say it again."

And he did.